West African Folktales

West African Folktales

General Editor: Jake Jackson
Associate Editor: Catherine Taylor

**FLAME TREE
PUBLISHING**

This is a FLAME TREE Book

FLAME TREE PUBLISHING
6 Melbray Mews
Fulham, London SW6 3NS
United Kingdom
www.flametreepublishing.com

First published 2021
Copyright © 2021 Flame Tree Publishing Ltd

23 25 24 22
3 5 7 9 8 6 4 2

ISBN: 978-1-83964-780-2
ebook ISBN: 978-1-83964-782-6
Special ISBN: 978-1-83964-829-8

The cover image is © copyright 2021 Flame Tree Publishing Ltd,
based on artwork courtesy of Shutterstock.com/serg_65.

All inside images courtesy of Shutterstock.com and the following:
serg_65, MicroOne, Miceking, Alvaro Cabrera Jimenez, Kristina Birukova.

Stories by Harold Courlander, as noted on their respective pages,
are copyright 1962, 1990 by Harold Courlander. Reprinted
by permission of The Emma Courlander Trust.

Contributors, authors, editors and sources for this series include:
Loren Auerbach, William H. Barker and Cecilia Sinclair, Norman Bancroft-Hunt, George W.
Bateman, James S. de Benneville, E.M. Berens, Katharine Berry Judson, W.H.I. Bleek and
L. C. Lloyd, Laura Bulbeck, J. F. Campbell, Harold Courlander, Jeremiah Curtin, F. Hadland
Davis, Elphinstone Dayrell, O.B. Duane, Dr Ray Dunning, W.W. Gibbings, William Elliot
Griffis, H. A. Guerber, Lafcadio Hearn, Stephen Hodge, James A. Honey M.D., Jake Jackson,
Joseph Jacobs, Judith John, Michael Kerrigan, J.W. Mackail, Alexander Mackenzie, Donald
Mackenzie, Chris McNab, Minnie Martin, A.B. Mitford (Lord Redesdale), Robert Hamill
Nassau, M.I. Ogumefu, Yei Theodora Ozaki, Robert Sutherland Rattray, Professor James
Riordan, Sara Robson, Lewis Spence, Henry M. Stanley, Capt. C.H. Stigand, Rachel Storm,
K.E. Sullivan, Percy Amaury Talbot, François-Marie Arouet a.k.a. Voltaire, E.A. Wallis Budge,
Dr Roy Willis, Epiphanius Wilson, E.T.C. Werner, Morris Meredith Williams.

A copy of the CIP data for this book is available from the British Library.

Printed and bound in the UK by Clays Ltd, Elcograf S.p.A

Contents

Series Foreword

STRETCHING BACK to the oral traditions of thousands of years ago, tales of heroes and disaster, creation and conquest have been told by many different civilizations in many different ways. Their impact sits deep within our culture even though the detail in the tales themselves are a loose mix of historical record, transformed narrative and the distortions of hundreds of storytellers.

Today the language of mythology lives with us: our mood is jovial, our countenance is saturnine, we are narcissistic and our modern life is hermetically sealed from others. The nuances of myths and legends form part of our daily routines and help us navigate the world around us, with its half truths and biased reported facts.

The nature of a myth is that its story is already known by most of those who hear it, or read it. Every generation brings a new emphasis, but the fundamentals remain the same: a desire to understand and describe the events and relationships of the world. Many of the great stories are archetypes that help us find our own place, equipping us with tools for self-understanding, both individually and as part of a broader culture.

For Western societies it is Greek mythology that speaks to us most clearly. It greatly influenced the mythological heritage of the ancient Roman civilization and is the lens through which we still see the Celts, the Norse and many of the other great peoples and religions. The Greeks themselves learned much from their neighbours, the Egyptians, an older culture that became weak with age and incestuous leadership.

It is important to understand that what we perceive now as mythology had its own origins in perceptions of the divine and the rituals of the sacred. The earliest civilizations, in the crucible of the Middle East, in the Sumer of the third millennium BC, are the source to which many of the mythic archetypes can be traced. As humankind collected together in cities for the first time, developed writing and industrial scale agriculture, started to irrigate the rivers and attempted to control rather than be at the mercy of its environment, humanity began to write down its tentative explanations of natural events, of floods and plagues, of disease.

Early stories tell of Gods (or god-like animals in the case of tribal societies such as African, Native American or Aboriginal cultures) who are crafty and use their wits to survive, and it is reasonable to suggest that these were the first rulers of the gathering peoples of the earth, later elevated to god-like status with the distance of time. Such tales became more political as cities vied with each other for supremacy, creating new Gods, new hierarchies for their pantheons. The older Gods took on primordial roles and became the preserve of creation and destruction, leaving the new gods to deal with more current, everyday affairs. Empires rose and fell, with Babylon assuming the mantle from Sumeria in the 1800s BC, then in turn to be swept away by the Assyrians of the 1200s BC; then the Assyrians and the Egyptians were subjugated by the Greeks, the Greeks by the Romans and so on, leading to the spread and assimilation of common themes, ideas and stories throughout the world.

The survival of history is dependent on the telling of good tales, but each one must have the 'feeling' of truth, otherwise it will be ignored. Around the firesides, or embedded in a book or a computer, the myths and legends of the past are still the living materials of retold myth, not restricted to an exploration of origins. Now we have devices and global communications that give us unparalleled access to a diversity of traditions. We can find out about Native American, Indian, Chinese and tribal African mythology in a way that was denied to our ancestors, we can find connections, match the archaeology, religion and the mythologies of the world to build a comprehensive image of the human experience that is endlessly fascinating.

The stories in this book provide an introduction to the themes and concerns of the myths and legends of their respective cultures, with a short introduction to provide a linguistic, geographic and political context. This is where the myths have arrived today, but undoubtedly over the next millennia, they will transform again whilst retaining their essential truths and signs.

Jake Jackson
General Editor

Introduction to West African Folktales

If one mythic figure exemplifies the character and spirit of West Africa more than any other, it is Anansi, the trickster spider. Quirky, mercurial and astonishingly quick-thinking, he is always ready with a way to turn adversity into advantage; setback into success. No region of the world has needed that ability more over the centuries than West Africa, perhaps: Anansi is irrepressibly upbeat. Not that he doesn't suffer his share of reverses (on occasion he embarrasses himself – he's by no means perfect), but he always comes back ready for the fray.

An enthusiastic storyteller himself, he is also an eager connoisseur and indefatigable collector. 'He longed to be the owner of all the stories known in the world,' we are told at one point. Anansi appreciates that myths encode the intelligence, the wit and humour of humankind, as do the wealth of West African Stories gathered here.

Doubtful Darkness

A sunny optimism prevails. As dismal as its history may have been at times, Africa was only ever the 'Dark Continent' because Europeans chose to close their eyes. To its inhabitants' humanity, in the first place; and then (it followed inevitably) to their achievements, the extraordinary civilizations that they had built. It was understandable that they should have found it a Confusing Continent, though, given the immense geographic, demographic and cultural complexity over which they were drawing their crisply clear-cut colonial map.

Nowhere was this more true than in that western corner between the Sahara's southern limit and the main body of central Africa. The first region to be visited by Europe's seaborne traders in the 'Age of Discovery' of the fifteenth century, it had been opened up well before that by Arab merchants from the Maghreb, who had come down here in camel caravans across the desert sand. The mineral and agricultural wealth which had attracted these outsiders had of course already fostered the growth of an array of important indigenous cities and states.

A World in One Region

West Africa is indeed a little world. The map may show an orderly series of small countries clustered round a curving coast, but this view is seriously misleading. A neat-looking little segment here, Ghana is actually only the tiniest bit smaller than the United Kingdom. Nigeria is almost four times that size. Moreover, these countries with their clear-cut borders encompass huge demographic diversity. Ghana's 100-plus indigenous ethnic communities speak some 79 languages, while Nigeria's 250-odd ethnic groups speak 500 tongues. Cameroon has 200 ethnic groups (and by some estimates up to 600 different languages). Even tiny Togo, only 57,000km² (22,000 square miles) in area, has 37 different recognized ethnicities; Sierra Leone lags well behind with 'just' sixteen. Liberia was famously colonized in the nineteenth century by freed slaves from the United States but it has seventeen indigenous ethnic groups as well.

Notoriously, national boundaries here were laid down arbitrarily by European negotiators. So Senegal was 'French', as was the Ivory Coast (or *Côte d'Ivoire*). So too were Togo and Benin; whereas Nigeria was 'British' – as, ultimately, was the 'Gold Coast' or Ghana. Even under colonialism, though, the real story was more complicated: Ghana had 'belonged' to the Portuguese and the Germans before the British made it theirs.

Indigenous Empires

The ancient homeland of the Yoruba, who built the great civilization around Ife, centred on the Niger delta but spilled across the borders of Nigeria into modern-day Togo and Benin. Their craftsmen created bronze sculptures of breathtaking beauty; their women worked miracles with textiles, developing sumptuous, tie-dyed indigo *adire* fabrics. The Yoruba believed that Ife was the centre of the world, and the place where human life had first begun. A naïve, parochial perspective, though no more so than the later one that saw the earth as being arranged around the Greenwich Meridian and Ife's stunning sculptures (in virtuosity and vision a match for anything being produced in Europe at the time) as 'primitive'.

As for the rich and powerful Kingdom of Benin, which flourished between the eleventh and fourteenth centuries (and also produced spectacular bronzes), that too was in Nigeria, a little way inland of the delta zone – not in the country we call Benin at all. Once again, the modern map misleads.

New states rose and fell in succession, village communities coalescing into states around charismatic rulers then slowly disintegrating as their power waned: the Ewe Kingdom of Ghana and Togo in the sixteenth century; the Fon Kingdom of Dahomey (in the south of what is now Benin) in the seventeenth.

Windows on the World

From about 1700, the Ashanti Confederacy, a grouping of communities of the Akan people, occupied areas across southern Ghana but also spread over into the Ivory Coast and Togo. Their wealth was originally founded in agriculture, like that of the Yoruba state, the Hausa Empire and the Kingdom of Benin before it. They built considerable cities, but seem to have commuted out to cultivate lands outside these centres.

Like other coastal communities, though, they also engaged in commerce with Europeans – first in precious resources (hence the labels 'Ivory Coast' and 'Gold Coast'); then subsequently in the brutal trade in slaves. Close relations with the colonial powers did not necessarily mean meek subservience: the Ashanti Confederacy resisted British settlement fiercely and scored several important victories.

Cultures of Quietness

Historically significant as these states were, they don't necessarily typify the trajectories of West Africa's peoples. Many lived modestly and quietly, never amassing great riches or acquiring empires. The Ekoi of southeastern Nigeria and Cameroon were experts in wood-carving, creating stunningly sculpted masks. Like the Ekoi, the Fang and Bulu of Cameroon also lived peacefully for centuries: all three groups were badly hit by the depredations of the slave trade.

Environmental considerations influenced the lifestyles – and hence the priorities – of different peoples. To take one obvious example: communities which lived near water, like Liberia's Jabo, who lived along their country's coast, or Ghana's Krachi, who had settled in the valley of the Volta River, subsisted by fishing as well as farming.

Pastoralist Preferences

Further north, in the 'Sahel', where the tropical forests started to give way to the grassland, scrub and semi-desert of the Saharan fringes, communities pursued a pastoralist way of life. Whilst some in the more fertile, southern zone grazed flocks from permanent villages, where they also farmed, others further north lived nomadically. They had to, given the scarcity of grazing and the unreliability of water sources: they needed to be ready to uproot at any moment and take their lives and flocks where the resources were.

The most famous of these peoples, perhaps, were the Fula, or Fulani. Herders of cattle and goats, they are believed to have originated near the coast in what is now Senegal. Over time, however, their nomadic pastoralist lifestyle took them deeper into the interior. But there were many other groups – including Akan communities living in more arid, northerly areas unsuited to the agrarian way of life their kinsfolk followed. These nomadic groups were the first to come into contact with Arab traders who over centuries came south over the Sahara to exchange salt and silks for precious metals, ivory and other luxuries. The Arabs also brought Islam to the region.

Demarcation Disputes

'West Africa', as a geographical or political category, is of course quite vague. Where it begins and ends is a matter of debate – with, ultimately, no right answer. The compiler of a collection of folktales has to make some fairly arbitrary decisions. Not so much with regard to the region's northern frontier: the Sahara Desert is seen as setting a 'natural' limit. Neither Mauritania nor Mali, Niger nor Burkina Faso really look like they belong.

To the southeast the limits are a lot less clear. Geographers generally exclude countries like Equatorial Guinea, Gabon, Cameroon and the Republic of the Congo. Demographically, it is more difficult to say. For this collection, it has been decided to include Cameroon. The westernmost of this group, it shows obvious continuities with the other countries we've included in its ethnic and linguistic communities. Its mythology clearly complements theirs as well.

Bantu Beginnings?

To make an already highly complex question all but impossible to resolve, there's the fact that so much of Eastern and Southern Africa seems to have been formed, culturally and linguistically, by West Africa. If humankind as a whole came 'out of Africa', as most experts believe, then a great deal of Africa came out of this one little corner. Albeit far, far more recently, it must be said.

To this day, by far the majority of West Africa's peoples speak languages belonging to the Niger-Congo group, which for many years was known to scholars as 'Bantu'. This title is avoided now, since it is generally associated with languages and peoples found in central and southern Africa. The label is logical enough, though, given that the more southerly Bantu languages are believed to have been distributed through the continent by a large-scale migration which took place almost a thousand years ago and appears to have originated in roughly this area of West Africa.

But the migrants didn't just take their language with them. They took all sorts of skills, assumptions and ideas; their beliefs and rituals; their traditions and (surely) their myths. Though these inevitably developed and changed as new communities settled further south and east and came by new histories and new identities, they were still shaped by their remoter origins. Which makes it even harder than it already was to establish a firm frontier for 'West Africa' and a clear canon of 'West African Folktales'.

A Crowded Cosmos

Despite these difficulties, and the great diversity of the region, clear themes do emerge as we read these stories. As in just about all the world's mythologies, cosmological questions are addressed, with attempts to explain how the universe was formed, the earth, the moon and stars; how nature was created and how humanity came to be.

It may be contradictory but it seems consistent, somehow, given the lively and colourful character of their mythology more generally, that the Yoruba were unable to imagine an actually empty universe. Even when the waters extended all over the earth, and the world was yet to be created, it was, their creation-story suggests, already peopled. (Contrast this with the seven-day story of the biblical Genesis account, in which the making of man and woman is God's final task.)

Other West African peoples took a different view, of course, but they generally concur in depicting the newly-created world as an extremely lively scene. And a strongly anthropomorphized one: the sun and moon are not just heavenly bodies but engaging (if sometimes semi-comic) personalities. Again, the contrast with the portentous impersonality of the biblical account is strong.

Animal Energy

Animals are well to the fore in a great many of these stories, though they too are strongly anthropomorphized in many cases. They are fierce and frightening on occasion, naturally; but at other times more loving, helpful, kind.

And of course cunning. Many of these tales of Anansi and the Tortoise trickster were to have sparkling second lives as 'Brer Rabbit' stories in the

United States, to whose southern plantations this lore was carried by the first slaves. Their descendants found themselves more in need of the put-upon trickster's resourcefulness than their forebears in West Africa could ever have imagined, perhaps, though the latter didn't go short of challenges themselves. Flood and famine, war and violence are among the disasters featured here. Overall, though, the upbeat mood prevails.

Design for Living

Which takes us to another point: these stories often seem to have been designed not just to delight but to inspire. Clever and enterprising as they are, the really important quality the tricksters here represent is their indomitability; their refusal to be beaten; their readiness to reimagine an apparently impossible situation in such a way as to secure a favourable outcome. What is most deceptive about them is that they seem defeated in the first place: they are entirely honest in their determination to win out.

These myths are also clearly intended to educate: a remarkable proportion of them could reasonably be classed as 'fables'. Though seldom stern or moralistic, they nevertheless offer clear moral lessons. We could all do with a bit more of the industry and patience of the ants; the lion's courage and integrity; the rueful self-awareness of King Chameleon as represented here. Whatever our rank, we would all do well to learn the lesson the King of Sedo has to about pride; to secure the devotion her loyal suitor 'Thinker' has for the beautiful maiden Morning Sunshine.

Some of these stories set out to explain how important principles of life and law came into being. We read of how the Hausa think the first person went mad, for instance; why it is important that a murderer should hang, however strongly we may be tempted towards mercy, and why it is ill-advised to offer help to one we know has criminal intent. Evil deeds, we find, have a way of coming back to bite us, however indirectly; a good one has a way of paying dividends.

Tales of Origin, Life & Death

AN ACCOUNT of where we come from, how we were brought into being, is pretty much a first requirement of any mythological tradition. West Africa's are certainly no exception. Such stories do not simply suggest a 'first cause' – important as that is. Nor do they just explain creation, revealing why and how we came to have the animals, trees and flowers; the forests and the seas; the rain, the sun, the seasons. As important – in some ways more so – they encode the cultural values of those who tell them; establish their relationship with Nature and the world. And with one another, for these tales tell us just as much about the ways in which human life has traditionally been ordered in everything from social hierarchies to gender roles.

All things considered, then, these stories carry quite some weight. The issues they address could hardly matter more. In tone, though, they are anything but portentous. Quirky, even comic at times, they treat the mysteries of existence with the most wry of wit; the challenges of life with droll amusement and the final fear of death with stoic good-humour.

The Kingdom of the Yorubas
(From the Yoruba people, southern Nigeria)

Φ

THE ANCIENT KING Oduduwa had a great many grandchildren, and on his death he divided among them all his possessions. But his youngest grandson, Oranyan, was at that time away hunting, and when he returned home he learnt that his brothers and cousins had inherited the old King's money, cattle, beads, native cloths, and crowns, but that to himself nothing was left but twenty-one pieces of iron, a cock, and some soil tied up in a rag.

At that time the whole earth was covered with water, on the surface of which the people lived. The resourceful Oranyan spread upon the water his pieces of iron, and upon the iron he placed the scrap of cloth, and upon the cloth the soil, and on the soil the cock. The cock scratched with his feet and scattered the soil far and wide, so that the ocean was partly filled up and islands appeared everywhere. The pieces of iron became the mineral wealth hidden under the ground.

Now Oranyan's brothers and cousins all desired to live on the land, and Oranyan allowed them to do so on payment of tribute. He thus became King of all the Yorubas, and was rich and prosperous through his grandfather's inheritance.

How All Stories and All History
Came Among Men
(By Agra of Mbeban, of the Ekoi people, Nigeria and Cameroon)

Φ

MOUSE GOES EVERYWHERE. Through rich men's houses she creeps, and visits even the poorest. At night, with her little bright eyes, she watches the doing of secret things, and no

21

treasure-chamber is so safe but she can tunnel through and see what is hidden there.

In old days she wove a story-child from all that she saw, and to each of these she gave a gown of different colours – white, red, blue, or black. The stories became her children, and lived in her house and served her, because she had no children of her own.

* * *

Now in olden days a sheep and a leopard lived in the same town. In course of time Leopard became enceinte and Sheep also. Sheep bore a daughter and Leopard a son.

There was a famine in all the land, so Leopard went to Sheep and said, "Let us kill our children and eat them." Sheep thought, "If I do not agree, she may kill my child in spite of me," so she answered "Good."

Then Sheep went and hid her own babe, and took all that she had and sold for a little dried meat. This she cooked and set before Leopard, and they both ate together. Leopard killed her own child, and ate that also.

In another year they both became enceinte once more. This time again the townsfolk were hungry. Leopard came as before and said, "Let us kill these children also." Sheep agreed, but she took her second child and hid her in the little room where the first child was, then went out, and begged till someone gave her a few pieces of dried meat. These she cooked and set before Leopard as she had done before, in place of her babe. Leopard ate and said nothing.

Some years afterwards Leopard sent to Sheep and said, "Come; to-day you shall feast with me."

Sheep went, and found a great calabash on the table. She opened it, and found it full of food, and by it three spoons laid ready.

She was astonished and questioned Leopard. "Formerly we used two spoons, you and I. Why should there be three to-day?"

Leopard laughed, opened the door of the inner room, and called, "Come, daughter, let us eat." Her daughter came, and they all ate together. Then the mother said, "When my first child came, I killed and ate him because we were very hungry; but when I learned how you had saved your child, I thought, 'Next time I also will play such a trick on Sheep.' Therefore I saved my daughter alive."

After that Sheep went home, and tended her two children. Years passed by, and all the daughters began to grow up. Leopard put her child into the fatting-house. Then she went to Sheep and said, "Give me one of your daughters to stay with mine in the fatting-house. She is alone and cannot eat."

Now Sheep and both her daughters were quite black, but there were some young goats in the house which served them as slaves. These were white, so before Sheep sent her daughter to Leopard's house she rubbed her all over with white chalk, then dyed one of the young goats black, and sent them together.

When they both arrived at the house, Leopard thought that the goat was Sheep's daughter. All three of the young ones were placed in the fatting-house. During the night Leopard entered the room, took Goat and killed her, then cooked the meal and gave to her own daughter to eat, thinking it was the daughter of Sheep whom she had slain.

Next day Leopard went to Sheep and said, "Give me your other child, that our three daughters may be in the fatting-house together."

Sheep consented, but before this child went she advised her what to do.

When therefore the second lamb reached the fatting-house she took out a bottle of rum and gave it to Leopard's daughter, saying "Drink this. It is a present which my mother has sent you." So Leopard's child drank and fell asleep. The two young sheep kept awake until their companion slept. They then got up, carried her from her own bed, and laid her on one of those prepared for themselves.

It was very dark in the room, and, when Leopard came in to kill one of the young sheep, she killed her own daughter instead. She was pleased and thought, "Now I have finished with the children whom Sheep hid from me." Next morning, very early, she went out to the bush to get palm wine that she might drink it with her daughter while they feasted on the young sheep.

No sooner had she left the house than the two sheep ran out. One of them went home to her mother's house, but the other followed after Leopard. The latter was at the top of a high palm tree, so Sheep's child stopped some way off and called in a loud voice:

"Last night you tried to kill me as you did the young goat, but you made a mistake, and killed your own child instead."

No sooner had Leopard heard this than she jumped from the tree and ran after the young sheep.

The latter ran to the cross-roads, and when Leopard reached the place she could not tell which way Sheep had gone. After thinking a while she took the wrong road and ran on.

Now when Sheep had run a long way she met the Nimm woman walking along with her Juju round her waist. The woman looked as if she had come a long way, and Sheep said, "Let me carry your Juju for you."

To this the Nimm woman agreed. When they came to her house she was very tired and her head hurt her.

Sheep said, "Let me fetch water and firewood while you rest."

The Nimm woman was very thankful, and went into her house to lie down.

When the young Sheep had done as she promised, she went into the other part of the house where the Nimm shrine was. On it she saw the "medicine." This she took and rubbed over herself.

Next day the Nimm woman said, "Will you go and fetch me my 'medicine' which stands on the shrine of Nimm?"

Sheep asked her, "Do you not know that I was 'born' into your medicine last night?"

At this the Nimm woman was very angry and sprang up. Sheep ran, and the Nimm woman followed her. In her hurry to escape, Sheep ran against the door of the house where Mouse lived. The door was old and it broke, and all the stories on earth, and all the histories ran out. After that they never went back to dwell with Mouse any more, but remained running up and down over all the earth.

The Gods Descend from the Sky
(From the Fon people, Benin)

NANA BALUKU, the mother of all creation, fell pregnant before she finally retired from the universe. Her offspring was androgynous, a being with one body and two faces. The face

that resembled a woman was called Mawu and her eyes were the moon. She took control of the night and all territories to the west. The male face was called Lisa and his eyes were the sun. Lisa controlled the east and took charge of the daylight.

At the beginning of the present world, Mawu-Lisa was the only being in existence, but eventually the moon was eclipsed by the sun and many children were conceived. The first fruits of the union were a pair of twins, a male called Da Zodji and a female called Nyohwè Ananu. Another child followed shortly afterwards, a male and female form joined in one body, and this child was named Sogbo. The third birth again produced twins, a male, Agbè, and a female, Naètè. The fourth and fifth children were both male and were named Agè and Gu. Gu's torso was made of stone and a giant sword protruded from the hole in his neck where his head would otherwise have been. The sixth offspring was not made of flesh and blood. He was given the name Djo, meaning air, or atmosphere. Finally, the seventh child born was named Legba, and because he was the youngest, he became Mawu-Lisa's particular favourite.

When these children had grown to adulthood and the appropriate time had arrived to divide up the kingdoms of the universe among them, Mawu-Lisa gathered them together. To their first-born, the twins Da Zodji and Nyohwè Ananu, the parents gave the earth below and sent them, laden with heavenly riches, down from the sky to inhabit their new home. To Sogbo, who was both man and woman, they gave the sky, commanding him to rule over thunder and lightning. The twins Agbè and Naètè were sent to take command of the waters and the creatures of the deep, while Agè was ordered to live in the bush as a hunter where he could take control of all the birds and beasts of the earth.

To Gu, whom Mawu-Lisa considered their strength, they gave the forests and vast stretches of fertile soil, supplying him also with the tools and weapons mankind would need to cultivate the land. Mawu-Lisa ordered Djo to occupy the space between the earth and the sky and entrusted him with the life-span of human beings. It was also Djo's role to clothe the other sky gods, making them invisible to man.

To each of their offspring, Mawu-Lisa then gave a special language. These are the languages still spoken by the priests and mediums of the gods in their songs and oracles. To Da Zodji and Nyohwè Ananu, Mawu-Lisa gave the language of the earth and took from them all memory of the sky language. They gave to Sogbo, Agbè and Naètè, Agè and Gu the languages they would speak. But to Djo, they gave the language of men.

Then Mawu-Lisa said to Legba: "Because you are my youngest child, I will keep you with me always. Your work will be to visit all the kingdoms ruled over by your brothers and sisters and report to me on their progress."

And that is why Legba knows all the languages of his siblings, and he alone knows the language of Mawu-Lisa. You will find Legba everywhere, because all beings, human and gods, must first approach Legba before Mawu-Lisa, the supreme deity, will answer their prayers.

God Abandons the Earth
(From Ghana)

IN THE BEGINNING, God was very proud of the human beings he had created and wanted to live as close as possible to them. So he made certain that the sky was low enough for the people to touch and built for himself a home directly above their heads. God was so near that everyone on earth became familiar with his face and every day he would stop to make conversation with the people, offering a helping hand if they were ever in trouble.

This arrangement worked very well at first, but soon God observed that the people had started to take advantage of his closeness. Children began to wipe their greasy hands on the sky when they had finished their meals and often, if a woman was in search of an extra ingredient for dinner, she would simply reach up, tear a piece off the sky and add it to her cooking pot. God remained tolerant through all of this, but he knew his patience would not last forever and hoped that his people would not test its limit much further.

Then one afternoon, just as he had lain down to rest, a group of women gathered underneath the sky to pound the corn they had harvested. One old woman among them had a particularly large wooden bowl and a very long pestle, and as she thumped down on the grains, she knocked violently against the sky. God arose indignantly from his bed and descended below, but as he approached the woman to chastise her, she suddenly jerked back her arm and hit him in the eye with her very long pestle.

God gave a great shout, his voice booming like thunder through the air, and as he shouted, he raised his powerful arms above his head and pushed upwards against the sky with all his strength, flinging it far into the distance.

As soon as they realized that the earth and the sky were separated, the people became angry with the old woman who had injured God and pestered her day and night to bring him back to them. The woman went away and although she was not very clever, she thought long and hard about the problem until she believed she had found the solution. Returning to her village, she ordered her children to collect all the wooden mortars that they could find. These she piled one on top of the other until they had almost bridged the gap between the earth and the heavens. Only one more mortar was needed to complete the job, but although her children searched high and low, they could not find the missing object. In desperation, the old woman told them to remove the lowest mortar from the bottom of the pile and place it on the top. But as soon as they did this, all the mortars came crashing down, killing the old woman, her children and the crowd who had gathered to admire the towering structure.

Ever since that day, God has remained in the heavens where mankind can no longer approach him as easily as before. There are some, however, who say they have caught a glimpse of him and others who offer up sacrifices calling for his forgiveness and asking him to make his home among them once more.

The Coming of Darkness
(From the Kono people, Sierra Leone)

WHEN GOD FIRST MADE THE WORLD, there was never any darkness or cold. The sun always shone brightly during the day, and at night, the moon bathed the earth in a softer light, ensuring that everything could still be seen quite clearly.

But one day God sent for the Bat and handed him a mysterious parcel to take to the moon. He told the Bat it contained darkness, but as he did not have the time to explain precisely what darkness was, the Bat went on his way without fully realizing the importance of his mission.

He flew at a leisurely pace with the parcel strapped on his back until he began to feel rather tired and hungry. He was in no great hurry he decided, and so he put down his load by the roadside and wandered off in search of something to eat.

But while he was away, a group of mischievous animals approached the spot where he had paused to rest and, seeing the parcel, began to open it, thinking there might be something of value inside of it. The Bat returned just as they were untying the last piece of string and rushed forward to stop them. But too late! The darkness forced its way through the opening and rose up into the sky before anyone had a chance to catch it.

Quickly the Bat gave chase, flying about everywhere, trying to grab hold of the darkness and return it to the parcel before God discovered what had happened. But the harder he tried, the more the darkness eluded him, so that eventually he fell into an exhausted sleep lasting several hours.

When the Bat awoke, he found himself in a strange twilight world and once again, he began chasing about in every direction, hoping he would succeed where he had failed before.

But the Bat has never managed to catch the darkness, although you will see him every evening just after the sun has set, trying to trap it and deliver it safely to the moon as God first commanded him.

Why the Moon and the Stars Receive Their Light from the Sun
(From the Akan peoples, Ghana)

ONCE UPON A TIME there was great scarcity of food in the land. Father Anansi and his son, Kweku Tsin, being very hungry, set out one morning to hunt in the forest. In a short time Kweku Tsin was fortunate enough to kill a fine deer – which he carried to his father at their resting-place. Anansi was very glad to see such a supply of food, and requested his son to remain there on guard, while he went for a large basket in which to carry it home. An hour or so passed without his return, and Kweku Tsin became anxious. Fearing lest his father had lost his way, he called out loudly, "Father, father!" to guide him to the spot. To his joy he heard a voice reply, "Yes, my son," and immediately he shouted again, thinking it was Anansi. Instead of the latter, however, a terrible dragon appeared. This monster breathed fire from his great nostrils, and was altogether a dreadful sight to behold. Kweku Tsin was terrified at his approach and speedily hid himself in a cave near by.

The dragon arrived at the resting-place, and was much annoyed to find only the deer's body. He vented his anger in blows upon the latter and went away. Soon after, Father Anansi made his appearance. He was greatly interested in his son's tale, and wished to see the dragon for himself. He soon had his desire, for the monster, smelling human flesh, hastily returned to the spot and seized them both. They were carried off by him to his castle, where they found many other unfortunate creatures also awaiting their fate. All were left in charge of the dragon's servant – a fine, white cock – which always crowed to summon his master, if anything unusual happened in the latter's absence. The dragon then went off in search of more prey.

Kweku Tsin now summoned all his fellow-prisoners together, to arrange a way of escape. All feared to run away – because of the wonderful powers of the monster. His eyesight was so keen that he could detect a fly moving miles away. Not only that, but he could move over the ground so swiftly that none could outdistance him. Kweku Tsin, however, being exceedingly clever, soon thought of a plan.

Knowing that the white cock would not crow as long as he has grains of rice to pick up, Kweku scattered on the ground the contents of forty bags of grain which were stored in the great hall. While the cock was thus busily engaged, Kweku Tsin ordered the spinners to spin fine hempen ropes, to make a strong rope ladder. One end of this he intended to throw up to heaven, trusting that the gods would catch it and hold it fast, while he and his fellow-prisoners mounted.

While the ladder was being made, the men killed and ate all the cattle they needed – reserving all the bones for Kweku Tsin at his express desire. When all was ready the young man gathered the bones into a great sack. He also procured the dragon's fiddle and placed it by his side.

Everything was now ready. Kweku Tsin threw one end of the ladder up to the sky. It was caught and held. The dragon's victims began to mount, one after the other, Kweku remaining at the bottom.

By this time, however, the monster's powerful eyesight showed him that something unusual was happening at his abode. He hastened his return. On seeing his approach, Kweku Tsin also mounted the ladder – with the bag of bones on his back, and the fiddle under his arm. The dragon began to climb after him. Each time the monster came too near the young man threw him a bone, with which, being very hungry, he was obliged to descend to the ground to eat.

Kweku Tsin repeated this performance till all the bones were gone, by which time the people were safely up in the heavens. Then he mounted himself, as rapidly as possible, stopping every now and then to play a tune on the wonderful fiddle. Each time he did this, the dragon had to return to earth, to dance – as he could not resist the magic music. When Kweku was quite close to the top, the dragon had very nearly reached him again. The brave youth bent down and cut the ladder away below his own feet. The dragon was dashed to the ground but Kweku was pulled up into safety by the gods.

The latter were so pleased with his wisdom and bravery in giving freedom to his fellowmen, that they made him the sun the source of all light and heat to the world. His father, Anansi, became the moon, and his friends the stars. Thereafter, it was Kweku Tsin's privilege to supply all these with light, each being dull and powerless without him.

How the Moon First Came into the Sky
(By Okun Asere of Mfamosing, of the Ekoi people, Nigeria and Cameroon)

IN A CERTAIN TOWN there lived Njomm Mbui (Juju sheep). He made great friends with Etuk (antelope), whose home was in the "bush."

When the two animals grew up they went out and cut farms. Njomm planted plantains in his, while Etuk set his with coco-yams.

When the time came round for the fruits to ripen, Njomm went to his farm and cut a bunch of plantains, while Etuk dug up some of his coco.

Each cleaned his food and put it in the pot to cook. When all was ready they sat down and ate.

Next morning Etuk said, "Let us change. I saw a bunch of plantains in your farm which I would like to get. Will you go instead to mine and take some coco?"

This was arranged, and Etuk said to Njomm, "Try to beat up fu-fu." Njomm tried, and found it very good. He gave some to Etuk. The latter ate all he wanted, then took the bunch of plantains and hung it up in his house.

Next morning he found that the fruit had grown soft, so he did not care to eat it. He therefore took the plantains and threw them away in the bush.

During the day Mbui came along and smelt plantains. He looked round till he found them, then picked up one and began to eat. They were very sweet. He ate his fill, then went on, and later met a crowd of the Nshum people (apes). To them he said, "To-day I found a very sweet thing in the bush."

In course of time Etuk grew hungry again, and Njomm said to him, "If you are hungry, why don't you tell me?"

He went to his farm and got four bunches of plantains. As he came back he met the monkey people. They begged for some of his fruit, so he gave it to them.

After they had eaten all there was, they in their turn went on, and met a herd of wild boars (Ngumi). To these they said, "There is very fine food to be got from Njomm and Etuk."

The Ngumi therefore came and questioned Etuk, "Where is coco to be had?" and Etuk answered, "The coco belongs to me."

The boars begged for some, so Etuk took a basket, filled it at his farm, and gave it to them.

After they were satisfied, they went on their way and next morning met Njokk (elephant).

To him they said, "Greetings, Lord! Last night we got very good food from the farms over there."

Njokk at once ran and asked the two friends, "Whence do you get so much food?" They said, "Wait a little."

Njomm took his long matchet and went to his farm. He cut five great bunches of plantains and carried them back. Etuk also got five baskets full of coco, which he brought to

Elephant. After the latter had eaten all this, he thanked them and went away.

All the bush-beasts came in their turn and begged for food, and to each the two friends gave willingly of all that they had. Lastly also came Mfong (Bush-cow).

Now not far from the two farms there was a great river called Akarram (the One which goes round). In the midst of it, deep down, dwelt Crocodile. One day Mfong went down into the water to drink, and from him crocodile learned that much food was to be had near by.

On this crocodile came out of the water and began walking towards the farms. He went to Njomm and Etuk and said:

"I am dying of hunger, pray give me food."

Etuk said, "To the beasts who are my friends I will give all I have, but to you I will give nothing, for you are no friend of mine; "but Njomm said:

"I do not like you very much, yet I will give you one bunch of plantains."

Crocodile took them and said, "Do not close your door to-night when you lie down to sleep. I will come back and buy more food from you at a great price."

He then went back to the water and sought out a python, which dwelt there. To the latter he said:

"I have found two men on land, who have much food." Python said, "I too am hungry. Will you give me to eat?"

So crocodile gave him some of the plantains which he had brought. When Python had tasted he said, "How sweet it is! Will you go back again and bring more?" Crocodile said, "Will you give me something with which to buy?" and Python answered, "Yes. I will give you something with which you can buy the whole farm."

On this he took from within his head a shining stone and gave it to crocodile. The latter started to go back to the farm. As he went, night fell and all the road grew dark, but he held in his jaws the shining stone, and it made a light on his path, so that all the way was bright. When he neared the dwelling of the two friends he hid the stone and called:

"Come out and I will show you something which I have brought."

It was very dark when they came to speak with him. Slowly the crocodile opened his claws, in which he held up the stone, and it began to glimmer between them. When he held it right out, the whole place became so bright that one could see to pick up a needle or any small thing. He said, "The price of this that I bring is one whole farm."

Etuk said, "I cannot buy. If I give my farm, nothing remains to me. What is the use of this great shining stone if I starve to death?" But Njomm said, "I will buy – oh, I will buy, for my farm full of plantains, for that which you bring fills the whole earth with light. Come let us go. I will show you my farm. From here to the water-side all round is my farm. Take it all, and do what you choose with it, only give me the great shining stone that, when darkness falls, the whole earth may still be light."

Crocodile said, "I agree."

Then Njomm went to his house with the stone, and Etuk went to his. Njomm placed it above the lintel, that it might shine for all the world; but Etuk closed his door and lay down to sleep.

In the morning Njomm was very hungry, but he had nothing to eat, because he had sold all his farm for the great white stone.

Next night and the night after he slept full of hunger, but on the third morning he went to Etuk and asked, "Will you give me a single coco-yam?" Etuk answered:

"I can give you nothing, for now you have nothing to give in exchange. It was not I who told you to buy the shining thing. To give something, when plenty remains, is good; but none but a fool would give his all, that a light may shine in the dark!"

Njomm was very sad. He said, "I have done nothing bad. Formerly no one could see in the night time. Now the python stone shines so that everyone can see to go wherever he chooses."

All that day Njomm still endured, though nearly dying of hunger, and at night time he crept down to the water, very weak and faint.

By the river-side he saw a palm tree, and on it a man trying to cut down clusters of ripe kernels; but this was hard to do, because it had grown very dark.

Njomm said, "Who is there?" and the man answered, "I am Effion Obassi."

The second time Njomm called, "What are you doing?" and EfBon replied:

"I am trying to gather palm kernels, but I cannot do so, for it is very dark amid these great leaves."

Njomm said to him, "It is useless to try to do such a thing in the dark. Are you blind?"

Effion answered, "I am not blind. Why do you ask?"

Then Njomm said, "Good; if you are not blind, I beg you to throw me down only one or two palm kernels, and in return I will show you a thing more bright and glorious than any you have seen before."

Effion replied, "Wait a minute, and I will try to throw a few down to you. Afterwards you shall show me the shining thing as you said."

He then threw down three palm kernels, which Njomm took, and stayed his hunger a little. The latter then called, "Please try to climb down. We will go together to my house."

Effion tried hard, and after some time he stood safely at the foot of the tree by the side of Njomm.

So soon as they got to his house, Njomm said, "Will you wait here a little while I go to question the townspeople?"

First he went to Etuk and asked, "Will you not give me a single coco to eat? See, the thing which I bought at the price of all that I had turns darkness to light for you, but for me, I die of hunger."

Etuk said, "I will give you nothing. Take back the thing for which you sold your all, and we will stay in our darkness as before."

Then Njomm begged of all the townsfolk that they would give him ever so little food in return for the light he had bought for them. Yet they all refused.

So Njomm went back to his house and took the shining stone, and gave it to Effion Obassi, saying:

"I love the earth folk, but they love not me. Now take the shining thing for which I gave my whole possessions. Go back to the place whence you came, for I know that you belong to the sky people, but when you reach your home in the heavens, hang up my stone in a place where all the earth folk may see its shining, and be glad."

Then Effion took the stone, and went back by the road he had come. He climbed up the palm tree, and the great leaves raised themselves upwards, pointing to the sky, and lifted him, till, from their points, he could climb into heaven.

When he reached his home, he sent and called all the Lords of the Sky and said, "I have brought back a thing to-day which can shine so that all the earth will be light. From now on everyone on earth or in heaven will be able to see at the darkest hour of the night."

The chiefs looked at the stone and wondered. Then they consulted together, and made a box. Effion said, "Make it so that the stone can shine out only from one side."

When the box was finished, he set the globe of fire within, and said, "Behold the stone is mine. From this time all the people must bring me food. I will no longer go to seek any for myself."

For some time they brought him plenty, but after a while they grew tired. Then Effion covered the side of the box, so that the stone could not shine till they brought him more. That is the reason why the moon is sometimes dark, and people on earth say "It is the end of the month. The sky people have grown weary of bringing food to Effion Obassi, and he will not let his stone shine out till they bring a fresh supply."

How All the Stars Came
(By Okun Asere of Mfamosing, of the Ekoi people, Nigeria and Cameroon)

EBOPP (THE LEMUR) and Mbawf (the Dormouse) were making a tour in the bush. They looked for a good place to cut farm. When one was found they cut down the trees, and took two days to clear enough ground. After this they went back to the town where the other animals were living. Next morning Ebopp said, "Let us go back to our new farms and build a small house." This they did. Ebopp made bis, and Mbaw his.

Now before a new town is begun, a little shed called Ekpa Ntan (House without Walls) is made where the Egbo house is to stand. Ebopp and Mbaw accordingly set to work and built an Ekpa Ntan. Then they went back to their old town and rested for two days.

On the third day they went to work again. Ebopp worked on his farm, Mbaw on his. That night they slept in the huts they had built, and at dawn started to work once more. When night came, Ebopp lighted a lamp and said, "I do not want to sleep here. If we sleep here we shall sleep hungry. Let us go back to our old town."

When they got there their wives cooked for them. Ebopp said to Mbaw, "Come and join together with me in eating." So his friend came and ate with him.

Afterwards Mbaw said, "Let us go to my house and have food too." So they went thither.

After they had eaten up all that Mbaw had cooked, Ebopp went home.

Next morning he went to call his friend and said, "Go and get young plantains to plant in the farm." Both of them collected a great basket full of these, and went to the place where the new farms were; Ebopp to his, and Mbaw to his.

Both worked hard. At midday Ebopp said, "Let us rest a little while, and eat the food we have brought." To this Mbaw agreed, but after some time they set to work again.

About five o'clock Ebopp called, "Let us go back now to the old town, for it is very far off."

So they left off working and went back, but before they could get there night fell.

Next morning they took more young plantains, and again worked hard all day. When it was time to go back, Ebopp, asked, "How many remain to plant of the young plantains?" Mbaw answered "About forty." On which Ebopp said, "Of mine also there remain about forty."

At dawn next day they went to their old farms to get some more plantain cuttings. Then they went on to the new farms and began planting. So soon as he had finished, Ebopp said "I have finished mine." To which Mbaw replied, "Mine also are finished."

Ebopp said, "My work is done, I need only come here for the hunting."

Then they both went back to the old town and told their wives:

"We have finished setting the plantains. We hope that you will go and plant coco-yams to-morrow. Try, both of you, to get baskets full of coco-yams for the planting."

To this the women agreed, and when they had collected as many as were necessary they set out for the new farms.

When they arrived, Mbaw's wife asked the wife of Ebopp, "Do you think we can finish planting all these to-day?" Ebopp's wife answered, "Yes, we can do it."

All day they worked hard, and at night went home and said, "We have finished planting all the coco-yams." Ebopp said, "Good, you have done well."

Now his wife's name was Akpan Anwan (Akpan means first-born). She and her sister Akandem were the daughters of Obassi Osaw. When she got home she started to cook the evening meal for her husband. When it was ready she placed it upon the table, set water also in a cup, and laid spoons near by.

They were eating together when a slave named Umaw ran in. He had just come from the town of Obassi Osaw. He said, "I would speak to Ebopp alone." When Akpan Anwan had left the room, the messenger said, "You are eating, but I bring you news that Akandem is dead."

Ebopp called out aloud in his grief, and sent a messenger to call his friend Mbaw.

So soon as the latter heard he came running and said, "What can we do? We are planting new farms and beginning to build a new town. There is hardly any food to be got. How then can we properly hold the funeral customs?"

Ebopp said, "Nevertheless, I must try my best." When Umaw got ready to return, Ebopp said:

"Say to Obassi Osaw 'Wait for me for six days, then I will surely come.'"

Next morning he said to Mbaw, "Come now, let us do our utmost to collect what is necessary for the rites of my sister-in-law."

They went round the town and bought all the food which they could find. Then Ebopp went back and said to his wife, "I did not wish to tell you before about the death of your sister, but to-day I must tell you. Get ready. In five days' time I will take you back to your Father's town to hold the funeral feast."

Akpan Anwan was very grieved to hear of this and wept. Ebopp said to Mbaw, "We must get palm wine for the feast, also rum for libations. How can we get these? I have no money and you also have none." Mbaw said, "Go round among the townsfolk and see if any of them will lend you some."

Ebopp said "Good," and began to walk up and down, begging from all his friends, but none would give to him, though it was a big town. At last he went down to the place where they were making palm oil by the river. Near to this lived Iku (Water Chevrotain). Ebopp told his trouble and begged help, but Iku said, "I am very sorry for you, but I have nothing to give."

Ebopp was quite discouraged by now, and turned to go away full of sorrow. When Iku saw this he said, "Wait a minute, there is one thing I can do. You know that I have the 'four eyes.' I will give you two, and with them you can buy all that you need."

From out of his head he took the two eyes with which he used to see in the dark. They shone so brightly that Ebopp knew they were worth a great price. He took them home and showed them to his wife and his friend Mbaw.

The latter said, "From to-day you are freed from all anxiety. With those you can buy all that is needed."

Next morning they gathered together all that had been collected, the plantains and the two shining eyes. Ebopp, Mbaw and Akpan carried the loads between them. They set out for the dwelling-place of Obassi Osaw.

When they got to the entrance of the town, Akpan Anwan began to weep bitterly. She threw down her burden, and ran to the spot where her sister lay buried. Then she lay down on the grave and would not rise again.

Ebopp carried his own load into the house where the dead woman had dwelt. Then he went back and got his wife's load which she had left behind.

The townsfolk said to Ebopp, "You have come to keep your sister-in-law's funeral customs to-day. Bring palm wine. Bring rum also for the libations, and let us hold the feast."

Ebopp said, "I have brought nothing but plantains. All else that is necessary I mean to buy here."

Now there was a famine in Obassi Osaw's town, so Ebopp put all his plantains in the Egbo house. Next day he sent to Obassi Osaw to bring his people, so that the food might be divided among them. Each man got one.

Then Osaw said, "All that you brought is eaten. If you can give us no more, you shall not take my daughter back with you to your country."

Ebopp went to find his friend, and told him what Obassi had said.

"Shall I sell the two eyes?" he asked. "They are worth hundreds and hundreds of plantains, and many pieces of cloth, but if I sell them now, the people are so hungry, they will only give a small price."

Mbaw said, "Do not mind. See, I will teach you how to get more sense."

"You hold one in your hand, and it is a big thing like a great shining stone, but if you put it in a mortar and grind it down, it will become, not one, but many, and some of the small pieces you can sell."

This Ebopp did, and ground up the great bright stones which had been Iku's eyes till they became like shining sand.

Then they went and got a black cap, which they filled with the fragments.

Mbaw said, "Now go and look round the town till you find someone who can sell what we need."

Ebopp did so, and in the house of Effion Obassi he saw great stores hidden – food and palm wine, palm oil in jars, and rum for the sacrifice.

Ebopp said to Effion, "If you will sell all this to me I will give you in exchange something which will make all the townsfolk bow down before you."

Effion said, "I will not sell all, but half of what I have I will sell you."

So Ebopp said, "Very well. I will take what you give me, only do not open the thing I shall leave in exchange till I have got back to my own country.

When you do open it, as I said before, all the townsfolk will bow down before you."

So the funeral feast was made, and the people were satisfied.

When the rites were finished, Obassi said, "It is good. You can go away now with your wife."

So Ebopp said to Mbaw and Akpan An wan, "Come, let us go back to our own town. We must not sleep here to-night."

When they had reached home once more, Ebopp sent a slave named Edet to Effion Obassi with the message:

"You can open the cap now. I have reached my town again." It was evening time, but Effion at once sent to call the townspeople and said, "I have a thing here which is worth a great price." They cried, "Let us see it." He answered, "My thing is a very good thing, such as you have never seen before."

He brought the cap outside and opened it before them. All the shining things fell out. As they fell a strong breeze came and caught them and blew them all over the town. They lay on the roads and on the floors of the compounds, each like a little star.

All the children came round and began picking them up. They gathered and gathered. In the daytime they could not see them, but every night they went out and sought for the shining things. Each one that they picked up they put in a box. At length many had been got together and shone like a little sun in the box. At the end of about a month nearly all had been collected. They could not shut down the lid, however, because the box was too full, so when a great breeze came by it blew all the shining things about again. That is why sometimes we have a small moon and plenty of stars shining round it, while sometimes we have a big moon and hardly any stars are to be seen. The children take a month to fill the box again.

When the sparkles were scattered about the town, Effion sent a messenger to Ebopp to ask, "Can you see the things shining from your town?"

At that time earth and sky were all joined together, like a house with an upstairs.

Ebopp went out and looked upward to the blue roof overhead. There he saw the small things sparkling in the darkness.

Next day he went to Iku and said:

"Will you please go into a deep hole? I want to look at your eyes."

Iku went inside the hole. Ebopp looked at his eyes. They were very bright, just like the sparkles which shone in the sky.

The cause of all the stars is therefore Ebopp, who took Iku's eyes to Obassi's town.

Iku's eyes are like the stars.

The moon shines when all the fragments are gathered together. When he shines most brightly it is because the children have picked up nearly all the fragments and put them into the box.

How the Two Biggest Stars
Came into the Sky
(From the Ekoi people, Nigeria and Cameroon)

O BASSI OSAW had three sons. Two of these he loved, but Ndifemm, the third, he did not love. One day the three brothers went out to see what had been caught in the traps they had set. The two favourite sons found nothing, but Ndifemm found an animal in each of his six traps. Four of the beasts he "dashed" between his two brothers, and the other two he took home to his father. Obassi refused them, but accepted from his other two sons those which Ndifemm had given them.

Another day Obassi ordered his three children each to dig a hole. They did so. He went and examined the work, and said "I find the two holes well done," but to Ndifemm he said, "Your hole is not deep enough."

The boy began to dig deeper, but one of his brothers went to him very softly and said, "Our father is attempting to kill you. Will you go to consult the charm? That will tell you what you should do."

Ndifemm, therefore, went to Nyopp (Porcupine) and asked him to practise the charm.

Nyopp said, u Go and bring me a piece of yam and some palm oil."

Ndifemm fetched these and gave them to Porcupine. The latter practised the charm, and told him, "Go and ask the Dassie to dig a run from your mother's house to the hole you have made."

When all this was done, Obassi sent one day and said, "Go down into the hole you have dug."

Ndifemm obeyed, but so soon as he reached the bottom he passed through the little tunnel and reached his mother's house. Next Obassi ordered the people to throw stones into the hole. The pit was soon filled up by these, but Ndifemm was there no longer. After a time Obassi began to cry out for the mourning of his son, and called all the people together to make a great play for Ndifemm's death.

On hearing this, the mother sent to her husband and said, "The Juju image will now come out." She dressed her son in the Egbo robes and took him before Obassi. Then she showed him that it was his own son whom he had thought dead. At that the father remained full of vexation.

One day Obassi called to his unloved son, and said, "Go to Nsann (the Thunder town) and bring me my cow from thence."

Ndifemm went to his mother and told her of this new order. She took a horn, and gave to her son saying, "When you get to Nsann town take this and blow upon it. You will see cows standing under a tree. When one answers the sound of the horn you will know that that is the very one for which your father sent you."

Ndifemm set forth, and did all that she had said. In a few days he brought back the cow to his father.

Obassi thought within himself, "I sent this boy to Nsann town that he might die, but he has returned home full of life." He therefore took thought for a way in which he might surely kill his son.

Ndifemm saw that his father's heart was steadfastly set against him, so he went to his mother and said:

"I know that it is my time to die. Will you die with me?"

The woman answered, "My husband loves me no more. In this world I have no one but you, therefore if you die I will die also."

Then, by cunning, Ndifemm made a hole in his father's eyes while the latter slept, and entered into them with his mother.

There they both died, and became stars in the sky.

Obassi opened his eyes, which are the heavens, and there they shone! Those are the two biggest stars which you see in the sky. They are Ndifemm, son of Obassi, and his mother.

How the Sun Came into the Sky

(By Okun Asere of Mfamosing, of the Ekoi people, Nigeria and Cameroon)

ONCE THERE LIVED a man named Agbo and his wife named Nchun. They had a daughter called Afion. When the latter was about fifteen years old, her father and mother agreed that it was time to put her in the fatting-house. So they sent for an old woman named Umaw, who was very wise in such matters, and told her to prepare everything. She came and made all ready, and then said, "There is nothing more to be done. I will go back to my own place."

The parents "dashed" her two bottles of palm oil and two pieces of dried meat. To the townsfolk also the father gave many demi-johns of palm wine. He took ten pieces of dried meat, cooked them and called all the people to a feast, because his daughter had entered the fatting-house that day.

After about four months the mother, Nchun, said to Afion, "You have stayed long enough. You may come out to-morrow."

Then the father got together several demi-johns of palm wine, the kind that is drawn from the tops of the palm trees, and five pieces of dried meat. The mother also took the same amount of meat and drink. The father announced to the townsfolk:

"My daughter is going to clean her face to-morrow. Let all men stay in the town." Next morning the parents cooked ten calabashes full of chop for the people, who feasted all that day.

In the evening the father took his daughter into the other part of the house, and said to her, "To-day you have cleaned your face. From to-day if a man should call you into his house you can go."

Next morning the mother cooked for the girl. Then the parents went to their farm and left her with a small boy who was as yet too young to work.

Now at that time Eyo (the Sun) dwelt upon earth, in the place that lies towards the great water. His body was redder than fire. He was very tall and thin. He lay in the bush, so that all his body up to the waist was hidden by the bush trees, but he stretched out his head and arms right into the room where the fatting-girl was. He said to her:

"I want to keep sweethearts with you," but she answered:

"You are so tall, your head, hands and arms alone fill my room. I cannot keep friends with you."

When he heard this the Sun was very angry, and said, "If you are not willing to become my sweetheart I will take my length away, but first I will kill you and leave you here."

Anon said to him:

"I do not care so much if you kill me. I would rather die than wed such a terrible being as you."

As soon as Eyo heard this he stretched out his hands, and killed her for true.

All this time the small boy had hidden himself where he could see everything that happened. He watched the terrible visitor draw the body into the middle room. Next he saw him go into the inner place where Nchun kept the fine mats. He took four of these and covered the fatting-girl. Next he went into another place where the fine cloths were kept. Of these again he took four, with four blankets and two small loin cloths. All these he laid over the dead girl.

After this Eyo left the house and stood in the little courtyard at the back. He began to lift his body up to the sky. He was so long that, though he tried all day, six o'clock in the evening was come and he had not quite finished. Some of him was in the sky and some still stayed upon earth.

When Agbo and Nchun came back from their farm, the small boy crept out from his hiding place, and said to them:

"The man who killed your daughter is a very tall man."

Father and mother began to weep. They took the body and called all the townsfolk together for the burial.

The people came with four guns. They wished to shoot the man who had killed the fatting-girl. At the back of the house they found him. They could not see all his body, but the feet only. With their four guns they shot at these. Then he gave a great spring and drew his feet up, after the rest of him, into the sky.

A fine house was standing there ready. Eyo entered and closed the door that he might be safe from the guns of the townsmen. In the morning, about six o'clock, he opened a window, and looked out a little way, very cautiously. When no one shot at him, he felt safer, and put his face right out. All day he looked down in case Anon should not be dead and he might see her once more. The people were busy away at their farms. At six o'clock they came back, so he drew in his face again, lest they should begin to shoot once more.

That is the reason why you only see the sun in the daytime. In the evening he draws back into his house and shuts the windows and doors.

How Sun and Moon Went up to the Sky
(By Ite Okonni of Akingrom, of the Ekoi people, Nigeria and Cameroon)

OBASSI NSI had three sons, named Eyo (Sun), Ejirum (Darkness), and 'Mi (Moon). The first two he loved, but the last he did not love. One day Nsi called to 'Mi and said:

"Go into the bush, catch a leopard, and bring him to me."

'Mi went sadly away, and as he reached the outskirts of the town began to weep. A man named Isse saw him and called "What is the matter?" 'Mi answered, "My father does not love me, and is sending me to catch a leopard in the bush, in order to destroy me."

The man said "Take comfort; I will give you a 'medicine 'which will make you successful." He went away, but soon returned with what he had promised, and rubbed the "medicine" on the boy's hands.

'Mi went into the bush, and almost at once saw a leopard lying down asleep. He cut strong lianes, and tied up the beast, so that it could not move, then dragged it along till he reached home once more, and stood before his father.

45

Nsi was astonished, but concealed his vexation, and said in a cunning way, "This my son is indeed a good son because he has done this thing."

Some time afterwards Nsi married another wife. Obassi Osaw came down to the wedding feast with his sons and daughters and a great retinue of sky people. These started to play with the earthfolk, who had also gathered together for the festival. After a while they took a cloth and tied it up in a bundle. To this a rope was fastened, and one of Nsi's sons caught the end, and began to draw it along the ground. All got sticks and tried to hit the bundle as it was dragged hither and thither. Ejirum also tried to hit it, but a splinter sprang from his stick as it struck the ground, and wounded the eye of one of Osaw's sons, so that the latter was blinded.

Osaw was angry, and said, "I myself will blind the eyes of Obassi Nsi."

The townspeople crowded round, and begged him to show mercy, but he would not relent. So they took Nsi and hid him away, where Osaw could not find him. After the latter had searched in vain he was still angry, and said:

"Now I am going back to my town, but Nsi will not escape me."

After two days he sent down ten men to fetch Obassi Nsi. They said, "We have been sent to bring you up," but the townsfolk said, "Here are great gifts of cows, bulls, and goats. Take them before your master, and perhaps he will not be angry any more."

When the men returned to the sky they said, "Here is a message from Obassi Nsi. He wants to beg you very much. He says, "It was not I who told anyone to hurt your son's eye.""

Osaw would not listen, but sent down three other men, and said:

"Even if you yourself did not break my son's eye yet you must come up to me."

When Nsi heard this, he called his people together. To his son Eyo (Sun) he said:

"Here are forty pieces of cloth. Will you take them to Osaw and beg him for me?"

Eyo started on his journey, and had reached about half way when he saw five beautiful women standing at the entrance to a town. No sooner had he seen them, than he forgot all about his errand, and began to sell the cloth for plantains, palm oil and palm wine, with which he made a feast for the beautiful women. There he stayed for some weeks, then took what was left of the goods and went on a little further till he came to another town, where he found two more women, as beautiful as the first. For four years he stayed at one or other of the towns, journeying to and fro between them.

After four years, when Nsi found that Eyo did not come back nor send any message, he called to his son 'Mi and said:

"The case which I have before Obassi Osaw has taken a long time to finish. Go to Nsann (Thunder town) and fetch hence a cow which you will find. When you have brought it away take it as a gift to Obassi Osaw, and settle my case for me."

'Mi answered, "Very well;" and his mother called to him, and said:

"Do what you can for your father, who is guiltless as to Obassi Osaw, but take care for yourself when you reach Nsann town. Let no one know the place where you sleep, lest you should perish in the night time."

'Mi answered, "I will do what I can."

Next morning he set forth, and before evening had reached Nsann. The people asked him:

"Where will you sleep to-night?" He answered, "I will sleep among the goats." When all was still he left the goat pen in the darkness, and went to the Egbo house, where he lay down and slept.

At midnight a thunderbolt struck the shed where the goats were herded, and killed them all.

Early in the morning the people came together and opened the door. When they saw the dead goats, but could not find the boy they were much astonished. As they stood wondering 'Mi came forward and said:

"If I were not a smart boy, the bolt would have killed me. As it is, I have saved myself."

Everybody in the town was sorry for the lad, and said "Let us give him the cow to take to his father." So the boy set out homeward, well content.

When 'Mi reached his father's house and led the cow before him, Nsi said, very softly to himself, so that he thought no one could hear:

"What can I do to kill this son of mine?"

'Mi heard, and next morning took the gun which his mother had given him, and went into the bush to hunt. First he shot Ise, the little grey duiker, and next Ngumi (the wild boar). These he carried home, and brought before his father, but the latter said:

"I will not eat of them."

So 'Mi took his kill away sadly, and gave it to his mother.

The woman cooked the meat in a delicate way, and then took it to her husband, who ate gladly of what he had before refused; but when he learned what she had done, he said:

"From to-day take your son away from here. Neither of you shall live in my town any more."

When 'Mi learned this he also was very angry. He took his gun and his matchet and went to find his friend Isse, who had given him the "leopard medicine "years before. To his grief he heard that this good friend had died while he himself was away at Nsann. So he went sadly out into the bush to hunt, that his mother might not starve. After a while he saw an Ikomme (squirrel) standing between the thick branches. He raised his gun to shoot, but in a moment all the place grew dark. A voice called behind him out of the darkness, "'Mi 'Mi," and he answered, "Who calls?" The voice cried, "I am your dead friend. Tell me, now, which do you choose, to die or to live?" 'Mi answered, "I am willing to die. Why should I live when my father seeks to kill me?"

After he had spoken, a deep sleep fell upon him. When he awoke the whole place was clear of trees. The sun was shining brightly, and before him stood a long table, on which were set dried meat, biscuits, rum, and palm wine, and all kinds of gin. Then he saw Isse walking up and down as in life, and directing everything, while many people were busily working round about.

They worked hard, and as they worked more and more men came out of the bush, till in a little space the whole house was finished. Then Isse said:

"This is your house, and all these are your people. Now, your father's case is a very long one. I will give you goods so that you may go and arrange it."

'Mi agreed, and next morning called together seven companions. He gave them that Isse had provided, many heads of tobacco, and countless demi-johns of palm wine.

Then 'Mi himself set out at their head for Obassi's town.

When he reached the entrance he called a meeting of the townsfolk, and said to them:

"I have come to try to settle my father's case, which has already been a very long one. I wish to hear from you how many goods I must pay."

The people said, "Let us see what you have brought."

So he showed them all, and they went before Obassi and begged him to take the gifts in payment, and settle the affair. Obassi answered, "Good. I accept what you have brought. The case is finished."

Then 'Mi went back to his father's town to fetch his mother. He met her wandering about at the entrance to the town, and was about to lead her away, when Nsi himself came by.

"Whither are you going?" he asked.

'Mi answered, "I am leading my mother away to my own town, which is a long way from here, and is full of rich things."

On hearing this Nsi said, "I should like to see So he followed his outcast wife and son till they came to that part of the bush where the new town stood.

Nsi was amazed at what he saw, and still more so when he found that 'Mi had been to Obassi Osaw and arranged his case. On this he sent a great company of men to seize Eyo and bring the latter before him. When they returned Nsi called both his sons, and said:

"From to-day you, Eyo, are my unloved son. You are too hot; no one will like you any more. You are careless sometimes, and burn up all tender plants in the farms." But to 'Mi he said:

"You, 'Mi, are my good son. In the night you can shine softly, so that men may see to walk safely when they are away from home."

When Eyo heard this he thought, "Now my father will hate me as he used to hate 'Mi. Perhaps he will try to kill me also. I will not stay here on earth, but will go up to the sky to Osaw."

'Mi also thought, "Perhaps my father is deceiving me, or, at at any rate, he may grow to hate me again. It is better to go up to the sky and stay with Obassi Osaw. From thence I can see what passes both in his land and in that of my father. Also I can shine the brighter on high, so that heaven and earth will be full of my light." Thus Nsi lost both of these sons, and remained on earth alone with his third boy, Ejirum (Darkness).

Why the Sunset Is Sometimes Red and Stormy
(From the Ekoi people, Nigeria and Cameroon)

IN THE BEGINNING of things, Obassi Osaw and Obassi Nsi lived in towns some distance apart. The former had no sons, but the latter had three. The first of them was a great thief, the second was the same, and when they stole anything their Father had to pay for it.

Now Obassi had great farms and plantations outside the town. Sometimes cows ate his yams; so one day he came home and put powder in his gun but no shot, meaning to frighten the beasts away next time they came. During his absence the two bad sons went and put shot in the gun. So when he fired at the cows one of them died.

Obassi Nsi cried out, and went back to the town. When he reached it he told the owner, "I shot your cow by accident; "but the man replied:

"Then I must kill you, just the same as my cow."

A meeting was held, and the townsfolk begged the man to accept another cow in exchange for the one he had lost, but he refused to do so, and still said that Obassi must die.

Next morning, therefore, Obassi said to his third son, "I have to die to-day; "but the latter cried:

"How can you die. First son and second son are fully grown, but I am still small. Do not leave me till I am grown up."

Obassi said, "Here is a key. The room to which it belongs shall be your own, so that you have somewhere to run to, and be safe from your brothers."

In the evening he called the boy again, and said:

"Do no evil thing in the town, and when I am dead kill a cow and give it to the people." That night he died.

The third son killed the cow as he had been bidden, but the first and second sons were very angry, and beat him, and said, "The cow belonged to us." They took away the key of his room, so that small boy had nowhere to go, and they seized all the goods for themselves, so he was left penniless. After that they went away from their father's land.

The boy went out sadly and walked through the town. He met an old woman, who asked "Whither are you going?" He said, "I am the small son of Obassi Nsi, and I have nowhere to go."

The old woman answered, "Do not trouble. Stay here with me," and to this the boy agreed. One day he found an old knife in the ground; this he cleaned and sharpened till it became all right again. Next morning he went to the bush and set native traps. In one of these he caught an Iku (water chevrotain), which he brought home and gave to the old woman. She said, "I cannot eat this meat; perhaps you have stolen it; "but he answered, "No, I will take you to the place where the traps are set." She went with him, and saw that it was as he had said; so agreed to eat the meat.

Next morning the boy said, "I wish to go and clear my farm." When he got to the plantation he saw some slaves of Obassi Osaw coming towards him. When they arrived they said:

"We have come to take charge of the goods of Obassi Nsi." On this the boy answered, "They are not in my hands. First and second sons have taken everything." So the men returned empty-handed.

Next day six more came and asked the same thing, but the lad said, "Wait a minute and I will see what can be done.' Then he went to the old woman and told her what had happened. She said, "Go to Porcupine, and get him to practise the charm."

When this was done the Diviner said, "Go to the middle compound of your father's town, and under the floor of the inner room you will find what will content the messengers."

The boy did as he was told, dug up the goods and gave them to the men to carry to Obassi Osaw.

When Obassi saw that his slaves brought back the goods, but not the boy, he was angry and said, "I told you to bring me the young son also. Why have you not done this?"

Next day, therefore, two more men were sent to bring the boy. No sooner did he arrive than the sky people brought him fruits, and all kinds of rich gifts, together with some very beautiful slaves. In spite of all that Osaw could do, however, the boy was not happy, but said, "I wish I could go back to earth once more."

Then Obassi Osaw was vexed, and his eyes began to glow, and from their gleam the sky grew red and stormy. That is the reason why we see Tornado sunsets. Obassi grows angry and his eyes become red. The storm always follows, for Tornados are the sound of the wrath of Obassi Osaw.

The Story of the Lightning and the Thunder
(From southern Nigeria)

☒

IN THE OLDEN DAYS the thunder and lightning lived on the earth amongst all the other people, but the king made them live at the far end of the town, as far as possible from other people's houses.

The thunder was an old mother sheep, and the lightning was her son, a ram. Whenever the ram got angry he used to go about and burn houses and knock down trees; he even did damage on the farms, and sometimes killed people. Whenever the lightning did these things, his mother used to call out to him in a very loud voice to stop and not to do any more damage; but the lightning did not care in the least for what his mother said, and when he was in a bad temper used to do a very large amount of damage. At last the people could not stand it any longer, and complained to the king.

So the king made a special order that the sheep (Thunder) and her son, the ram (Lightning), should leave the town and live in the far bush. This did not do much good, as when the ram got angry he still burnt the forest, and the flames sometimes spread to the farms and consumed them.

So the people complained again, and the king banished both the lightning and the thunder from the earth and made them live in the sky, where they could not cause so much destruction. Ever since, when the lightning is angry, he commits damage as before, but you can hear his mother, the thunder, rebuking him and telling him to stop. Sometimes, however, when the mother has gone away some distance from her naughty son, you can still see that he is angry and is doing damage, but his mother's voice cannot be heard.

A Story About a Giant, and the Cause of Thunder

(From the Hausa people, southern Niger and northern Nigeria)

Ϙ

THIS STORY is about a forest giant – about him and a man called, A-Man-among-Men. There was a certain man by name, A-Man-among-Men, always when he came from the bush he used to lift up a tree and come and throw it down, and say, "I am A-Man-among-Men." His wife said, "Come now, leave off saying you are a-man-among-men; if you saw a-man-among-men you would run." But he said, "It is a lie."

Now it was always so, if he has brought in wood, then he would throw it down with force and say, "I am A-Man-among-Men." The wife said, "Come now, leave off saying so; if you have seen a man-among-men, you would run." But he said, "It is a lie."

Now one day his wife went to the stream. She came to a certain well; the well bucket, ten men were necessary to draw it up. She came, but had to do without the water, so she turned back. She was going home, when she met another woman who said, "Where are you going with a calabash, with no water?" She said, "I have come and seen a bucket there. I could not draw it; that is what caused me to turn back home." And this second woman, who had a son, said, "Let us return that you may find water." She said, "All right."

So they returned together to the well. This woman, who had the son, told the boy to lift the bucket and draw water. Now the boy was small, not past the age when he was carried on his mother's back. Then he lifted the bucket then and there, and put it in the well, and drew up the water. They filled their large water-pots, they bathed, they washed their clothes, they lifted up the water to go home. This one was astonished.

Then she saw that one who had the boy has turned off the path and was entering the bush. Then the wife of him called A-Man-among-Men said, "Where are you going?" She said to her, "I am going home, where else?" She said, "Is that the way to your home?" She said, "Yes." She said, "Whose home is it?" She said,

53

"The home of A-Man-among-Men." Then she was silent; she did not say anything till she got home. She told her husband. He said that to-morrow she must take him there. She replied, "May Allah give us a to-morrow." Next morning he was the first to get up from sleep. He took the weapons of the chase and slung them over his shoulder. He put his axe on his shoulder and wakened his wife from sleep. He said, "Get up, let us go. Take me that I may see, that I may see the one called A-Man-among-Men."

She got up, lifted her large water-pot, and passed on in front. He was following her until they got to the edge of the well. Now they found what they sought indeed. As they were coming, the wife of A-Man-among-Men came up, both she and her son. They greeted her, and the wife of this one showed him the bucket and said, "Lift it and draw water for me."

So he went and lifted the bucket in a rage and let it down the well; but the bucket pulled him, and he would have fallen into the well, when the little boy seized him, both him and the bucket, and drew out and threw them on one side. Then the boy lifted up the bucket, put it in the well, drew water, and filled their water-pots.

His wife said, "You have said you are going to see him called A-Man-among-Men. You have seen this is his wife and son. If you still want to go you can go together. As for me, I am not going." The boy's mother said, "Oh, what is the matter? You had better not come." But he said he would come; and she said, "Let us be off." They set out.

When they arrived at the house she showed him a place for storing meat, and he got inside. Now he, the master of the house, was not at home; he has gone to the bush. His wife said, "You have seen he has gone to the bush; but you must not stir if he has come." He sat inside till evening came.

The master of the house came. He keeps saying, "I smell the smell of a man." His wife said, "Is there another person here? It is not is not I." Thus, if he said he smelled the smell of a man, then she would say, "Is there another person here. Is it not I? If you want to eat me up, well and good, for there is no one else but I."

Now he was a huge man, his words like a tornado; ten elephants he would eat. When dawn came, he made his morning meal of one; then he went to the bush, and if he should see a person there he would kill him.

Now he (A Man-among-Men) was in the store-house, hidden. The man's wife told him, saying, "You must not move till he is asleep. If you have seen the place dark, he is not asleep; if you have seen the place light, that is a sign he is asleep; come out and fly." Shortly after he saw the place has become light like day, so he came out.

He was running, he was running, until dawn, he was running, till the sun rose he was running, he did not stand. Then that man woke up from sleep and he said, "I smell the smell of a man, I smell the smell of a man." He rose up, he followed where the man had gone. He was running. He also, the other one, was running till he met some people who were clearing the ground for a farm, and they asked what had happened. And he said, "Some one is chasing me." They said, "Stand here till he comes."

A short time passed, and the wind caused by him came; it lifted them and cast them down. And he said, "Yes, that is it, the wind he makes running; he himself has not yet come. If you are able to withstand him tell me. If you are not able, say so." And they said, "Pass on."

So he ran off, and came and met some people hoeing. They said, "What is chasing you?" He replied, "Some one is pursuing me." They said, "What kind of a man is chasing one such as you." He said, "Some one who says he is A-Man-among-Men." They said, "Not a man-among-men, a man-among-women. Stand till he comes."

He stood. Here he was when the wind of him came, it was pushing about the men who were hoeing. So he said, "You have seen, that is the wind he makes; he has not yet come himself If you are a match for him tell me; if not say so." And they said, "Pass on"; and off he ran. He was running. He came across some people sowing; they said, "What are you running for?" He said, "Some one is chasing me." And they said, "What kind of a man is it who is chasing the like of you?" He said, "His name is A-Man-among-Men." They said, "Sit here till he comes." He sat down.

In a short time the wind he made came and it lifted them and cast them down. And they said, "What kind of wind is that?" He, the man who was being pursued, said, "It is his wind." And they said, "Pass on." They threw away the sowing implements, and went into the bush and hid, but that one was running on.

He came and met a certain huge man; he was sitting alone at the foot of a baobab tree. He had killed elephants and was roasting them, as for him, twenty elephants he could eat; in the morning he broke his fast with five. His name was "The Giant of the Forest."

Then he questioned him and said, "Where are you going in all this haste?" And he said, "A-Man-among-Men is chasing me." And the Giant of the Forest said, "Come here, sit down till he comes." He sat down. They waited a little while. Then a wind made by A-Man-among-Men came, and lifted him, and was about to carry him off, when the Giant of the Forest shouted to him to come back. And he said, "It is not I myself who am going off, the wind caused by the man is taking me away." At that the Giant of the Forest got in a rage, he got up and caught his hand, and placed it under his thigh.

He was sitting until A-Man-among-Men came up and said, "You sitting there, are you of the living, or of the dead?" And the Giant of the Forest said, "You are interfering." And A-Man-among-Men said, "If you want to find health give up to me what you are keeping there." And the Giant of the Forest said, "Come and take him." And at that he flew into a rage and sprang and seized him. They were struggling together.

When they had twisted their legs round one another they leaped up into the heavens. Till this day they are wrestling there; when they are tired out they sit down and rest; and if they rise up to struggle that is the thunder you are wont to hear in the sky; it is they struggling.

He also, that other one, escaped, and went home, and told the tale. And his wife said, "That is why I was always telling you whatever you do, make little of it. Whether it be you excel in strength, or in power, or riches, or poverty, and are puffed up with pride, it is all the same; some one is better than you. You said, it was a lie. Behold, your own eyes have seen."

How the First Rain Came
(By Okun Asere of Mfamosing; Ekoi people, Nigeria and Cameroon)

ONCE, LONG AGO, a daughter was born to Obassi Osaw, and a son to Obassi Nsi. When both had come to marriageable age, Nsi sent a message to say "Let us exchange children. I will send

my son that he may wed one of your maidens. Send your daughter down to my town, that she may become my wife."

To this Obassi Osaw agreed. So the son of Nsi went up to the heavens carrying many fine gifts, and Ara, the sky maiden, came down to dwell on earth. With her came seven men-slaves and seven women-slaves, whom her father sent that they might work for her, so that she should not be called upon to do anything herself.

One day, very early in the morning, Obassi Nsi said to his new wife, "Go, work in my farm!" She answered, "My Father gave me the slaves so that they should work instead of me. Therefore send them." Obassi Nsi was very angry and said, "Did you not hear that I gave my orders to you. You yourself shall work in my farm. As for the slaves, I will tell them what to do."

The girl went, though very unwillingly, and when she returned at night, tired out, Nsi said to her:

"Go at once to the river and bring water for the household."

She answered, "I am weary with working in the farm; may not my slaves at least do this while I rest?"

Again Nsi refused, and drove her forth, so she went backward and forward many times, carrying the heavy jars. Night had fallen long before she had brought enough.

Next morning Nsi bade her do the most menial services, and all day long kept her at work, cooking, fetching water, and making lire. That night again she was very weary before she might lie down to rest. At dawn on the third morning he said, "Go and bring in much firewood." Now the girl was young and unused to work, so as she went she wept, and the tears were still falling when she came back carrying her heavy burden.

As soon as Nsi saw her enter he called to her, "Come here and lie down before me.... I wish to shame you in the presence of all my people...." On that the girl wept still more bitterly.

No food was given her till midday on the morrow, and then not enough. When she had finished eating up all there was, Nsi said to her:

"Go out and bring in a great bundle of fish poison."

The girl went into the bush to seek for the plant, but as she walked through the thick undergrowth a thorn pierced her foot. She lay down alone. All day long she lay there in pain, but as the sun sank she began to feel better. She got up and managed to limp back to the house.

When she entered, Nsi said to her, "Early this morning I ordered you to go and collect fish poison. You have stayed away all day and done nothing." So he drove her into the goat pen, and said, "To-night you shall sleep with the goats; you shall not enter my house."

That night she ate nothing. Early next morning one of the slaves opened the door of the goat pen, and found the girl lying within, with her foot all swollen and sore. She could not walk so for five days she was left with the goats. After that her foot began to get better.

So soon as she could walk again at all, Nsi called her and said:

"Here is a pot. Take it to the river, and bring it back filled to the brim."

She set out, but when she reached the water-side, she sat down on the bank and dipped her foot in the cool stream. She said to herself, "I will never go back; it is better to stay here alone."

After a while one of the slaves came down to the river. He questioned her:

"At dawn this morning you were sent to fetch water. Why have you not returned home?"

The girl said, "I will not come back."

When the slave had left her she thought, "Perhaps he will tell them, and they will be angered and may come and kill me. I had better go back after all." So she filled her pot and tried to raise it on to her head, but it was too heavy. Next she lifted it on to a tree trunk that lay by the side of the river, and, kneeling beneath, tried to draw it, in that way, on to her head, but the pot fell and broke, and in falling a sharp sherd cut off one of her ears. The blood poured down from the wound, and she began to weep again, but suddenly thought:

"My Father is alive, my mother is alive, I do not know why I I stay here with Obassi Nsi. I will go back to my own Father."

Then she set out to find the road by which Obassi Osaw had sent her to earth. She came to a high tree, and from it saw a long rope hanging. She said to herself:

"This is the way by which my Father sent me."

She caught the rope and began to climb. Before she reached half-way she grew very weary, and her sighs and tears mounted up to the kingdom of Obassi Osaw. When she reached mid-way she stayed and rested a while. Afterwards she climbed on again.

After a long time she reached the top of the rope, and found herself on the border of her Father's land. Here she sat down almost worn out with weariness, and still weeping.

Now, one of the slaves of Obassi Osaw had been sent out to collect firewood. He chanced to stray on and on, and came to the place near where the girl was resting. He heard her sobs mixed with broken words, and ran back to the town, crying out, "I have heard the voice of Ara. She is weeping about a mile from here."

Obassi heard but could not believe, yet he said:

"Take twelve slaves, and, should you find my daughter as you say, bring her here."

When they reached the place they found that it was Ara for true. So they carried her home.

When her Father saw her coming he called out:

"Take her to the house of her mother."

There one of the lesser wives, Akun by name, heated water and bathed her. Then they prepared a bed, and covered her well with soft skins and fine cloths.

While she was resting, Obassi killed a young kid and sent it to Akun, bidding her prepare it for his daughter. Akun took it, and after she had washed it, cooked it whole in a pot. Also Obassi sent a great bunch of plantains and other fruits, and these also they set, orderly upon a table before the girl. Next they poured water into a gourd, and brought palm wine in a native cup, bidding her drink.

After she had eaten and drunk, Obassi came with four slaves carrying a great chest made of ebony. He bade them set it before her, opened it and said, "Come here; choose anything you will from this box."

Ara chose two pieces of cloth, three gowns, four small loin cloths, four looking-glasses, four spoons, two pairs of shoes (at £1), four cooking pots, and four chains of beads.

After this Obassi Osaw's storekeeper, named Ekpenyon, came forward and brought her twelve anklets. Akun gave her two gowns, a fu-fu stick and a wooden knife. Her own mother brought her five gowns, richer than all the rest, and five slaves to wait upon her.

After this Obassi Osaw said; "A house has been got ready for you, go there that you may be its mistress."

Next he went out and called together the members of the chief "club "of the town. This was named Angbu. He said to the men:

"Go; fetch the son of Obassi Nsi. Cut off both his ears and bring them to me. Then flog him and drive him down the road to his Father's town, with this message from me:

"I had built a great house up here in my town. In it I placed your son, and treated him kindly. Now that I know what you have done to my child, I send back your son to you earless, in payment for Ara's ear, and the sufferings which you put upon her."

When the Angbu Club had cut off the ears of the son of Obassi Nsi, they brought them before Obassi Osaw, and drove the lad back on the earthward road, as they had been ordered.

Osaw took the ears and made a great Juju, and by reason of this a strong wind arose, and drove the boy earthward. On its wings it bore all the sufferings of Ara, and the tears which she had shed through the cruelty of Obassi Nsi. The boy stumbled along, half-blinded by the rain, and as he went he thought:

"Obassi Osaw may do to me what he chooses. He had never done any unkind thing before. It is only in return for my Father's cruelty that I must suffer all this."

So his tears mixed with those of Ara and fell earthward as rain.

Up till that time there had been no rain on the earth. It fell for the first time when Obassi Osaw made the great wind and drove forth the son of his enemy.

How All the Rivers First Came on Earth
(By Okun Asere of Mfamosing; Ekoi people, Nigeria and Cameroon)

I N THE VERY, VERY, VERY OLDEN TIME, an old man named Etim 'Ne (old person) came down from the sky; he alone with his old wife Ejaw (wild cat). At that time there were no people on the earth. This old couple were the very first to go down to dwell there.

Now up to this time all water was kept in the kingdom of Obassi Osaw. On earth there was not a single drop.

Etim 'Ne and his wife stayed for seven days, and during that time they had only the juice of plantain stems to drink or cook with.

At the end of that time the old man said to his old wife, "I will go back to Obassi Osaw's town and ask him to give us a little water."

When he arrived at the old town where they used to dwell, he went to the house of Obassi and said:

"Since we went down to earth we have had no water, only the juice which we sucked from the plantain stems. For three nights I will sleep in your town, then when I return to earth I hope that you will give me some water to take with me. Should my wife have children they will be glad for the water, and what they offer to you in thanksgiving I myself will bring up to your town."

On the third morning, very early, Obassi Osaw put the water charm in a calabash, and bound it firmly with tie-tie. Then he gave it to Etim 'Ne, and said, "When you wish to loose this, let no one be present. Open it, and you will find seven good gifts inside. Wherever you want water, take out one of these and throw it on the ground."

Etim 'Ne thanked Lord Obassi, and set out on his way earthward. Just before he came to the place where he had begun to cut farm, he opened the calabash, and found within seven stones, clear as water. He made a small hole and laid one of the stones within it. Soon a little stream began to well out, then more and more, till it became a broad lake, great as from here to Ako.

Etim 'Ne went on and told his wife. They both rejoiced greatly, but he thought, "How is this? Can a man be truly happy, yet have no child?"

After two days his wife came to him and said, "Obassi is sending us yet another gift. Soon we shall be no longer alone on earth, you and I."

When the due months were passed, she bore him seven children, all at one time. They were all sons. Later she became enceinte again, and this time bore seven daughters. After that she was tired, and never bore any more children.

In course of time the girls were all sent to the fatting-house. While they were there Etim 'Ne pointed out to his seven sons where he would like them to build their compounds. When these were finished, he gave a daughter to each son and said, "Do not care that she is your sister. Just marry her. There is no one else who can become your wife."

The eldest son dwelt by the first water which Etim 'Ne had made, but to each of the others he gave a lake or river – seven in all.

After one year, all the girls became enceinte. Each of them had seven children, three girls and four boys. Etim 'Ne said, "It is good." He was very happy. As the children grew up he sent them to other places.

Now the seven sons were all hunters. Three of them were good, and brought some of their kill to give to their father, but four were very bad, and hid all the meat, so that they might keep everything for themselves.

When Etim 'Ne saw this, he left the rivers near the farms of his three good sons, but took them away from the four bad boys. These latter were very sad when they found their water gone, so they consulted together and went and got palm wine. This they carried before their father and said:

"We are seven, your children. First you gave the water to all. Now you have taken it away from us four. What have we done?"

Etim 'Ne answered, "Of all the meat you killed in the bush you brought none to me. Therefore I took away your rivers. Because you have come to beg me I will forgive you, and will give you four good streams. As your children grow and multiply I will give you many."

After another year the sons had children again. When the latter grew up they went to different places and built their houses.

When these were ready Etim 'Ne sent for all the children and said, "At dawn to-morrow let each of you go down to the stream which flows by the farm of his father. Seek in its bed till you find seven smooth stones. Some must be small and some big like the palm of your hand. Let each one go in a different direction, and after walking about a mile, lay a stone upon the ground. Then walk on again and do the same, till all are finished. Where you set a big stone a river will come, and where you set a small stone a stream will come."

All the sons did as they were bidden, save one alone. He took a great basket and filled it with stones. Then he went to a place in the bush near his own farm. He thought, "Our father told us, if you throw a big stone a big river will come. If I throw down all my stones together, so great a water will come that it will surpass the waters of all my brothers." Then he emptied his basket of stones all in one place, and, behold! water flowed from every side, so that all his farm, and all the land round about became covered with water. When he saw that it would not stop but threatened to overflow the whole earth he grew very much afraid. He saw his wife running, and called to her, "Let us go to my father." Then they both ran as hard as they could toward the house of Etim 'Ne.

Before they reached it the other children, who had been setting the smooth stones in the bush, as their father had told them, heard the sound of the coming of the waters. Great fear fell upon them, and they also dropped what remained and ran back to Etim 'Ne.

He also had heard the rushing of the water and knew what the bad son had done. He took the magic calabash in his hand and ran with his wife to a hill behind their farm. On this there grew many tall palm trees. Beneath the tallest of these he stood, while his children gathered round one after the other as they got back from the bush. Etim 'Ne held on high the calabash which Obassi had given him, and prayed:

"Lord Obassi, let not the good thing which you gave for our joy turn to our hurt."

As he prayed the water began to go down. It sought around till it found places where there had been no water. At each of these it made a bed for itself, great or small, some for broad rivers, and some for little streams. Only where the bad son had emptied his basket it did not go back, but remained in a great lake covering all his farm, so that he was very hungry, and had to beg from his brothers till the time came for the fruits to ripen in the new farm which he had to cut.

After many days Etim 'Ne called all his children around, and told them the names of all the rivers, and of every little stream. Then he said, "Let no one forget to remember me when I shall have left you, for I it was who gave water to all the earth, so that every one shall be glad."

Two days afterwards he died. In the beginning there were no people on the earth and no water. Etim 'Ne it was who first came down to dwell with his old wife Ejaw, and he it was who begged water from Obassi Osaw.

How Palm Trees and Water Came on Earth
(From the Ekoi people, Nigeria and Cameroon)

Φ

IN THE BEGINNING of all things Obassi made a man and a woman and brought them down to earth. There for a while he left them, but came again a little later, and asked what they had found to

eat and drink. They answered that they neither ate nor drank, so Obassi made a trench in the ground

Then from a fold of his robe he took out a vessel containing water, and poured it into the trench. This became a stream. Afterwards he took a palm kernel, and planted it. He then told the couple to use water for cooking their food, for washing and drinking. He also said they must carefully tend the palm tree which he had planted. When ripe clusters appeared upon it, they should cut these down, and take great care of them, for they would provide food as well as medicine. The outer cover or rind should be used as food, while the kernel makes good medicine.

How Death First Entered the World
(From the Krachi people)

MANY YEARS AGO, a great famine spread throughout the land, and at that time, the eldest son of every household was sent out in search of food and instructed not to return until he had found something for the family to eat and drink.

There was a certain young man among the Krachi whose responsibility it was to provide for the family, and so he wandered off in search of food, moving deeper and deeper into the bush every day until he finally came to a spot he did not recognize. Just up ahead of him, he noticed a large form lying on the ground. He approached it cautiously, hoping that if the creature were dead, it might be a good source of food, but he had taken only a few steps forward when the mound began to stir, revealing that it was not an animal at all, but a ferocious-looking giant with flowing white hair stretched out for miles on the ground around him, all the way from Krachi to Salaga.

The giant opened one eye and shouted at the young man to explain his presence. The boy stood absolutely terrified, yet after some minutes, he managed to blurt out that he had never intended to disturb the giant's rest, but had come a great distance in search of food.

"I am Owuo," said the giant, "but people also call me Death. You, my friend, have caught me in a good mood and so I will give you some food and water if you will fetch and carry for me in return."

The young man could scarcely believe his luck, and readily agreed to serve the giant in exchange for a few regular meals. Owuo arose and walked towards his cave where he began roasting some meat on a spit over the fire. Never before had the boy tasted such a fine meal, and after he had washed it down with a bowl of fresh water, he sat back and smiled, well pleased that he had made the acquaintance of the giant.

For a long time afterwards, the young man happily served Owuo, and every evening, in return for his work, he was presented with a plate of the most delicious meat for his supper.

But one day the boy awoke feeling terribly homesick and begged his master to allow him to visit his family, if only for a few days.

"You may visit your family for as long as you wish," said the giant, "on the condition that you bring another boy to replace you."

So the young man returned to his village where he told his family the whole story of his meeting with the giant. Eventually he managed to persuade his younger brother to go with him into the bush and here he handed him over to Owuo, promising that he would himself return before too long.

Several months had passed, and soon the young man grew hungry again and began to yearn for a taste of the meat the giant had cooked for him. Finally, he made up his mind to return to his master, and leaving his family behind, he returned to Owuo's hut and knocked boldly on the door.

The giant himself answered, and asked the young man what he wanted.

"I would like some more of the good meat you were once so generous to share with me," said the boy, hoping the giant would remember his face.

"Very well," replied Owuo, "you can have as much of it as you want, but you will have to work hard for me, as you did before."

The young man consented, and after he had eaten as much as he could, he went about his chores enthusiastically. The work lasted many weeks and every day the boy ate his fill of roasted meat. But to his surprise he never saw anything of his brother, and whenever he asked about him, the giant told him, rather aloofly, that the lad had simply gone away on business.

Once more, however, the young man grew homesick and asked Owuo for permission to visit his village. The giant agreed on condition that this time, he bring back a girl to carry out his duties while he was away. The young man hurried home and there he pleaded with his sister to go into the bush and keep the giant company for a few months. The girl agreed, and after she had waved goodbye to her brother, she entered the giant's cave quite merrily, accompanied by a slave companion her own age.

Only a short time had passed before the boy began to dream of the meat again, longing for even a small morsel of it. So he followed the familiar path through the bush until he found Owuo's cave. The giant did not seem particularly pleased to see him and grumbled loudly at the disturbance. But he pointed the way to a room at the back and told the boy to help himself to as much meat as he wanted.

The young man took up a juicy bone which he began to devour. But to his horror, he recognized it at once as his sister's thigh and as he looked more closely at all the rest of the meat, he was appalled to discover that he had been sitting there, happily chewing on the body of his sister and her slave girl.

As fast as his legs could carry him, he raced back to the village and immediately confessed to the elders what he had done and the awful things he had seen. At once, the alarm was sounded and all the people hurried out into the bush to investigate the giant's dwelling for themselves. But as they drew nearer, they became fearful of what he might do to them and scurried back to the village to consult among themselves what steps should be taken. Eventually, it was agreed to go to Salaga, where they knew the giant's long hair came to an end, and set it alight. The chief of the village carried the torch, and when they were certain that the giant's hair was burning well, they returned to the bush, hid themselves in the undergrowth, and awaited the giant's reaction.

Presently, Owuo began to sweat and toss about inside his cave. The closer the flames moved towards him, the more he thrashed about and grumbled until, at last, he rushed outside, his head on fire, and fell down screaming in agony.

The villagers approached him warily and only the young man had the courage to venture close enough to see whether the giant was still breathing. And as he bent over the huge form, he noticed a bundle of medicine concealed in the roots of Owuo's hair. Quickly he seized it and called to the others to come and see what he had found.

The chief of the village examined the bundle, but no one could say what power the peculiar medicine might have. Then one old man among the crowd suggested that no harm could be done if they took some of the medicine and sprinkled it on the bones and meat in the giant's hut. This was done, and to the delight of everyone gathered, the slave girl, her mistress and the boy's brother returned to life at once.

A small quantity of the medicine-dust remained, but when the young man proposed that he should put it on the giant and restore him to life, there was a great uproar among the people. Yet the boy insisted that he should help the giant who had once helped him, and so the chief, by way of compromise, allowed him to sprinkle the left-over dust into the eye of the dead giant.

The young man had no sooner done this when the giant's eye opened wide, causing the people to flee in great terror.

But it is from this eye that death comes. For every time that Owuo shuts that eye, a man dies, and unfortunately for mankind, he is forever blinking and winking, trying to clear the dust from his eye.

Why Dead People are Buried
(From southern Nigeria)

I N THE BEGINNING OF THE WORLD when the Creator had made men and women and the animals, they all lived together in the creation land. The Creator was a big chief, past all men, and being very kind-hearted, was very sorry whenever anyone died. So one day he sent for the dog, who was his head messenger, and told him to go out into the world and give his word to all people that for the future whenever anyone died the body was to be placed in the compound, and wood ashes were to be thrown over it; that the dead body was to be left on the ground, and in twenty-four hours it would become alive again.

When the dog had travelled for half a day he began to get tired; so as he was near an old woman's house he looked in, and seeing a bone with some meat on it he made a meal off it, and then went to sleep, entirely forgetting the message which had been given him to deliver.

After a time, when the dog did not return, the Creator called for a sheep, and sent him out with the same message. But the sheep was a very foolish one, and being hungry, began eating the sweet grasses by the wayside. After a time, however, he remembered that he had a message to deliver, but forgot what it was exactly; so as he went about among the people he told them that the message the Creator had given him to tell the people, was that whenever anyone died they should be buried underneath the ground.

A little time afterwards the dog remembered his message, so he ran into the town and told the people that they were to place wood ashes on the dead bodies and leave them in the compound, and that they would come to life again after twenty-four hours. But the people would not believe him, and said, "We have already received the word from the Creator by the sheep, that all dead bodies should be buried." In consequence of this the dead bodies are now always buried, and the dog is much disliked and not trusted as a messenger, as if he had not found the bone in the old woman's house and forgotten his message, the dead people might still be alive.

How the Lame Boy Brought Fire from Heaven
(By Okon Asere of Mfamosing; Ekoi people, Nigeria and Cameroon)

IN THE BEGINNING OF THE WORLD, Obassi Osaw made everything, but he did not give fire to the people who were on earth. Etim 'Ne said to the Lame Boy, "What is the use of Obassi Osaw sending us here without any fire? Go therefore and ask him to give us some." So the Lame Boy set out.

Obassi Osaw was very angry when he got the message, and sent the boy back quickly to earth to reprove Etim 'Ne for what he had asked. In those days the Lame Boy had not become lame, but could walk like other people.

When Etim 'Ne heard that he had angered Obassi Osaw, he set out himself for the latter's town and said:

"Please forgive me for what I did yesterday. It was by accident." Obassi would not pardon him, though he stayed for three days begging forgiveness. Then he went home.

When Etim reached his town the boy laughed at him. "Are you a chief," said he, "yet could get no fire? I myself will go and bring it to you. If they will give me none I will steal it."

That very day the lad set out. He reached the house of Obassi at evening time and found the people preparing food. He helped with the work, and when Obassi began to eat, knelt down humbly till the meal was ended.

The master saw that the boy was useful and did not drive him out of the house. After he had served for several days, Obassi called to him and said, "Go to the house of my wives and ask them to send me a lamp."

The boy gladly did as he was bidden, for it was in the house of the wives that fire was kept. He touched nothing, but waited until the lamp was given him, then brought it back with all speed. Once, after he had stayed for many days among the servants, Obassi sent him again, and this time one of the wives said, "You can light the lamp at the fire." She went into her house and left him alone.

The boy took a brand and lighted the lamp, then he wrapped the brand in plantain leaves and tied it up in his cloth, carried the lamp to his master and said, "I wish to go out for a certain purpose." Obassi answered, "You can go."

The boy went to the bush outside the town where some dry wood was lying. He laid the brand amongst it, and blew till it caught alight. Then he covered it with plantain stems and leaves to hide the smoke, and went back to the house. Obassi asked, "Why have you been so long?" and the lad answered, "I did not feel well."

That night when all the people were sleeping, the thief tied his cloth together and crept to the end of the town where the fire was hidden. He found it burning, and took a glowing brand and some firewood and set out homeward.

When earth was reached once more the lad went to Etim and said:

"Here is the fire which I promised to bring you. Send for some wood, and I will show you what we must do."

So the first fire was made on earth. Obassi Osaw looked down from his house in the sky and saw the smoke rising. He said to his eldest son Akpan Obassi, "Go, ask the boy if it is he who has stolen the fire."

Akpan came down to earth, and asked as his father had bidden him. The lad confessed, "I was the one who stole the fire. The reason why I hid it was because I feared."

Akpan replied, "I bring you a message. Up till now you have been able to walk. From to-day you will not be able to do so any more."

That is the reason why the Lame Boy cannot walk. He it was who first brought fire to earth from Obassi's home in the sky.

Why Women Have Long Hair
(From the Yoruba people, southern Nigeria)

TWO WOMEN QUARRELLED, and one of them went out secretly at night and dug a deep pit in the middle of the path leading from her enemy's house to the village well.

Early next morning, when all were going to the well for water with jars balanced on their heads, this woman fell into the pit and cried loudly for help.

Her friends ran to her and, seizing her by the hair, began to pull her out of the pit. To their surprise, her hair stretched as they pulled, and by the time she was safely on the path, her hair was as long as a man's arm.

This made her very much ashamed, and she ran away and hid herself.

But after a while she realized that her long hair was beautiful, and then she felt very proud and scorned all the short-haired women, jeering at them. When they saw this, they were consumed with jealousy, and began to be ashamed of their short hair. "We have men's hair," they said to one another. "How beautiful it would be to have long hair!"

So one by one they jumped into the pit, and their friends pulled them out by the hair.

And in this way they, and all women after them, had long hair.

How Human Beings Got Knee-caps
(From the Ekoi people, Nigeria and Cameroon)

Ⓕ

ONCE, LONG AGO, a woman named Nka Yenge went fishing in the river. With her were many other women. They all went into the water, some down stream and some up. Now deep down in one of the pools a smooth white stone was lying, something like a Nimm stone. As the women went by, several of them said, "What a beautiful stone!" but when Nka Yenge came, she stood looking at it for a long time and said, "I wish I could get that stone!" When she came back she said the same thing, and as she passed a third time she said:

"I must have that stone."

Suddenly the stone sprang out of the water and struck against her knee. There it stayed and she could not loosen it; so she went home weeping with pain. On the way thither, she met a man, who asked, "Why do you weep?"

The woman could not speak for tears, but the stone answered, "I was lying in the water. When the woman passed up and down, she said that she wished to have me. Her wish was so strong that it drew me up out of the water. Now I have joined myself to her, and shall never leave her again."

The man was very sorry, and called to the woman, "Come here. We will go to my house, and I will try what I can do." When they reached his house, he got a strong knife and tried to chop off the stone, but it was no use. The stone had gone inside.

That is the reason why we have knee-caps. Formerly we did not have any.

How Brothers and Sisters First Came to Quarrel and Hate Each Other
(From the Hausa people, southern Niger and northern Nigeria)

THIS TALE is about a maiden. A certain man had three children, two boys and a girl, and it was the girl he loved. Then one day their big brother went with them to the forest, telling them to come for sticks. And when they had reached the forest, he seized the girl, climbed a tree with her, and tied her on to the tree, and came and said, "The maiden has been lost in the forest," and they said they did not see her, so they came home.

They were weeping. Then their father asked them what had happened, and they said, "Our young sister she was lost in the forest and we did not see her. We searched until we were tired, but we did not see her."

Then their father said, "It cannot be helped." Then one day traders came and were passing in the forest. The girl heard their voices and she sang, "You, you, you, who are carrying kola nuts, if you have come to the village on the hill, greet my big brother Hallabau, greet my big brother Tanka-baka, and greet my big brother Shadusa." When the traders heard this they said that birds were the cause of this singing. Then again she repeated the song. Then the leader of the caravan said he would go and see what it was that was singing thus.

So he went off and came across the maiden fastened to the tree. And he said, "Are you alive or dead?" The maiden said, "Alive, alive." So the leader of the caravan himself climbed up the tree and untied her. Now long ago the caravan leader had wished for offspring, but he was childless. Then he said, "Where is the maiden from?"

And the maiden said, "Our father begat us, we were three, two boys by one mother, I also alone, by my mother. Our father and mother loved me, but did not love my brothers. And because of that our big brother brought me here,

72

deceiving me by saying we were going for sticks. He came with me here, tied me to a tree and left me. Our father is a wealthy man, and because of that, my brother did this to me." Then the leader of the caravan said, "As for me, you have become my daughter."

So the leader of the caravan took her home and nursed her till she recovered. She remained with him until she reached a marriageable age, and grew into a maid whose like was nowhere. And whenever she was heard of, people came to look on her, until a day when her elder brother reached manhood. He had not found a wife. Then he heard the report which said that a certain wealthy man had a daughter in such and such a village; in all the country there was not her like. Then he went to his father and said he had heard about the daughter of a certain wealthy man and it was her he wished to marry.

So his father gave him gifts, and he came to seek a wife in marriage. And Allah blessed his quest and he found what he sought, and the maid was wedded to him. They came home, but when he would consummate their union, she would not give herself to him; and it was always thus. Only, when they all went off to the farms she would lift her mortar and golden pestle which her father had given her, saying she was going to make 'fura' cakes. And she poured the grain into the mortar of gold and pounded and sung, "Pound, pound, mortar, father has become the father of my husband, alas for me! Mother has become the mother of my husband, alas, my mortar!" And so on till she had finished pounding. She was weeping and singing.

Now a certain old woman of the place heard what she was saying. It was always so, until one day she told the mother of the girl's husband, and she said, "When you are all about to go to the farm, do you, mother of the husband, come out, give her grain, and bid her pound 'fura', as you are going to the farm. When you get outside steal away and come back, enter the house, and remain silent and hear what she says." So the mother of the man came out, their father came out, the boys and the woman all came out, and said they were off to the farm.

A little while after the man's mother came back and entered the hut and crouched down. Then the maiden lifted her mortar and golden pestle. She was singing and saying, "Pound, pound, my mortar, father has become my husband's father, alas, my mortar! Mother has become my husband's mother, alas for me!" She was singing thus and shedding tears, the mother also was in the room and was watching her until she had done all she had to do.

When the people of the house who had gone to the farms came back, the mother did not say anything. When night came, then she told her husband; she said, "Such and such the maid did." The father said, "Could it possibly be the maid who was lost?" Then they said, "But if it is she there is a certain mark on her back ever since she was an infant, she had been left in a house with a fire and it had burned her."

She was summoned. They adjured her by Allah and the Prophet and said, "This man who gave you in marriage, is he your father or were you given to him to be brought up only?" But the maiden refused to answer. Try as they could they could not get an answer. Then the father said, "Present your back that I may see."

She turned her back, and they saw the scar where the fire had burned her when she was an infant. Then they said, "Truly it is so. From the first when you came why did you refuse to tell us?" And they knew it was their daughter. And they sent to her foster father, the one who had found her, and he was told what had happened. And he said, "There is no harm done. I beg you give me the maiden. If I have found another I shall give her to the husband." But the girl's real father and mother refused to consent to this.

As for the husband, when he heard this he took his quiver and bow. He went into the forest and hanged himself. He died. And this was the beginning of hatred among the children of one father by different mothers.

How the First Hippopotami Came
(From the Ekoi people, Nigeria and Cameroon)

ONCE, LONG AGO, Elephant had a beautiful daughter, whom all the beasts wished to wed. Now at that time a very great fish named Njokk Mbonn (Elephant fish) dwelt in the river, and one evening he came to Elephant and said, "I should like to marry your daughter."

74

Next morning Leopard came too, and said, "Do not let anyone marry the girl but me." When he heard that the King of the fishes had also asked her in marriage he was very angry, and went home to call all his family together to fight. Nsun (antelope) happened to pass by while they were arranging the matter, and he went at once and said to Fish:

"Listen to what I have heard to-day. Leopard and all his people are coming to fight you."

When Njokk Mbonn heard this he said nothing, but only took a yam and roasted it. When it was ready he ate part, and put the rest on one side. Just then he heard the sound of his enemies coming in the distance, and close at hand he saw Elephant also with his daughter.

Then Fish went down into the water. By magic he made a big wave rise up and overflow the bank. As this ebbed it drew Elephant and his daughter down to the depths beneath, where Fish lay waiting.

When the other animals saw what had happened they all fled, crying to one another:

"If we try to fight with Njokk Mbonn he will kill us all. Let us go back at once."

Fish thought to himself, "I must kill Leopard, or he will come back again some day."

At dawn, therefore, he came up to the bank, and lay there cleaning his teeth, which were very white and shining.

When Leopard came along he stood looking at his enemy and thought, "My teeth are not so fine as his. What can I do?" So he said, "Will you kindly clean my teeth also?"

When Fish heard this he answered, "Very well, but I cannot do it unless you will lie down. If you are willing to do this I will clean your mouth."

Leopard lay down; Fish sent his wave once more, and swept his enemy down to the depths of the river. Instead of finding a fine house there, as Elephant and his daughter had done, Leopard found only a strong prison, where he soon died.

Njokk Mbonn married the daughter of Elephant, and they lived happily for many years. Their children were the Water-Elephants (i.e., Hippopotami). If Fish had not wedded this wife there would have been no Hippo in our rivers.

How Mushrooms First Grew
(From the Akan peoples, Ghana)

Φ

LONG, LONG AGO there dwelt in a town two brothers whose bad habits brought them much trouble. Day by day they got more deeply in debt. Their creditors gave them no peace, so at last they ran away into the woods. They became highway robbers.

But they were not happy. Their minds were troubled by their evil deeds. At last they decided to go home, make a big farm, and pay off their debts gradually.

They accordingly set to work and soon had quite a fine farm prepared for corn. As the soil was good, they hoped the harvest would bring them in much money.

Unfortunately, that very day a bushfowl came along. Being hungry, it scratched up all the newly planted seeds and ate them.

The two poor brothers, on arriving at the field next day, were dismayed to find all their work quite wasted. They put down a trap for the thief. That evening the bushfowl was caught in it. The two brothers, when they came and found the bird, told it that now all their debts would be transferred to it because it had robbed them of the means of paying the debts themselves.

The poor bird – in great trouble at having such a burden thrust upon it made a nest under a silk-cotton tree. There it began to lay eggs, meaning to hatch them and sell the young birds for money to pay off the debts.

A terrible hurricane came, however, and a branch of the tree came down. All the eggs were smashed. As a result, the bushfowl transferred the debts to the tree, as it had broken the eggs.

The silk-cotton tree was in dismay at having such a big sum of money to pay off. It immediately set to work to make as much silk cotton as it possibly could, that it might sell it.

An elephant, not knowing all that had happened, came along. Seeing the silk cotton, he came to the tree and plucked down all its bearings. By this means the debts were transferred to the poor elephant.

The elephant was very sad when he found what he had done. He wandered away into the desert, thinking of a way to make money. He could think of none.

As he stood quietly under a tree, a poor hunter crept up. This man thought he was very lucky to find such a fine elephant standing so still. He at once shot him.

Just before the animal died, he told the hunter that now the debts would have to be paid by him. The hunter was much grieved when he heard this, as he had no money at all.

He walked home wondering what he could do to make enough money to pay the debts. In the darkness he did not see the stump of a tree which the overseers had cut down in the road. He fell and broke his leg. By this means the debts were transferred to the tree-stump.

Not knowing this, a party of white ants came along next morning and began to eat into the tree. When they had broken it nearly to the ground, the tree told them that now the debts were theirs, as they had killed it.

The ants, being very wise, held a council together to find out how best they could make money. They decided each to contribute as much as possible. With the proceeds one of their young men would go to the nearest market and buy pure linen thread. This they would weave and sell and the profits would go to help pay the debts.

This was done. From time to time all the linen in stock was brought and spread out in the sunshine to keep it in good condition. When men see this linen lying out on the ant-hills, they call it "mushroom," and gather it for food.

Tales of Anansi, the Spider Trickster

THE FIGURE OF THE TRICKSTER is central to a great many mythological traditions, from Indra and Narada in Indian legend to the Coyote in Native American myth (and of course the fox in European fairy tale). Jacob in the Bible serves the same sort of function in the Bible as Odysseus does in Homer or as Maui does in the stories of Hawaii.

And why not? The whole world loves a quick-witted corner-cutter. There's a reason why we do, though, and it goes well beyond our enjoyment of the unexpected narrative twist; the satisfaction of seeing a problem solved; a quandary cleverly avoided or neatly finessed. The reality is that we want to see rules broken because this implies possibility and freedom but also want to be reminded that there are rules. Without a stable, accommodating order, we know, we are never really going to feel at home, but we want to have a 'hall pass' of some sort. This is where the trickster comes in, an exemplar of what we might attain with talent, ingenuity and daring: Anansi the Spider embodies all these things.

How Anansi Became a Spider
(From the Dagomba people)

A VERY LONG TIME AGO, there lived a king who had amongst his possessions a very magnificent ram, larger and taller than any other specimen in the entire country. The ram was more precious to him than anything else he owned and he made it quite clear to his subjects that the animal must be allowed to roam wherever it chose, and be allowed to eat as much food as it desired, even if the people themselves were forced to go hungry. If anyone should ever hit or injure the king's ram, that man should certainly die.

Every citizen of the kingdom obeyed the king's orders without a great deal of complaint, but there was one among them, a wealthy farmer named Anansi, who was particularly proud of the crops he raised. Everyone suspected that he would not tolerate a visit from the king's ram and they prayed amongst themselves that such an event might never happen.

One day, however, when the rains had begun to fall, and his crops were already as tall as his waist, Anansi went out to make a final inspection of his fields. He was very pleased with what he saw and was just about to return to his farmhouse when he noticed in the distance an area of land where the corn had been trampled underfoot and the young shoots eaten away. There in the middle of the field, still munching away quite happily, stood the king's ram. Anansi was so furious he hurled a large pebble at the animal intending only to frighten him away. But the stone hit the ram right between the eyes and before he had quite realized what he had done, the animal lay dead at his feet.

Anansi did not know what he should do. Like everybody else in the village, he was only too familiar with the king's orders and knew he would face certain death if his crime was discovered. He leaned back against a shea-butter tree wondering how to resolve the dreadful mess. Suddenly a nut fell on his head from one of the branches above. Anansi picked it up and ate it. He liked the taste of it very much and so he shook the tree until several more nuts fell to the ground. Then the most fantastic idea entered his head. He picked up the nuts and put them in his pocket. He quickly lifted the ram and climbed the tree with him. As soon as he had tied the animal to a strong bough he descended once more and headed off towards the house of his friend, Kusumbuli, the spider.

Anansi found his friend at home and the two sat down and began to chat. After a few moments, Anansi took one of the shea-nuts from his pocket and handed it to his friend.

"This nut has an excellent flavour," said Kusumbuli, as he sat chomping on the ripe flesh, "tell me, where did you come across such a fine crop?"

Anansi promised to show the spider the exact spot and led him to the tree where the nuts were growing in large clusters.

"You'll have to shake quite hard to loosen them," Anansi advised Kusumbuli, "don't be afraid, the trunk is a strong one."

So the spider began shaking the tree violently and as he did so, the dead ram fell to the ground.

"Oh, my friend," cried Anansi at once, "what have you done? Look, the king's ram is lying at your feet and you have killed him."

Kusumbuli turned pale as a wave of panic swept over him.

"There is only one thing you can do now," Anansi urged the spider, "go and unburden your conscience at once. Tell the king precisely what has happened and with any luck he will understand that the whole affair was a most unfortunate accident."

Kusumbuli thought that this was good advice, so he picked up the dead ram and set off to confess his crime, hoping the king would be in a good mood.

The road towards the king's palace brought him past his own home and the spider went indoors to bid a sad farewell to his wife and children, believing that he might never set eyes on them again. Anansi stood at the entrance while Kusumbuli went into the back room and told his wife everything that had happened. She listened attentively to what he said and immediately saw that there was some trick involved.

"I have never seen a ram climb a tree before, Kusumbuli," she said to him. "Use your head. Anansi has something to do with this and you are taking the blame for him. Hear me now and do exactly as I say."

So she advised her husband that he must leave Anansi behind and pretend to go alone in search of the king. After he had gone some distance, she told him, he was to rest and then return home and announce that all had turned out well in the end. The spider agreed to do this and asked Anansi if he would be so good as to look after his wife and children. His friend promised to watch over them faithfully and the spider set off on his travels winking at his wife as he moved away.

Several hours later, Kusumbuli returned to his home, smiling from ear to ear as he embraced his family.

"Come and celebrate with us, Anansi," he cried excitedly, "I have been to see the king and he was not at all angry with me. In fact, he said he had no use for a dead ram and insisted that I help myself to as much of the meat as I wanted."

At this, Anansi became enraged and shouted out:

"What! You have been given all that meat when it was I who took the trouble to kill that ram. I should have been given my fair share, you deserved none of it."

Kusumbuli and his wife now leaped upon Anansi and bound his hands and legs. Then they dragged him to the king's palace and reported to their ruler the whole unpleasant affair.

Anansi squirmed on the floor and begged for the king's mercy. But the king could not control his fury and he raised his foot to kick Anansi as he lay on the ground. The king kicked so hard that Anansi broke into a thousand pieces that scattered themselves all over the room.

And that is how Anansi came to be such a small spider. And that is why you will find him in every corner of the house, awaiting the day when someone will put all the pieces together again.

Anansi Obtains the Sky God's Stories
(From the Ashanti people)

KWAKU ANANSI had one great wish. He longed to be the owner of all the stories known in the world, but these were kept by the Sky God, Nyame [The Ashanti refer to God as 'Nyame'. The Dagomba call him 'Wuni', while the Krachi refer to him as 'Wulbari'.], in a safe hiding-place high above the clouds.

One day, Anansi decided to pay the Sky God a visit to see if he could persuade Nyame to sell him the stories.

"I am flattered you have come so far, little creature," the Sky God told Anansi, "but many rich and powerful men have preceded you and none has been able to purchase what they came here for. I am willing to part with my stories, but the price is very high. What makes you think that you can succeed where they have all failed?"

"I feel sure I will be able to buy them," answered Anansi bravely, "if you will only tell me what the price is."

"You are very determined, I see," replied Nyame, "but I must warn you that the price is no ordinary one. Listen carefully now to what I demand of you.

"First of all, you must capture Onini, the wise old python, and present him to me. When you have done this, you must go in search of the Mmoboro, the largest nest of hornets in the forest, and bring them here also. Finally, look for Osebo, the fastest of all leopards and set a suitable trap for him. Bring him to me either dead or alive.

"When you have delivered me these three things, all the stories of the world will be handed over to you."

"I shall bring you everything you ask for," Anansi declared firmly, and he hastened towards his home where he began making plans for the tasks ahead.

That afternoon, he sat down with his wife, Aso, and told her all about his visit to the Sky God.

"How will I go about trapping the great python, Onini?" he asked her.

His wife, who was a very clever woman, instructed her husband to make a special trip to the centre of the woods:

"Go and cut yourself a long bamboo pole," she ordered him, "and gather some strong creeper-vines as well. As soon as you have done this, return here to me and I will tell you what to do with these things."

Anansi gathered these objects as his wife had commanded and after they had spent some hours consulting further, he set off enthusiastically towards the house of Onini.

As he approached closer, he suddenly began arguing with himself in a loud and angry voice:

"My wife is a stupid woman," he pronounced, "she says it is longer and stronger. I say it is shorter and weaker. She has no respect. I have a great deal. She is stupid. I am right."

"What's all this about?" asked the python, suddenly appearing at the door of his hut. "Why are you having this angry conversation with yourself?"

"Oh! Please ignore me," answered the spider. "It's just that my wife has put me in such a bad mood. For she says this bamboo pole is longer and stronger than you are, and I say she is a liar."

"There is no need for the two of you to argue so bitterly on my account," replied the python, "bring that pole over here and we will soon find out who is right."

So Anansi laid the bamboo pole on the earth and the python stretched himself out alongside it.

"I'm still not certain about this," said Anansi after a few moments. "When you stretch at one end, you appear to shrink at the other end. Perhaps if I tied you to the pole I would have a clearer idea of your size."

"Very well," answered the python, "just so long as we can sort this out properly."

Anansi then took the creeper-vine and wrapped it round and round the length of the python's body until the great creature was unable to move.

"Onini," said Anansi, "it appears my wife was right. You are shorter and weaker than this pole and more foolish into the bargain. Now you are my prisoner and I must take you to the Sky God, as I have promised."

The great python lowered his head in defeat as Anansi tugged on the pole, dragging him along towards the home of Nyame.

"You have done well, spider," said the god, "but remember, there are two more, equally difficult quests ahead. You have much to accomplish yet, and it would not be wise to delay here any longer."

So Anansi returned home once more and sat down to discuss the next task with his wife.

"There are still hornets to catch," he told her, "and I cannot think of a way to capture an entire swarm all at once."

"Look for a gourd," his wife suggested, "and after you have filled it with water, go out in search of the hornets."

Anansi found a suitable gourd and filled it to the brim. Fortunately, he knew exactly the tree where the hornets had built their nest. But before he approached too close, he poured some of the water from the gourd over himself so that his clothes were dripping wet. Then, he began sprinkling the nest with the remaining water while shouting out to the hornets:

"Why do you remain in such a flimsy shelter Mmoboro, when the great rains have already begun? You will soon be swept away, you foolish people. Here, take cover in this dry gourd of mine and it will protect you from the storms."

The hornets thanked the spider for this most timely warning and disappeared one by one into the gourd. As soon as the last of them had entered, Anansi plugged the mouth of the vessel with some grass and chuckled to himself:

"Fools! I have outwitted you as well. Now you can join Onini, the python. I'm certain Nyame will be very pleased to see you."

Anansi was delighted with himself. It had not escaped his notice that even the Sky God appeared rather astonished by his success and it filled him with great excitement to think that very soon he would own all the stories of the world.

Only Osebo, the leopard, stood between the spider and his great wish, but Anansi was confident that with the help of his wife he could easily ensnare the creature as he had done all the others.

"You must go and look for the leopard's tracks," his wife told him, "and then dig a hole where you know he is certain to walk."

Anansi went away and dug a very deep pit in the earth, covering it with branches and leaves so that it was well-hidden from the naked eye. Night-time closed in around him and soon afterwards, Osebo came prowling as usual and fell right into the deep hole, snarling furiously as he hit the bottom.

At dawn on the following morning, Anansi approached the giant pit and called to the leopard:

"What has happened here? Have you been drinking, leopard? How on earth will you manage to escape from this great hole?"

"I have fallen into a silly man-trap," said the leopard impatiently. "Help me out at once. I am almost starving to death in this wretched place."

"And if I help you out, how can I be sure you won't eat me?" asked Anansi. "You say you are very hungry, after all."

"I wouldn't do a thing like that," Osebo reassured him. "I beg you, just this once, to trust me. Nothing bad will happen to you, I promise."

Anansi hurried away from the opening of the pit and soon returned with a long, thick rope. Glancing around him, he spotted a tall green tree and bent it towards the ground, securing it with a length of the rope so that the top branches hung over the pit. Then he tied another piece of rope to these branches, dropping the loose end into the pit for the leopard to tie to his tail.

"As soon as you have tied a large knot, let me know and I will haul you up," shouted Anansi.

Osebo obeyed the spider's every word, and as soon as he gave the signal that he was ready, Anansi cut the rope pinning the tree to the ground. It sprung upright at once, pulling the leopard out of the hole in one swift motion. Osebo hung upside down, wriggling and twisting helplessly, trying with every ounce of his strength to loosen his tail from the rope. But Anansi was not about to take any chances and he plunged his knife deep into the leopard's chest, killing him instantly. Then he lifted the leopard's body from the earth and carried it all the way to the Sky God.

Nyame now called together all the elders of the skies, among them the Adonten, the Oyoko, the Kontire and Akwam chiefs, and informed them of the great exploits of Anansi, the spider:

"Many great warriors and chiefs have tried before," the Sky God told the congregation, "but none has been able to pay the price I have asked of them. Kwaku Anansi has brought me Onini the python, the Mmoboro nest and the body of the mighty Osebo. The time has come to repay him as he deserves. He has won the right to tell my stories. From today, they will no longer be called stories of the Sky God, but stories of Anansi, the spider."

And so, with Nyame's blessing, Anansi became the treasurer of all the stories that have ever been told. And even now, whenever a man wishes to tell a story for the entertainment of his people, he must acknowledge first of all that the tale is a great gift, given to him by Anansi, the spider.

How Wisdom Became the Property of the Human Race
(From the Akan peoples, Ghana)

THERE ONCE LIVED, in Fanti-land, a man named Father Anansi. He possessed all the wisdom in the world. People came to him daily for advice and help.

One day the men of the country were unfortunate enough to offend Father Anansi, who immediately resolved to punish them. After much thought he decided that the severest penalty he could inflict would be to hide all his wisdom from them. He set to work at once to gather again all that he had already given. When he had succeeded, as he thought, in collecting it, he placed all in one great pot. This he carefully sealed, and determined to put it in a spot where no human being could reach it.

Now, Father Anansi had a son, whose name was Kweku Tsin. This boy began to suspect his father of some secret design, so he made up his mind to watch carefully. Next day he saw his father quietly slip out of the house, with his precious pot hung round his neck. Kweku Tsin followed. Father Anansi went through the forest till he had left the village far behind. Then, selecting the highest and most inaccessible-looking tree, he began to climb. The heavy pot, hanging in front of him, made his ascent almost impossible. Again and again he tried to reach the top of the tree, where he intended to hang the pot. There, he thought, Wisdom would indeed be beyond the reach of every one but himself. He was unable, however, to carry out his desire. At each trial the pot swung in his way.

For some time Kweku Tsin watched his father's vain attempts. At last, unable to contain himself any longer, he cried out: "Father, why do you not hang the pot on your back? Then you could easily climb the tree."

Father Anansi turned and said: "I thought I had all the world's wisdom in this pot. But I find you possess more than I do. All my wisdom was

insufficient to show me what to do, yet you have been able to tell me."
In his anger he threw the pot down. It struck on a great rock and broke.
The wisdom contained in it escaped and spread throughout the world.

How Beasts and Serpents Came into the World
(From the Akan peoples, Ghana)

THE FAMINE had lasted nearly three years. Anansi's son, Kweku
Tsin, being very hungry, looked daily in the forest in the hope
of finding food. One day he was fortunate enough to discover
three palm-kernels lying on the ground. He picked up two stones
with which to crack them. The first nut, however, slipped when he
hit it, and fell into a hole behind him. The same thing happened
to the second and to the third. Very much annoyed at his loss,
Kweku determined to go down the hole to see if he could find his
lost nuts.

To his surprise, however, he discovered that this hole was really the
entrance to a town, of which he had never before even heard. When he
reached it he found absolute silence everywhere. He called out, "Is there
nobody in this town?" and presently heard a voice in answer. He went in
its direction and found an old woman sitting in one of the houses. She
demanded the reason of his appearance – which he readily gave.

The old woman was very kind and sympathetic, and promised to help
him. "You must do exactly as I tell you," said she. "Go into the garden and
listen attentively. You will hear the yams speak. Pass by any yam that says,
'Dig me out, dig me out!' But take the one that says, 'Do not dig me out!'
Then bring it to me."

When he brought it, she directed him to remove the peel from the yam
and throw the latter away. He was then to boil the rind, and while boiling,
it would become yam. It did actually do so, and they sat down to eat some
of it. Before beginning their meal the old woman requested Kweku not to

look at her while she ate. Being very polite and obedient, he did exactly as he was told.

In the evening the old woman sent him into the garden to choose one of the drums which stood there. She warned him: "If you come to a drum which says 'Ding-ding' on being touched – take it. But be very careful not to take one which sounds 'Dong-dong.'" He obeyed her direction in every detail. When he showed her the drum, she looked pleased and told him, to his great delight, that he had only to beat it if at any time he were hungry. That would bring him food in plenty. He thanked the old woman heartily and went home.

As soon as he reached his own hut, he gathered his household together, and then beat the drum. Immediately, food of every description appeared before them, and they all ate as much as they wished.

The following day Kweku Tsin gathered all the people of the village together in the Assembly Place, and then beat the drum once more. In this way every family got sufficient food for their wants, and all thanked Kweku very much for thus providing for them.

Kweku's father, however, was not at all pleased to see his son thus able to feed the whole village. Anansi thought he, too, ought to have a drum. Then the people would be grateful to him instead of to Kweku Tsin. Accordingly, he asked the young man where the wonderful drum had come from. His son was most unwilling to tell him, but Anansi gave him no peace until he had heard the whole story. He then wasted no time, but set off at once toward the entrance hole. He had taken the precaution to carry with him an old nut which he pretended to crack. Then throwing it into the hole, he jumped in after it and hurried along to the silent village. Arrived at the first house, he shouted, "Is there no one in this town?" The old woman answered as before, and Anansi entered her house.

He did not trouble to be polite to her, but addressed her most rudely, saying, "Hurry up, old woman, and get me something to eat." The woman quietly directed him to go into the garden and choose the yam which should say, "Do not dig me out." Anansi laughed in her face and said, "You surely take me for a fool. If the yam does not want me to dig it out I will certainly not do so. I will take the one which wants to be gathered." This he did.

When he brought it to the old woman she told him, as she told his son, to throw away the inside and boil the rind. Again he refused to obey. "Who ever heard of such a silly thing as throwing away the yam? I will do nothing of the sort. I will throw away the peel and boil the inside." He did so, and the yam turned into stones. He was then obliged to do as she first suggested, and boil the rind. The latter while boiling turned into yam. Anansi turned angrily to the old woman and said, "You are a witch." She took no notice of his remark, but went on setting the table. She placed his dinner on a small table, lower than her own, saying. "You must not look at me while I eat." He rudely replied, "Indeed, I will look at you if I choose. And I will have my dinner at your table, not at that small one." Again she said nothing – but she left her dinner untouched. Anansi ate his own, then took hers and ate it also.

When he had finished she said, "Now go into the garden and choose a drum. Do not take one which sounds 'Dong-dong'; only take one which says 'Ding-ding.'" Anansi retorted, "Do you think I will take your advice, you witch? No, I will choose the drum which says 'Dong-dong.' You are just trying to play a trick on me."

He did as he wished. Having secured the drum he marched off without so much as a Thank you to the old woman.

No sooner had he reached home, than he longed to show off his new power to the villagers. He called all to the Assembly Place, telling them to bring dishes and trays, as he was going to provide them with food. The people in great delight hurried to the spot. Anansi, proudly taking his position in the midst of them, began to beat his drum. To his horror and dismay, instead of the multitude of food-stuffs which Kweku had summoned, Anansi saw, rushing toward him, beasts and serpents of all kinds. Such creatures had never been seen on the earth before.

The people fled in every direction – all except Anansi, who was too terrified to move. He speedily received fitting punishment for his disobedience. Fortunately, Kweku, with his mother and sisters, had been at the outer edge of the crowd, so easily escaped into shelter. The animals presently scattered in every direction, and ever since they have roamed wild in the great forests.

Anansi and Nothing
(From the Akan peoples, Ghana)

NEAR ANANSI'S miserable little hut there was a fine palace where lived a very rich man called Nothing. Nothing and Anansi proposed, one day, to go to the neighbouring town to get some wives. Accordingly, they set off together.

Nothing, being a rich man, wore a very fine velvet cloth, while Anansi had a ragged cotton one. While they were on their way Anansi persuaded Nothing to change clothes for a little while, promising to give back the fine velvet before they reached the town. He delayed doing this, however, first on one pretext, then on another – till they arrived at their destination.

Anansi, being dressed in such a fine garment, found no difficulty in getting as many wives as he wished. Poor Nothing, with his ragged and miserable cloth, was treated with great contempt. At first he could not get even one wife. At last, however, a woman took pity on him and gave him her daughter. The poor girl was laughed at very heartily by Anansi's wives for choosing such a beggar as Nothing appeared to be. She wisely took no notice of their scorn.

The party set off for home. When they reached the cross-roads leading to their respective houses the women were astonished. The road leading to Anansi's house was only half cleared. The one which led to Nothing's palace was, of course, wide and well made. Not only so, but his servants had strewn it with beautiful skins and carpets, in preparation for his return. Servants were there, awaiting him, with fine clothes for himself and his wife. No one was waiting for Anansi.

Nothing's wife was queen over the whole district and had everything her heart could desire, Anansi's wives could not even get proper food; they had to live on unripe bananas with peppers. The wife of Nothing heard of her friends' miserable state and invited them to a great feast in her palace. They came, and were so pleased with all they saw that they agreed to stay there. Accordingly, they refused to come back to Anansi's hut.

He was very angry, and tried in many ways to kill Nothing, but without success. Finally, however, he persuaded some rat friends to dig a deep tunnel in front of Nothing's door. When the hole was finished Anansi lined it with knives and broken bottles. He then smeared the steps of the palace with okro to make them very slippery, and withdrew to a little distance.

When he thought Nothing's household was safely in bed and asleep, he called to Nothing to come out to the courtyard and see something. Nothing's wife, however, dissuaded him from going. Anansi tried again and again, and each time she bade her husband not to listen. At last Nothing determined to go and see this thing. As he placed his foot on the first step, of course he slipped, and down he fell into the hole. The noise alarmed the household. Lights were fetched and Nothing was found in the ditch, so much wounded by the knives that he soon died. His wife was terribly grieved at his untimely death. She boiled many yams, mashed them, and took a great dishful of them round the district. To every child she met she gave some, so that the child might help her to cry for her husband. This is why, if you find a child crying and ask the cause, you will often be told he is "crying for nothing."

Thunder and Anansi
(From the Akan peoples, Ghana)

THERE HAD BEEN a long and severe famine in the land where Anansi lived. He had been quite unable to obtain food for his poor wife and family. One day, gazing desperately out to sea, he saw rising from the midst of the water, a tiny island with a tall palm-tree upon it. He determined to reach this tree – if any means proved possible – and climb it, in the hope of finding a few nuts to reward him. How to get there was the difficulty.

This, however, solved itself when he reached the beach, for there lay the means to his hand, in the shape of an old broken boat. It certainly did not look very strong, but Anansi decided to try it.

His first six attempts were unsuccessful – a great wave dashed him back on the beach each time he tried to put off. He was persevering, however, and at the seventh trial was successful in getting away. He steered the battered old boat as best he could, and at length reached the palm-tree of his desire. Having tied the boat to the trunk of the tree – which grew almost straight out of the water – he climbed toward the nuts. Plucking all he could reach, he dropped them, one by one, down to the boat. To his dismay, every one missed the boat and fell, instead, into the water until only the last one remained. This he aimed even more carefully than the others, but it also fell into the water and disappeared from his hungry eyes. He had not tasted even one and now all were gone.

He could not bear the thought of going home empty-handed, so, in his despair, he threw himself into the water, too. To his complete astonishment, instead of being drowned, he found himself standing on the sea-bottom in front of a pretty little cottage. From the latter came an old man, who asked Anansi what he wanted so badly that he had come to Thunder's cottage to seek it. Anansi told his tale of woe, and Thunder showed himself most sympathetic.

He went into the cottage and fetched a fine cooking-pot, which he presented to Anansi – telling him that he need never be hungry again. The pot would always supply enough food for himself and his family. Anansi was most grateful, and left Thunder with many thanks.

Being anxious to test the pot at once, Anansi only waited till he was again seated in the old boat to say, "Pot, pot, what you used to do for your master do now for me." Immediately good food of all sorts appeared. Anansi ate a hearty meal, which he very much enjoyed.

On reaching land again, his first thought was to run home and give all his family a good meal from his wonderful pot. A selfish, greedy fear prevented him. "What if I should use up all the magic of the pot on them, and have nothing more left for myself! Better keep the pot a secret – then I can enjoy a meal when I want one." So, his mind full of this thought, he hid the pot.

He reached home, pretending to be utterly worn out with fatigue and hunger. There was not a grain of food to be had anywhere. His wife and poor children were weak with want of it, but selfish Anansi took no notice of that. He congratulated himself at the thought of his magic pot, now safely hidden in his room. There he retired from time to time when he felt hungry, and enjoyed a good meal. His family got thinner and thinner, but he grew plumper and plumper. They began to suspect some secret, and determined to find it out. His eldest son, Kweku Tsin, had the power of changing himself into any shape he chose; so he took the form of a tiny fly, and accompanied his father everywhere. At last, Anansi, feeling hungry, entered his room and closed the door. Next he took the pot, and had a fine meal. Having replaced the pot in its hiding-place, he went out, on the pretence of looking for food.

As soon as he was safely out of sight, Kweku Tsin fetched out the pot and called all his hungry family to come at once. They had as good a meal as their father had had. When they had finished, Mrs. Anansi – to punish her husband – said she would take the pot down to the village and give everybody a meal. This she did – but alas! in working to prepare so much food at one time, the pot grew too hot and melted away. What was to be done now? Anansi would be so angry! His wife forbade every one to mention the pot.

Anansi returned, ready for his supper, and, as usual, went into his room, carefully shutting the door. He went to the hiding-place – it was empty. He looked around in consternation. No pot was to be seen anywhere. Some one must have discovered it. His family must be the culprits; he would find a means to punish them.

Saying nothing to any one about the matter, he waited till morning. As soon as it was light he started off towards the shore, where the old boat lay. Getting into the boat, it started of its own accord and glided swiftly over the water – straight for the palm-tree. Arrived there, Anansi attached the boat as before and climbed the tree. This time, unlike the last, the nuts almost fell into his hands. When he aimed them at the boat they fell easily into it – not one, as before, dropping into the water. He deliberately took them and threw them over-board, immediately jumping after them. As before, he found himself in front of Thunder's cottage, with Thunder waiting to hear his tale. This he told, the old man showing the same sympathy as he had previously done.

This time, however, he presented Anansi with a fine stick and bade him good-bye. Anansi could scarcely wait till he got into the boat so anxious was he to try the magic properties of his new gift. "Stick, stick," he said, "what you used to do for your master do for me also." The stick began to beat him so severely that, in a few minutes, he was obliged to jump into the water and swim ashore, leaving boat and stick to drift away where they pleased. Then he returned sorrowfully homeward, bemoaning his many bruises and wishing he had acted more wisely from the beginning.

Why the Lizard Continually Moves His Head up and Down
(From the Akan peoples, Ghana)

IN A TOWN not very far from Anansi's home lived a great king. This king had three beautiful daughters, whose names were kept a secret from everybody except their own family. One day their father made a proclamation that his three daughters would be given as wives to any man who could find out their names. Anansi made up his mind to do so.

He first bought a large jar of honey, and set off for the bathing-place of the king's daughters. Arrived there, he climbed to the top of a tree on which grew some very fine fruit. He picked some of this fruit and poured honey over it. When he saw the princesses approaching he dropped the fruit on the ground and waited. The girls thought the fruit dropped of its own accord, and one of them ran forward to pick it up. When she tasted it, she called out to her sisters by name to exclaim on its sweetness. Anansi dropped another, which the second princess picked up – she, in her turn, calling out the names of the other two. In this fashion Anansi found out all the names.

As soon as the princesses had gone Anansi came down from the tree and hurried into the town. He went to all the great men and summoned them to a meeting at the King's palace on the morrow.

He then visited his friend the Lizard, to get him to act as herald at the Court next day. He told Lizard the three names, and the latter was to sound them through his trumpet when the time came.

Early next morning the King and his Court were assembled as usual. All the great men of the town appeared, as Anansi had requested.

Anansi stated his business, reminding the King of his promise to give his three daughters to the man who had found out their names. The King demanded to hear the latter, whereupon Lizard sounded them on his trumpet.

The King and courtiers were much surprised. His Majesty, however, could not break the promise he had made of giving his daughters to the man who named them. He accordingly gave them to Mr. Lizard. Anansi was very angry, and explained that he had told the names to Lizard, so that he ought to get at least two of the girls, while Lizard could have the third. The King refused. Anansi then begged hard for even one, but that was also refused. He went home in a very bad temper, declaring that he would be revenged on Lizard for stealing his wives away.

He thought over the matter very carefully, but could not find a way of punishing Lizard. At last, however, he had an idea.

He went to the King and explained that he was setting off next morning on a long journey. He wished to start very early, and so begged the King's help. The King had a fine cock, which always crowed at daybreak to waken the King if he wished to get up early. Anansi begged that the King would command the cock to crow next morning, that Anansi might be sure of getting off in time. This the King readily promised.

As soon as night fell Anansi went by a back way to the cock's sleeping-place, seized the bird quickly, and killed it. He then carried it to Lizard's house, where all were in bed. There he quietly cooked the cock, placed the feathers under Lizard's bed, and put some of the flesh on a dish close to Lizard's hand. The wicked Anansi then took some boiling water and poured it into poor Lizard's mouth, thus making him dumb.

When morning came, Anansi went to the King and reproached him for not letting the cock crow. The King was much surprised to hear that it had not obeyed his commands.

He sent one of his servants to find and bring the cock to him, but, of course, the servant returned empty-handed. The King then ordered them to find the thief. No trace of him could be found anywhere. Anansi then cunningly said to the King: "I know Lizard is a rogue, because he stole my three wives from me. Perhaps he is the thief." Accordingly, the men went to search Lizard's house.

There, of course, they found the remnants of the cock, cooked ready to eat, and his feathers under the bed. They questioned Lizard, but the poor animal was unable to reply. He could only move his head up and down helplessly. They thought he was refusing to speak, so dragged him before the King. To the King's questions he could only return the same answer, and his Majesty got very angry. He did not know that Anansi had made the poor animal dumb. Lizard tried very hard to speak, but in vain.

He was accordingly judged guilty of theft, and as a punishment his wives were taken away from him and given to Anansi.

Since then lizards have always had a way of moving their heads helplessly backward and forward, as if saying, "How can any one be so foolish as to trust Anansi?"

Tit for Tat
(From the Akan peoples, Ghana)

THERE HAD BEEN a great famine in the land for many months. Meat had become so scarce that only the rich chiefs had money enough to buy it. The poor people were starving. Anansi and his family were in a miserable state.

One day, Anansi's eldest son – Kweku Tsin – to his great joy, discovered a place in the forest where there were still many animals. Knowing his father's wicked ways, Kweku told him nothing of the matter. Anansi, however, speedily discovered that Kweku was returning loaded, day after day, to the village. There he was able to sell the meat at a good price to the hungry villagers. Anansi immediately wanted to know the secret – but his son wisely refused to tell him. The old man determined to find out by a trick.

Slipping into his son's room one night, when he was fast asleep, he cut a tiny hole in the corner of the bag which Kweku always carried into the forest. Anansi then put a quantity of ashes into the bag and replaced it where he had found it.

Next morning, as Kweku set out for the forest, he threw the bag, as usual, over his shoulder. Unknown to him, at each step, the ashes were sprinkled on the ground. Consequently, when Anansi set out an hour later he was easily able to follow his son by means of the trail of ashes. He, too, arrived at the animals' home in the forest, and found Kweku there before him. He immediately drove his son away, saying that, by the law of the land., the place belonged to him. Kweku saw how he had been tricked, and determined to have the meat back.

He accordingly went home – made a tiny image and hung little bells round its neck. He then tied a long thread to its head and returned toward the hunting-place.

When about half-way there, he hung the image to a branch of a tree in the path, and hid himself in the bushes near by – holding the other end of the thread in his hand.

The greedy father, in the meantime, had killed as many animals as he could find, being determined to become rich as speedily as possible. He then skinned them and prepared the flesh – to carry it to the neighbouring villages to sell. Taking the first load, he set off for his own village. Half-way there, he came to the place where the image hung in the way. Thinking this was one of the gods, he stopped. As he approached, the image began to shake its head vigorously at him. He felt that this meant that the gods were angry. To please them, he said to the image, "May I give you a little of this meat?" Again the image shook its head. "May I give you half of this meat?" he then inquired. The head shook once more. "Do you want the whole of this meat?" he shouted fiercely. This time the head nodded, as if the image were well pleased. "I will not give you all my meat," Anansi cried. At this the image shook in every limb as if in a terrible temper. Anansi was so frightened that he threw the whole load on the ground and ran away. As he ran, he called back, "To-morrow I shall go to Ekubon – you will not be able to take my meat from me there, you thief."

But Kweku had heard where his father intended to go next day – and set the image in his path as before. Again Anansi was obliged to leave his whole load – and again he called out the name of the place where he would go the following day.

The same thing occurred, day after day, till all the animals in the wood were killed. By this time, Kweku Tsin had become very rich – but his father

Anansi was still very poor. He was obliged to go to Kweku's house every day for food.

When the famine was over, Kweku gave a great feast and invited the entire village. While all were gathered together, Kweku told the story of his father's cunning and how it had been overcome. This caused great merriment among the villagers. Anansi was so ashamed that he readily promised Kweku to refrain from his evil tricks for the future. This promise, however, he did not keep long.

Why White Ants Always Harm
Man's Property
(From the Akan peoples, Ghana)

THERE CAME ONCE such a terrible famine in the land that a grain of corn was worth far more than its weight in gold. A hungry spider was wandering through the forest looking for food. To his great joy he found a dead antelope.

Knowing that he would not be allowed to reach home in safety with it, he wrapped it up very carefully in a long mat and bound it securely.

Placing it on his head, he started for home. As he went, he wept bitterly, telling every one that this was his dead grandfather's body. Every one he met sympathized heartily with him.

On his way he met the wolf and the leopard. These two wise animals suspected that this was one of Spider's tricks. They knew that he was not to be trusted. Walking on a little way, they discussed what they could do to find out what was in the bundle.

They agreed to take a short cut across the country to a tree which they knew Cousin Spider must pass. When they reached this tree they hid themselves very carefully behind it and waited for him.

As he passed the place they shook the tree and uttered frightful noises. This so frightened Mr. Spider that he dropped his load and ran away.

The two gentlemen opened the bundle and, to their great joy, discovered the flesh of the antelope in it. They carried it off to their own home and began to prepare supper.

When Mr. Spider recovered from his fear he began to wonder who could have been at the tree to make the noises. He decided that his enemies must be Wolf and Leopard. He made up his mind he would get his meat back from them.

He took a small lizard and filed his teeth to fine, sharp points. He then sent him to spy upon the wolf and leopard – by begging fire from them. He was to get the fire and quench it as soon as he left their cottage. He could then return and ask a second time. If they asked him questions, he must smile and show his teeth.

The lizard did as he was told, and everything turned out just as Spider had expected. Wolf and Leopard eagerly asked the lizard where he had had his teeth filed so beauti- fully. He replied that "Filing Spider" had done it for him.

Wolf and Leopard discussed the matter and decided to have their teeth filed in the same way. They could then easily break the bones of their food.

Accordingly, they went to the house of the disguised spider and asked him to make their teeth like Lizard's. Spider agreed, but said that, to do it properly, he would first have to hang them on a tree. They made no objection to this.

When he had them safely hung, Spider and his family came and mocked them. Spider then went to their cottage and brought away the body of the antelope. The whole village was invited to the feast, which was held in front of the two poor animals on the tree. During this festival every one made fun of the wolf and leopard.

Next morning White Ant and his children passed the place on their way to some friends. Mr. Leopard begged them to set him and his friend free. White Ant and his family set to work, destroyed the tree and set them at liberty. Leopard and Wolf promised the ants that on their return they would spread a feast for them.

Unfortunately, Spider heard the invitation and made up his mind to benefit by it. On the third day (which was the very time set by the wolf and leopard) Spider dressed up his children like the ants. They set out, singing the ants' chorus, in order to deceive Leopard.

Wolf and Leopard welcomed them heartily and spread a splendid feast for them, which the spiders thoroughly enjoyed.

Soon after their departure the real ants arrived. The two hosts, thinking these must be Spider and his family, poured boiling water over them and killed them all except the father.

White Ant, on reaching home again, in great anger, vowed that he would never again help any one. He would take every opportunity to harm property. From that day to this white ants have been a perfect pest to man.

The Squirrel and the Spider
(From the Akan peoples, Ghana)

A HARD-WORKING SQUIRREL had, after much labour, succeeded in cultivating a very fine farm. Being a skilful climber of trees, he had not troubled to make a roadway into his farm. He used to reach it by the trees.

One day, when his harvests were very nearly ripe, it happened that Spider went out hunting in that neighbourhood. During his travels, he arrived at Squirrel's farm. Greatly pleased at the appearance of the fields, he sought for the roadway to it. Finding none, he returned home and told his family all about the matter. The very next day they all set out for this fine place, and set to work immediately to make a road. When this was completed Spider – who was very cunning – threw pieces of earthenware pot along the pathway. This he did to make believe that his children had dropped them while working to prepare the farm.

Then he and his family began to cut down and carry away such of the corn as was ripe. Squirrel noticed that his fields were being robbed, but could not at first find the thief. He determined to watch. Sure enough Spider soon reappeared to steal more of the harvest. Squirrel demanded to know what right he had on these fields. Spider immediately asked him the same question. "They are my fields," said Squirrel. "Oh, no! They are mine," retorted Spider. "I dug them and sowed them and planted them," said poor Squirrel. "Then where is your roadway to them?" said crafty Spider. "I need no roadway. I come by the trees," was Squirrel's reply. Needless to say, Spider laughed such an answer to scorn, and continued to use the farm as his own.

Squirrel appealed to the law, but the court decided that no one had ever had a farm without a road leading to it, therefore the fields must be Spider's.

In great glee Spider and his family prepared to cut down all the harvest that remained. When it was cut they tied it in great bundles and set off to the nearest market-place to sell it. When they were about half-way there, a terrible storm came on. They were obliged to put down their burdens by the roadside and run for shelter. When the storm had passed they returned to pick up their loads.

As they approached the spot they found a great, black crow there, with his broad wings outspread to keep the bundles dry. Spider went to him and very politely thanked him for so kindly taking care of their property. "Your property!" replied Father Crow. "Who ever heard of any one leaving bundles of corn by the roadside? Nonsense! These loads are mine." So saying, he picked them up and, went off with them, leaving Spider and his children to return home sorrowful and empty-handed. Their thieving ways had brought them little profit.

Why We See Ants Carrying Bundles as Big as Themselves
(From the Akan peoples, Ghana)

KWEKU ANANSI and Kweku Tsin – his son – were both very clever farmers. Generally they succeeded in getting fine harvests from each of their farms. One year, however, they were very unfortunate. They had sown their seeds as usual, but no rain had fallen for more than a month after and it looked as if the seeds would be unable to sprout.

Kweku Tsin was walking sadly through his fields one day looking at the bare, dry ground, and wondering what he and his family would do for food, if they were unable to get any harvest. To his surprise he saw a tiny dwarf seated by the roadside. The little hunchback asked the reason for his sadness, and Kweku Tsin told him. The dwarf promised to help him by bringing rain on the farm. He bade Kweku fetch two small sticks and tap him lightly on the hump, while he sang:

"O water, go up! O water, go up, And let rain fall, and let rain fall!"

To Kweku's great joy rain immediately began to fall, and continued till the ground was thoroughly well soaked. In the days following the seeds germinated, and the crops began to promise well.

Anansi soon heard how well Kweku's crops were growing – whilst his own were still bare and hard. He went straightway to his son and demanded to know the reason. Kweku Tsin, being an honest fellow, at once told him what had happened.

Anansi quickly made up his mind to get his farm watered in the same way, and accordingly set out toward it. As he went, he cut two big, strong sticks, thinking, "My son made the dwarf work with little sticks. I will make him do twice as much with my big ones." He carefully hid, the big sticks, however, when he saw the dwarf coming toward him. As before, the hunchback asked what the trouble was, and Anansi told him. "Take two small sticks, and beat me lightly on the hump," said the dwarf. "I will get rain for you."

But Anansi took his big sticks and beat so hard that the dwarf fell down dead. The greedy fellow was now thoroughly frightened, for he knew that the dwarf was jester to the King of the country, and a very great favourite of his. He wondered how he could fix the blame on some one else. He picked up the dwarf's dead body and carried it to a kola-tree. There he laid it on one of the top branches and sat down under the tree to watch.

By and by Kweku Tsin came along to see if his father had succeeded in getting rain for his crops. "Did you not see the dwarf, father?" he asked, as he saw the old man sitting alone. "Oh, yes!" replied Anansi; "but he has climbed this tree to pick kola. I am now waiting for him." "I will go up and fetch him," said the young man – and immediately began to climb. As soon as his head touched the body the latter, of course, fell to the ground. "Oh! what have you done, you wicked fellow?" cried his father. "You have killed the King's jester!" "That is all right," quietly replied the son (who saw that this was one of Anansi's tricks). "The King is very angry with him, and has promised a bag of money to any one who would kill him. I will now go and get the reward."

"No! No! No!" shouted Anansi. "The reward is mine. I killed him with two big sticks. I will take him to the King." "Very well," was the son's reply. "As you killed him, you may take him."

Off set Anansi, quite pleased with the prospect of getting a reward. He reached the King's court, only to find the King very angry at the death of his favourite. The body of the jester was shut up in a great box and Anansi was condemned – as a punishment – to carry it on his head for ever. The King enchanted the box so that it could never be set down on the ground. The only way in which Anansi could ever get rid of it was by getting some other man to put it on his head. This, of course, no one was willing to do.

At last, one day, when Anansi was almost worn out with his heavy burden, he met the Ant. "Will you hold this box for me while I go to market and buy some things I need badly?" said Anansi to Mr. Ant. "I know your tricks, Anansi," replied Ant. "You want to be rid of it." "Oh, no, indeed, Mr. Ant," protested Anansi. "Indeed I will come back for it, I promise."

Mr. Ant, who was an honest fellow, and always kept his own promises, believed him. He took the box on his head, and Anansi hurried off. Needless to say, the sly fellow had not the least intention of keeping his word. Mr. Ant waited in vain for his return – and was obliged to wander all the rest of his life with the box in his head. That is the reason we so often see ants carrying great bundles as they hurry along.

Why Spiders Are Always Found in the Corners of Ceilings
(From the Akan peoples, Ghana)

EGYA ANANSI was a very skilful farmer. He, with his wife and son, set to work one year to prepare a farm, much larger than any they had previously worked. They planted in it yams, maize, and beans – and were rewarded by a very rich crop. Their harvest was quite ten times greater than any they had ever had before.

Egya Anansi was very well pleased when he saw his wealth of corn and beans.

He was, however, an exceedingly selfish and greedy man, who never liked to share anything – even with his own wife and son. When he saw that the crops were quite ripe, he thought of a plan whereby he alone would profit by them. He called his wife and son to him and spoke thus: "We have all three worked exceedingly hard to prepare these fields. They have well repaid us. We will now gather in the harvest and pack it away in our barns. When that is done, we shall be in need of a rest. I propose that you and our son should go back to our home in the village and remain there at your ease for two or three weeks. I have to go to the coast on very urgent business. When I return we will all come to the farm and enjoy our well-earned feast."

Anansi's wife and son thought this a very good, sensible plan, and at once agreed to it. They went straight back to their village, leaving the cunning husband to start on his journey. Needless to say he had not the slightest intention of so doing.

Instead, he built himself a very comfortable hut near the farm – supplied it with all manner of cooking utensils, gathered in a large store of the corn and vegetables from the barn, and prepared for a solitary feast. This went on for a fortnight. By that time Anansi's son began to think it was time for him to go and weed the farm, lest the weeds should grow too high. He accordingly went there and worked several hours on it. While passing the barn, he happened to look in. Great was his surprise to see that more than half of their magnificent harvest had gone. He was greatly disturbed, thinking robbers had been at work, and wondered how he could prevent further mischief.

Returning to the village, he told the people there what had happened, and they helped to make a rubber-man. When evening came they carried the sticky figure to the farm, and placed it in the midst of the fields, to frighten away the thieves. Some of the young men remained with Anansi's son to watch in one of the barns.

When all was dark, Egya Anansi (quite unaware of what had happened) came, as usual, out of his hiding-place to fetch more food. On his way to the barn. he saw in front of him the figure of a man, and at first felt very frightened. Finding that the man did not move, however, he gained confidence and went up to him. "What do you want here?" said he. There was no answer. He repeated his question with the same result. Anansi then became very angry and dealt the figure a blow on the cheek with his right hand. Of course, his hand stuck fast to the rubber. "How dare you hold my hand!" he exclaimed. "Let me go at once or I shall hit you again." He then hit the figure with his left hand, which also stuck. He tried to disengage himself-by pushing against it with his knees and body, until, finally, knees, body, hands, and head were all firmly attached to the rubber-man. There Egya Anansi had to stay till daybreak, when his son came out with the other villagers to catch the robber. They were astonished to find that the evil-doer was Anansi himself. He, on the other hand, was so ashamed to be caught in the act of greediness that he changed into a spider and took refuge in a dark corner of the ceiling lest any one should see him. Since then spiders have always been found in dark, dusty corners, where people are not likely to notice them.

Anansi the Blind Fisherman
(From the Akan peoples, Ghana)

ANANSI, in his old age, became a fisherman. Very soon after that his sight began to fail. Finally, he grew quite blind. However, still being very strong, he continued his fishing – with the help of two men. The latter were exceedingly kind to him, and aided him in every possible way. They led him, each morning, to the beach and into the canoe. They told him where to spread his net and when to pull it in. When they returned to land they told him just where and when to step out, so that he did not even get wet.

Day after day this went on, but Anansi – instead of being in the least grateful to them – behaved very badly. When they told him where to spread his net, he would reply sharply, "I know. I was just about to put it there." When they were directing him to get out of the boat, he would say, "Oh, I know perfectly well we are at the beach. I was just getting ready to step out."

This went on for a long time, Anansi getting ruder and ruder to his helpers every day, until they could bear his treatment no longer. They determined when opportunity offered to punish him for his ingratitude.

The next day, as usual, he came with them to the beach. When they had got the canoe ready, they bade him step in. "Do you think I am a fool?" said he. "I know the canoe is there." They made no answer, but got in and patiently pulled toward the fishing-place. When they told him where to spread his net, he replied with so much abuse that they determined, there and then, to punish him.

By this time the canoe was full of fish, so they turned to row home. When they had gone a little way they stopped and said to him, "Here we are at the beach." He promptly told them that they were very foolish – to tell him a thing he knew so well. He added many rude and insulting remarks, which made them thoroughly angry. He then jumped proudly out, expecting to land on the beach. To his great astonishment he found himself sinking in deep water. The two men rowed quickly away, leaving him to struggle.

Like all the men of that country he was a good swimmer, but, of course, being blind, he was unable to see where the land lay. So he swam until he was completely tired out – and was drowned.

The Grinding-Stone that Ground
Flour by Itself
(From the Akan peoples, Ghana)

THERE HAD BEEN another great famine throughout the land. The villagers looked thin and pale for lack of food. Only one family appeared healthy and well. This was the household of Anansi's cousin. Anansi was unable to understand this, and felt sure his cousin was getting food in some way. The greedy fellow determined to find out the secret.

What had happened was this: Spider's cousin, while hunting one morning, had discovered a wonderful stone. The stone lay on the grass in the forest and ground flour of its own accord. Near by ran a stream of honey. Kofi was delighted. He sat down and had a good meal. Not being a greedy man, he took away with him only enough for his family's needs.

Each morning he returned to the stone and got sufficient food for that day. In this manner he and his family kept well and plump, while the surrounding villagers were starved and miserable-looking.

Anansi gave him no peace till he promised to show him the stone. This he was most unwilling to do – knowing his cousin's wicked ways. He felt sure that when Anansi saw the stone he would not be content to take only what he needed. However, Anansi troubled him so much with questions that at last he promised. He told Anansi that they would start next morning, as soon as the women set about their work. Anansi was too impatient to wait. In the middle of the night he bade his children get up and make a noise with the pots as if they were the women at work. Spider at once ran and wakened his cousin, saying, "Quick! It is time to start." His cousin, however, saw he had been tricked, and went back to bed again, saying he would not start till the women were sweeping. No sooner was he asleep again than Spider made his children take brooms and begin to sweep very noisily. He roused Kofi once more, saying, "It is time we had started." Once more his cousin refused to set off – saying it was only another trick of Spider's. He again returned to bed and to sleep. This time Spider slipped into his cousin's room and cut a hole in the bottom of his bag, which he then filled with ashes. After that he went off and left Kofi in peace.

When morning came the cousin awoke. Seeing no sign of Spider he very gladly set off alone to the forest, thinking he had got rid of the tiresome fellow. He was no sooner seated by the stone, however, than Anansi appeared, having followed him by the trail of ashes.

"Aha!" cried he. "Here is plenty of food for all. No more need to starve." "Hush," said his cousin. "You must not shout here. The place is too wonderful. Sit down quietly and eat."

They had a good meal, and Kofi prepared to return home with enough for his family. "No, no!" cried Anansi. "I am going to take the stone." In vain did his friend try to overcome his greed. Anansi insisted on putting the stone on his head, and setting out for the village.

"Spider, Spider, put me down, said the stone.
The pig came and drank and went away,
The antelope came and fed and went away:
Spider, Spider, put me down."

Spider, however, refused to listen. He carried the stone from village to village selling flour, until his bag was full of money. He then set out for home.

Having reached his hut and feeling very tired he prepared to put the stone down. But the stone refused to be moved from his head. It stuck fast there, and no efforts could displace it. The weight of it very soon grew too much for Anansi, and ground him down into small pieces, which were completely covered over by the stone. That is why we often find tiny spiders gathered together under large stones.

To Lose an Elephant for the Sake of a Wren Is a Very Foolish Thing to Do
(From the Akan peoples, Ghana)

IN THE OLDEN TIMES there stood in the King's town a very great tree. This tree was so huge that it began to overshadow the neighbouring fields. The King decided to have it cut down. He caused his servants to proclaim throughout the country that any one who succeeded in cutting down the tree with a wooden axe should have an elephant in payment.

People thought it would be impossible to cut down such a great tree with an axe of wood. Spider, however, decided to try by cunning to gain the elephant. He accordingly presented himself before the King and expressed his readiness to get rid of the tree.

A servant was sent with him to keep watch and to see that he only used the wooden axe given him. Spider, however, had taken care to have another, made of steel, hidden in his bag.

He now began to fell the tree. In a very few minutes, he said to the servant, "See, yonder is a fine antelope. If you are quick, you will be able to hit it with a stone. Run!" The lad did as he was bid, and ran a long way – but could see no sign of the antelope. In his absence, Spider seized the sharp axe and hastened to cut as much of the tree as he could, carefully hiding the axe in his bag before the servant's return.

This trick he repeated several times, till finally the tree was cut down. Spider went to the King to get the elephant, and took the servant to prove that he had used only the wooden axe. He got his promised reward, and started for home in great glee. On the way, however, he began to think over the matter. Shall I take this animal home?" thought he. "That would be foolish, for then I would be obliged to share it with my family. No! I will hide it in the forest, and eat it at my leisure. In that way I can have the whole of it for myself. Now what can I take home for the children's dinner?"

Thereupon he looked around and a little distance away saw a tiny wren sitting on a tree. "Exactly what I want," he said to himself. "That will be quite sufficient for them. I will tie my elephant to this tree while I catch the bird."

This he did, but when he tried to seize the latter, it flew off. He chased it for some time, without success. "Well! Well!" said he. "My family will just have to go without dinner. I will now go back and get my elephant." He returned to the spot where he had left the animal, but to his dismay the latter had escaped. Spider was obliged to go home empty-handed, and he, as well as his family, went dinnerless that day.

Tales of Tortoise, the Trickster

TORTOISE MAKES a most improbable trickster, it might be thought: unlike the quick and skilful spider, he is conspicuously slow and clumsy. Cautious in his movements, he is doggedly deliberate in his actions. A less mercurial creature we'd have difficulty imagining.

But then we recall that, even for European tradition, he has presented more paradoxical possibilities. In Aesop, of course, it was he who famously 'won the race' against the apparently far swifter and more agile hare. In some ways he does the same in West African myth. Not for the most part quite so literally, though. It's Tortoise's mind that moves quickly: physically, he's as slow and cumbersome as you would expect.

Actually, his sluggish movement and wrinkled skin make him seem a parody of human decrepitude; his scaly skin and stonelike shell suggest the closed-off thinking and inflexibility of the old. But his cunning and resourcefulness remind us of the wisdom and insight old age can bring. The bumps and ridges life's hard knocks have left on his shell underline the importance of all the experience our elders – and our ancestors, over generations – have accrued.

How the Tortoise Got Its Shell
(From the Akan peoples, Ghana)

A FEW HUNDRED YEARS AGO, the chief Mauri (God) determined to have a splendid yam festival. He therefore sent his messengers to invite all his chiefs and people to the gathering, which was to take place on Fida (Friday).

On the morning of that day he sent some of his servants to the neighbouring towns and villages to buy goats, sheep, and cows for the great feast. Mr. Klo (the tortoise), who was a tall and handsome fellow was sent to buy palm wine. He was directed to the palm-fields of Koklovi (the chicken).

At that time Klo was a very powerful traveller and speedily reached his destination although it was many miles distant from Mauri's palace.

When he arrived Koklovi was taking his breakfast. When they had exchanged polite salutations Koklovi asked the reason of Klo's visit. He replied, "I was sent by His Majesty Mauri, the ruler of the world, to buy him palm wine." "Whether he's ruler of the world or not," answered Koklovi, "no one can buy my wine with money. If you want it you must fight for it. If you win you can have it all and the palm-trees too."

This answer delighted Klo as he was a very strong fighter. Koklovi was the same, so that the fighting continued for several hours before Klo was able to overcome Koklovi. He was at last successful, however, and securely bound Koklovi before he left him.

Then, taking his great pot, he filled it with wine. Finding that there was more wine than the pot would hold, Klo foolishly drank all the rest. He then piled the palm-trees on his back and set out for the palace with the pot of wine. The amount which he had drunk, however, made him feel so sleepy and tired that he could not walk fast with his load. Added to this, a terrible rain began to fall, which made the ground very slippery and still more difficult to travel over.

By the time Klo succeeded in reaching his master's palace the gates were shut and locked. Mauri, finding it so late, had concluded that every one was inside.

There were many people packed into the great hall, and all were singing and dancing. The noise of the concert was so great that no one heard Klo's knocking at the gate, and there he had to stay with his great load of wine and palm-trees.

The rain continued for nearly two months and was so terrible that the people all remained in the palace till it had finished. By that time Klo had died, under the weight of his load – which he had been unable to get off his back. There he lay, before the gate, with the pile of palm-trees on top of him.

When the rain ceased and the gates were opened the people were amazed to see this great mound in front of the gate, where before there had been nothing. They fetched spades and began to shovel it away.

When they came to the bottom of the pile there lay Klo. His earthenware pot and the dust had caked together and formed quite a hard cover on his back.

He was taken into the palace – and by the use of many wonderful medicines he was restored to life. But since that date he has never been able to stand upright. He has been a creeping creature, with a great shell on his back.

The Hunter and the Tortoise
(From the Akan peoples, Ghana)

A VILLAGE HUNTER had one day gone farther afield than usual. Coming to a part of the forest with which he was unacquainted, he was astonished to hear a voice singing. He listened; this was the song:

> *"It is man who forces himself on things,*
> *Not things which force themselves on him."*

The singing was accompanied by sweet music – which entirely charmed the hunter's heart.

When the little song was finished, the hunter peeped through the branches to see who the singer could be. Imagine his amazement when he found it was none other than a tortoise, with a tiny harp slung in front of her. Never had he seen such a marvellous thing.

Time after time he returned to the same place in order to listen to this wonderful creature. At last he persuaded her to let him carry her back to his hut, that he might enjoy her singing daily in comfort. This she permitted, only on the understanding that she sang to him alone.

The hunter did not rest long content with this arrangement, however. Soon he began to wish that he could show off this wonderful tortoise to all the world, and thereby thought he would gain great honour. He told the secret, first to one, then to another, until finally it reached the ears of the chief himself. The hunter was commanded to come and tell his tale before the Assembly. When, however, he described the tortoise who sang and played on, the harp, the people shouted in scorn. They refused to believe him.

At last he said, "If I do not speak truth, I give you leave to kill me. To-morrow I will bring the tortoise to this place and you may all hear her. If she cannot do as I say, I am willing to die." "Good," replied the people, "and if the tortoise can do as you say, we give you leave to punish us in any way you choose."

The matter being then settled, the hunter returned home, well pleased with the prospect. As soon as the morrow dawned, he carried tortoise and harp down to the Assembly Place – where a table had been placed ready for her. Every one gathered round to listen. But no song came. The people were very patient, and quite willing to give both tortoise and hunter a chance. Hours went by, and, to the hunter's dismay and shame, the tortoise remained mute. He tried every means in his power to coax her to sing, but in vain. The people at first whispered, then spoke outright, in scorn of the boaster and his claims.

Night came on and brought with it the hunter's doom. As the last ray of the setting sun faded, he was beheaded. The instant this had happened the tortoise spoke. The people looked at one another in troubled wonder: "Our brother spoke truth, then, and we have killed him." The tortoise, however, went on to explain. "He brought his punishment on himself. I led a happy life in the forest, singing my little song. He was not content to come and listen to me, He had to tell my secret (which did not at all concern him) to all the world. Had he not tried to make a show of me this would never have happened."

> *"It is man who forces himself on things,*
> *Not things which force themselves on him."*

Tortoise and the Wisdom of the World
(From Nigeria)

TORTOISE WAS VERY ANGRY when he awoke one day to discover that other people around him had started to behave just as wisely as himself. He was angry because he was an ambitious fellow and wanted to keep all the wisdom of the world for his own personal use. If he succeeded in his ambition, he felt he would be so wise that everyone, including the great chiefs and elders of the people, would have to seek his advice before making any decision, no matter how small. He intended to charge a great deal of money for the privilege, and was adamant that nothing would upset his great plan.

And so he set out to collect all the wisdom of the world before anyone else decided to help himself to it. He hollowed out an enormous gourd for the purpose and began crawling along on his stomach through the bush, collecting the wisdom piece by piece and dropping it carefully into the large vessel. After several hours, when he was happy he had gathered every last scrap, he plugged the gourd with a roll of leaves and made his way slowly homewards.

But now that he had all the wisdom of the world in his possession, he grew fearful that it might be stolen from him. So he decided straight away that it would be best to hide the gourd in a safe place at the centre of the forest. He soon found a very tall palm tree which seemed suitable enough and prepared himself to climb to the top. First of all he took a rope and made a loop around the neck of the gourd. When he had done this, he hung the vessel from his neck so that it rested on his stomach. Then he took a very deep breath and began to climb the tree.

But he found that after several minutes he had not made any progress, for the gourd was so large it kept getting in his way. He slung it to one side and tried again. Still he could not move forward even an inch. He slung the gourd impatiently to the other side, but the same thing happened. Finally, he tried to stretch past it, but all these efforts came to nothing and he beat the tree with his fists in exasperation.

Suddenly he heard someone sniggering behind him. He turned around and came face to face with a hunter who had been watching him with great amusement for some time.

"Tortoise," said the hunter eventually, "why don't you hang the gourd over your back if you insist on climbing that tree?"

"What a good idea," replied the tortoise, "I'd never have thought of that on my own."

But he had no sooner spoken these words when it dawned on him that the hunter must have helped himself to some of the precious wisdom.

Tortoise now grew even more angry and frustrated and began scuttling up the tree to get away from the thieving hunter. He moved so fast, however, that the rope holding the gourd slipped from around his neck causing the vessel to drop to the ground where it broke into hundreds of little pieces.

All the wisdom of the world was now scattered everywhere. And ever since that time nobody else has attempted to gather it all together in one place.

But whenever he feels the need, Tortoise makes a special journey to the palm tree at the centre of the forest, for he knows that the little pieces are still there on the ground, waiting to be discovered by anyone who cares to search hard enough.

Tortoise and the King
(From the Yoruba people, southern Nigeria)

ONE YEAR the Elephant had done a great deal of damage, breaking down the trees, drinking up the water in a time of scarcity, and eating the first tender crops from the fields.

The King's hunters tried in vain to destroy him, for Elephant knew many charms, and always escaped from their traps.

At last the King offered the hand of his daughter in marriage to anyone who would rid the country of the pest.

Tortoise went to the palace and offered to catch Elephant, and then made his preparations. Outside the town a large pit was dug, and on the top of it was laid a thin platform covered with velvet cloths and leopard-skins, like a throne.

Then Tortoise set off into the forest, accompanied by slaves and drummers. Elephant was very much surprised to see his little friend Tortoise riding in such state, and suspected a trap; but Tortoise said that the old King was dead and the people all wished Elephant to rule over them, because he was the greatest of all animals. When he heard this, Elephant was flattered, and agreed to accompany Tortoise to the town. But when he went up on to the platform to be crowned King, the wood gave way beneath him, and he crashed down into the pit and was speedily slain by the King's hunters.

All the people rejoiced, and praised the cunning of Tortoise, who went to the palace to receive his bride. But the King refused to give his daughter to such an insignificant creature, and Tortoise determined to have a revenge. When the new crops were just ripening, he called together all the field-mice and elves, and asked them to eat up and carry away the corn. They were only too pleased with the idea, and the farmers in distress found the fields quite bare.

Now there was prospect of a famine in the land, and the King offered the same reward as before to anyone who would rid the country of the pests.

Tortoise once again appeared in the palace and offered his help. The King was eager enough to accept it, but Tortoise cautiously refused to do anything until the Princess became his bride.

The King was thus forced to consent to the marriage, and when it had taken place, Tortoise, true to his word, called together all the mice and elves and showed them a platform loaded with dainty morsels of food. He then addressed them as follows:

"The people are so distressed at the damage you have done, that they have prepared this feast for you, and they promise to do the same twice every year, before the harvesting of the first and second crops, if you will agree not to touch the corn in the fields."

The little creatures all consented, and marched in a great crowd to the platform, which they soon cleared.

The King and his people were not very pleased to hear of this arrangement, but they were so afraid of Tortoise that they could not complain, and after that the mice and elves never troubled the country again.

Tortoise and Mr. Fly
(From the Yoruba people, southern Nigeria)

Φ

ONCE Tortoise and his family fell on hard times and had nothing to eat, but they noticed that their neighbour, Mr. Fly, seemed to be very prosperous and feasted every night.

Tortoise was curious to know how he obtained so much money, and after watching him for some days he discovered that Mr. Fly flew away every morning early with a large empty sack on his back, and returned in the evening with the sack full, and after that his wife would prepare a feast.

One morning Tortoise hid in the sack and waited to see what would happen. Soon Mr. Fly came out of his house, lifted up the sack, and flew away.

He descended at last in the market-place of a large town, where drummers were beating the tones of the dance, and maidens were dancing before a crowd of people.

Mr. Fly laid his sack on the ground, and Tortoise saw him standing beside one of the drummers. When the people threw money, Mr. Fly picked the coins up and hid them in his sack, and by evening he had collected a great quantity. Then he took up the sack again and flew home. Tortoise quickly got out and took most of the money with him, so that poor Mr. Fly was surprised to find the sack almost empty.

This happened several times, until one day as he put money in the sack Mr. Fly caught sight of Tortoise hiding inside it. He was very angry at the trick, and going to the drummer asked him if he had missed any money.

"Yes," said the drummer. "For some days I have been losing coins."

"Look inside this sack," replied Mr. Fly, "and you will see the thief sitting among the money he has stolen."

The drummer peeped inside the sack and saw Tortoise.

"How shall the thief be punished?" he cried angrily.

"Just tie up the sack," said Mr. Fly, "and then beat upon it as if it were a drum."

So the drummer tied up the sack and beat upon it until Tortoise was black and blue, and this is why his back is covered with bruises.

Then Mr. Fly picked up the sack, and flew high up in the air and dropped it. By chance the sack fell down just outside Tortoise's house, and neighbours came to tell Nyanribo, his wife, that someone had left a present outside the door. But when she opened the sack in the presence of a crowd of people, she found only Tortoise inside, more dead than alive. Then Mr. Fly made a song and narrated the whole story, and the drummers also played it, and Tortoise and Nyanribo were so ashamed that they left the place and went to live in another country.

The Three Deaths of Tortoise
(From the Yoruba people, southern Nigeria)

TORTOISE HAD MANY ENEMIES, and they plotted together to kill him. One night when Tortoise was asleep in his hut, they set fire to it, and as they saw the flames leaping up, they said to one another:

"He cannot escape. He will die."

But Tortoise drew himself into his shell and was untouched by the fire, and in the morning his enemies were astonished to see him walking about as usual.

Soon they made another plan and threw Tortoise into a pool of water.

"The pool is deep. He will drown," said his enemies to one another.

But Tortoise had drawn himself into his shell and was secure, and at noon the sun shone fiercely and dried up the pool.

That evening Tortoise walked about the village as if nothing had happened, and his enemies were astonished.

The next day they made a third attempt to kill him. They made a deep hole in the ground and buried Tortoise, and this time they were quite sure he could not escape. To mark the place, they put a bamboo stake in the ground.

Meanwhile a man who was passing saw the bamboo stake, and thought, "Someone has buried a treasure here!" He called his friends, and they began to dig, but all they found was Tortoise fast asleep inside his shell.

Tortoise walked about the village again, looking very happy, and his enemies were filled with astonishment.

"He has a charm, and we shall never be able to kill him," they said to one another, and from that day they left him in peace.

Tortoise and the Cock
(From the Yoruba people, southern Nigeria)

ONE DAY Tortoise and Nyanribo felt very hungry, but they could not afford to buy food, and while they were discussing what might be done, Tortoise heard a cock crowing, and it gave him an idea. He went to the cock and said:

"I have come to warn you. I heard the farmer asking his wife to prepare chicken for dinner to-morrow."

At this all the fowls were in great distress and wondered which of them was to be killed. Tortoise replied:

"I heard the farmer's wife say that she will kill the first of you which she hears crowing or clucking in the morning."

Naturally the fowls decided to be absolutely silent.

Very early in the morning Tortoise went creeping among the fowls and stole all the eggs from the nests, taking them one by one to his house; but the cock was afraid to crow and the hens were afraid to cluck, and when the farmer's wife came to collect the eggs, she found that they had all been stolen.

At this she flew into a rage, and killed all the fowls instead of one, and while the farmer and his wife had a feast of chicken, Tortoise and Nyanribo invited their friends to a feast of eggs!

Tortoise and Crab
(From the Yoruba people, southern Nigeria)

EVERYONE KNOWS that Tortoise and Crab are enemies. One morning on the seashore they decided to fight to see which was the stronger, but, as both of them are protected by a hard shell, neither could succeed in injuring the other.

Finally they came to an agreement that they were equal in strength.

"We are so well protected by our armour," said Tortoise, "that no one can harm us."

"And thus," said Crab, "we are the strongest creatures in the world."

But at this moment a boy passed by and picked them both up. Tortoise was boiled in a pot and his shell was made into ornaments, while Crab was cooked in a stew for the boy's supper. Since that day the descendants of the two boasters have always been ashamed to meet, and that is why they always shun one another.

Tortoise and Pigeon
(From the Yoruba people, southern Nigeria)

TORTOISE AND PIGEON were often seen walking together, but unfortunately Tortoise treated his friend rather badly, and often played tricks on him. Pigeon never complained, and put up with everything in a good-humoured way. Once Tortoise came to him and said:

"I am going on a journey to-day to visit my cousins; will you come with me?"

Pigeon agreed to accompany him, and they set off. When they had go ne some distance they came to a river, and Pigeon was forced to take Tortoise upon his back and fly across with him.

Soon afterwards they reached the house of Tortoise's cousins. Tortoise left his friend standing at the door while he went inside and greeted his relatives. They had prepared a feast for him, and they all began to eat together.

"Will you not ask your friend to eat with us?" said the cousins; but Tortoise was so greedy that he did not wish Pigeon to share the feast, and replied:

"My friend is a silly fellow, he will not eat in a stranger's house, and he is so shy that he refuses to come in."

After some time Tortoise bade farewell to his cousins, saying, "Greetings to you on your hospitality," and came out of the house. But Pigeon, who was both tired and hungry, had heard his words and determined to pay him out for once.

When they reached the river-bank, he took Tortoise up once again on his back; when he had flown half-way across, he allowed Tortoise to fall off into the river. But, by chance, instead of falling into the water, he landed on the back of a crocodile which was floating on the surface, and when the crocodile came up to the bank, Tortoise quickly descended and hurried away.

Pigeon saw what had happened, and that Tortoise had safely reached the land; so he flew ahead of him until he came to a field where a dead horse was lying.

To trick Tortoise once more, Pigeon cut off the horse's head and stuck it in the ground, as if it grew there like a plant.

When Tortoise reached the field and saw the horse's head, he went straight away to the King of the country and told him that he knew of a place where horses' heads grew like plants.

"If this is true," said the King, "I will reward you with a great treasure; but if it is false, you must die."

The King and a large crowd of people accompanied Tortoise to the field, but meanwhile Pigeon had removed the head. Tortoise ran about looking for it, but in vain, and he was condemned to die. A large fire was made, and Tortoise was thrown on to it.

But now Pigeon repented of the trick he had done, and quickly called together all the birds of the air. They came like a wind, beating out the fire with their wings, and so rescued Tortoise.

When Pigeon had explained this trick, the King pardoned Tortoise, and allowed the two friends to depart in safety.

Tortoise and the Whip-Tree
(From the Yoruba people, southern Nigeria)

Ɵ

THERE WAS A FAMINE in the land, and everyone longed for food. Each day Tortoise went into the forest to see if he could find anything to eat, but in the evenings he came home discouraged with only a few herbs and dried-up nut-kernels for his family.

One day, as he walked through a grove, he saw two trees close together – a small stunted tree and a big tree with thick foliage and spreading branches. "What sort of tree are you?" he asked the little tree.

"I am the Chop-tree," was the reply.

"Well, Chop-tree, what can you produce?" asked Tortoise. And at the words the little tree waved its branches and a shower of food fell to the ground. Tortoise ate until nothing remained, and then turned to the tall and handsome tree.

"And what tree are you?" he asked, thinking that such a splendid tree must produce rich fruit. The tree told him that its name was Whip-tree, to which Tortoise replied: "Whip-tree, what can you produce?"

At these words the Whip-tree bent its branches and beat Tortoise until he cried for mercy. When the beating ceased, Tortoise went home, but, being of a greedy nature, he said nothing of the two trees, and showed his wife only a few poor nuts which he had found.

After that he went every day to the Chop-tree and feasted to his heart's content. While his family and all the people, even to the King, became thin and meagre, Tortoise appeared daily fatter and more prosperous, until Nyanribo, his wife, began to suspect.

One day Nyanribo resolved to follow him into the forest, and great was her surprise when she saw her husband stand under the little tree and say: "Tree, do your duty!" The branches waved, and rich titbits fell to the ground.

Nyanribo cried out in astonishment and reproached her husband for his greediness. She hastened back to the town and returned with the whole family of children and cousins. She stood under the Chop-tree and said: "Tree, do your duty!" When the food fell down, they all partook of the feast.

But spiteful Tortoise was displeased, and exclaimed:

"I wish you would stand under the other tree and receive your proper reward!"

Hearing this, they all went to stand under the Whip-tree, and Nyanribo again cried: "Tree, do your duty!" Alas! The branches began to beat them all soundly until they died.

Tortoise was alarmed at this and hastily returned to his house, but the neighbours soon noticed that his wife and family were absent, and the King ordered Tortoise to account for their disappearance.

Tortoise therefore led the King and all the nobles and the people into the forest, and when they were gathered under the Chop-tree he cried out: "Tree, do your duty!" and, as before, a feast appeared, which the hungry people soon devoured.

Tortoise then asked them to stand underneath the othet tree, and this they were eager to do. The King himself was the one to cry out: "Tree, do your duty!" and the branches began to beat all those who stood below until they cried out with pain.

In a great rage the people hunted for Tortoise, desiring to kill him; but he hid inside his shell, in a secret place, and they could not harm him.

He stayed in concealment until the King died and a new King was found, and then he thought it safe to appear in the town. But whenever he hears the two words "Chop" and "Whip," he hides in his shell, thinking himself in danger.

Tortoise and the Rain
(From the Yoruba people, southern Nigeria)

✪

TORTOISE AND A CLOUD once made the following agreement: Whenever Tortoise very much desired fine weather, he was to stand outside his house and call: "Pass! Pass!" and then the Cloud would roll away and allow the sun to shine. And when Tortoise desired rain, he was to cry: "Fall! Fall!" and the rain would pour down. In payment for this service, Tortoise was to place on the ground each time a certain number of cowries.

Tortoise was delighted with this arrangement, and at first he duly placed the sum of money on the ground every time he asked the Cloud for fine or wet weather.

One day, the occasion of a Chief's wedding, the sky was very cloudy, and it seemed likely to rain. Tortoise heard the Chief complaining: "We have promised the drummers a great deal of money, but if it rains nobody will come to see the maidens dance at my wedding!"

Tortoise went to the Chief and said: "If you will give me a certain sum, I will hold up the clouds on my hard back and there will be no rain."

The Chief readily agreed to pay the cowries Tortoise demanded, and Tortoise stood at the back of his hut and cried to the Cloud: "Pass! Pass!" The Cloud rolled back, the sun shone brightly, and the wedding took place with much rejoicing.

But Tortoise did not lay any money on the ground, and instead, he kept the whole amount for himself.

The next day a man came to Tortoise's house and offered him much money if he would cause the rain to fall. "For," he said, "my fishing-stakes are too high, but if it rains the river will swell and the fish will come into my baskets."

"Very well," replied Tortoise. "I will throw a spear into the clouds, and the rain will fall."

Then he stood at the back of his house, where he could not be seen, and cried to the Cloud: "Fall! Fall!" It began to pour with rain.

But again he neglected to lay money on the ground and kept it all for himself. Soon, in this way, he grew rich and famous, and almost every day someone asked for fine or rainy weather. He stored many bags of cowries in his house and gave nothing to the Cloud.

When two people asked him for rain and sunshine on the same day, Tortoise pretended that he had grown tired with holding up the clouds on his back, and so the rain fell.

But after some time, seeing how rich Tortoise became, the hard-working Cloud was angry and decided to punish him.

One day Tortoise wished to set out on a journey with his family, so he stood outside his house and cried: "Pass! Pass! Let the sun shine on my journey!"

But as soon as he had set out, the Cloud rolled back again and rain poured down in torrents, causing a great flood in which Tortoise and all his family were drowned.

The Leopard, the Squirrel and the Tortoise
(From southern Nigeria)

MANY YEARS AGO there was a great famine throughout the land, and all the people were starving. The yam crop had failed entirely, the plantains did not bear any fruit, the ground-nuts were all shrivelled up, and the corn never came to a head; even the palm oil nuts did not ripen, and the peppers and ocros also gave out.

The leopard, however, who lived entirely on 'beef', did not care for any of these things; and although some of the animals who lived on corn and the growing crops began to get rather skinny, he did not mind very much. In order to save himself trouble, as everybody was complaining of the famine, he called a meeting of all the animals and told them that, as they all knew, he was very powerful and must have food, that the famine did not affect him, as he only lived on flesh, and as there were plenty of animals about he did not intend to starve. He then told all the animals present at the meeting that if they did not wish to be killed themselves they must bring their grandmothers to him for food, and when they were finished he would feed off their mothers. The animals might bring their grandmothers in succession, and he would take them in their turn; so that, as there were many different animals, it would probably be some time before their mothers were eaten, by which time it was possible that the famine would be over. But in any case, he warned them that he was determined to have sufficient food for himself, and that if the grandmothers or mothers were not forthcoming he would turn upon the young people themselves and kill and eat them.

This, of course, the young generation, who had attended the meeting, did not appreciate, and in order to save their own skins, agreed to supply the leopard with his daily meal.

The first to appear with his aged grandmother was the squirrel. The grandmother was a poor decrepit old thing, with a mangy tail, and the leopard swallowed her at one gulp, and then looked round for more. In an angry voice he growled out: "This is not the proper food for me; I must have more at once."

Then a bush cat pushed his old grandmother in front of the leopard, but he snarled at her and said, "Take the nasty old thing away; I want some sweet food."

It was then the turn of a bush buck, and after a great deal of hesitation a wretchedly poor and thin old doe tottered and fell in front of the leopard, who immediately despatched her, and although the meal was very unsatisfactory, declared that his appetite was appeased for that day.

The next day a few more animals brought their old grandmothers, until at last it became the tortoise's turn; but being very cunning, he produced witnesses to prove that his grandmother was dead, so the leopard excused him.

After a few days all the animals' grandmothers were exhausted, and it became the turn of the mothers to supply food for the ravenous leopard. Now although most of the young animals did not mind getting rid of their grandmothers, whom they had scarcely even known, many of them had very strong objections to providing their mothers, of whom they were very fond, as food for the leopard. Amongst the strongest objectors were the squirrel and the tortoise. The tortoise, who had thought the whole thing out, was aware that, as everyone knew that his mother was alive (she being rather an amiable old person and friendly with all-comers), the same excuse would not avail him a second time. He therefore told his mother to climb up a palm tree, and that he would provide her with food until the famine was over. He instructed her to let down a basket every day, and said that he would place food in it for her. The tortoise made the basket for his mother, and attached it to a long string of tie-tie. The string was so strong that she could haul her son up whenever he wished to visit her.

All went well for some days, as the tortoise used to go at daylight to the bottom of the tree where his mother lived and place her food in the basket; then the old lady would pull the basket up and have her food, and the tortoise would depart on his daily round in his usual leisurely manner.

In the meantime the leopard had to have his daily food, and the squirrel's turn came first after the grandmothers had been finished, so he was forced to produce his mother for the leopard to eat, as he was a poor, weak thing and not possessed of any cunning. The squirrel was, however, very fond of his mother, and when she had been eaten he remembered that the tortoise had not produced his grandmother for the leopard's food. He therefore determined to set a watch on the movements of the tortoise.

The very next morning, while he was gathering nuts, he saw the tortoise walking very slowly through the bush, and being high up in the trees and able to travel very fast, had no difficulty in keeping the tortoise in sight without being noticed. When the tortoise arrived at the foot of the tree where his mother lived, he placed the food in the basket which his mother had let down already by the tie-tie, and having got into the basket and given a pull at the string to signify that everything was right, was hauled up, and after a time was let down again in the basket. The squirrel was watching all the time, and directly the tortoise had gone, jumped from branch to branch of the trees, and very soon arrived at the place where the leopard was snoozing.

When he woke up, the squirrel said:

"You have eaten my grandmother and my mother, but the tortoise has not provided any food for you. It is now his turn, and he has hidden his mother away in a tree."

At this the leopard was very angry, and told the squirrel to lead him at once to the tree where the tortoise's mother lived. But the squirrel said:

"The tortoise only goes at daylight, when his mother lets down a basket; so if you go in the morning early, she will pull you up, and you can then kill her."

To this the leopard agreed, and the next morning the squirrel came at cockcrow and led the leopard to the tree where the tortoise's mother was hidden. The old lady had already let down the basket for her daily supply of food, and the leopard got into it and gave the line a pull; but except a few small jerks nothing happened, as the old mother tortoise was not strong enough to pull a heavy leopard off the ground. When the leopard saw that he was not going to be pulled up, being an expert climber, he scrambled up the tree, and when he got to the top he found the poor old tortoise, whose shell was so tough that he thought she was not worth eating, so he threw her down on to the ground in a violent temper, and then came down himself and went home.

Shortly after this the tortoise arrived at the tree, and finding the basket on the ground gave his usual tug at it, but there was no answer. He then looked about, and after a little time came upon the broken shell of his poor old mother, who by this time was quite dead. The tortoise knew at once that the leopard had killed his mother, and made up his mind that for the future he would live alone and have nothing to do with the other animals.

The Leopard, the Tortoise
and the Bush Rat
(From southern Nigeria)

A T THE TIME of the great famine all the animals were very thin and weak from want of food; but there was one exception, and that was the tortoise and all his family, who were quite fat, and did not seem to suffer at all. Even the leopard was very thin, in spite of the arrangement he had made with the animals to bring him their old grandmothers and mothers for food.

In the early days of the famine (as you will remember) the leopard had killed the mother of the tortoise, in consequence of which the tortoise was very angry with the leopard, and determined if possible to be revenged upon him. The tortoise, who was very clever, had discovered a shallow lake full of fish in the middle of the forest, and every morning he used to go to the lake and, without much trouble, bring back enough food for himself and his family. One day the leopard met the tortoise and noticed how fat he was. As he was very thin himself he decided to watch the tortoise, so the next morning he hid himself in the long grass near the tortoise's house and waited very patiently, until at last the tortoise came along quite slowly, carrying a basket which appeared to be very heavy. Then the leopard sprang out, and said to the tortoise:

"What have you got in that basket?"

The tortoise, as he did not want to lose his breakfast, replied that he was carrying firewood back to his home. Unfortunately for the tortoise the leopard had a very acute sense of smell, and knew at once that there was fish in the basket, so he said:

"I know there is fish in there, and I am going to eat it."

The tortoise, not being in a position to refuse, as he was such a poor creature, said:

"Very well. Let us sit down under this shady tree, and if you will make a fire I will go to my house and get pepper, oil, and salt, and then we will feed together."

To this the leopard agreed, and began to search about for dry wood, and started the fire. In the meantime the tortoise waddled off to his house, and very soon returned with the pepper, salt, and oil; he also brought a long piece of cane tie-tie, which is very strong. This he put on the ground, and began boiling the fish. Then he said to the leopard:

"While we are waiting for the fish to cook, let us play at tying one another up to a tree. You may tie me up first, and when I say 'Tighten,' you must loose the rope, and when I say 'Loosen,' you must tighten the rope."

The leopard, who was very hungry, thought that this game would make the time pass more quickly until the fish was cooked, so he said he would play. The tortoise then stood with his back to the tree and said, "Loosen the rope," and the leopard, in accordance with the rules of the game, began to tie up the tortoise. Very soon the tortoise shouted out, "Tighten!" and the leopard at once unfastened the tie-tie, and the tortoise was free. The tortoise then said, "Now, leopard, it is your turn;" so the leopard stood up against the tree and called out to the tortoise to loosen the rope, and the tortoise at once very quickly passed the rope several times round the leopard and got him fast to the tree. Then the leopard said, "Tighten the rope;" but instead of playing the game in accordance with the rules he had laid down, the tortoise ran faster and faster with the rope round the leopard, taking great care, however, to keep out of reach of the leopard's claws, and very soon had the leopard so securely fastened that it was quite impossible for him to free himself.

All this time the leopard was calling out to the tortoise to let him go, as he was tired of the game; but the tortoise only laughed, and sat down at the fireside and commenced his meal. When he had finished he packed up the remainder of the fish for his family, and prepared to go, but before he started he said to the leopard:

"You killed my mother and now you want to take my fish. It is not likely that I am going to the lake to get fish for you, so I shall leave you here to starve."

He then threw the remains of the pepper and salt into the leopard's eyes and quietly went on his way, leaving the leopard roaring with pain.

All that day and throughout the night the leopard was calling out for someone to release him, and vowing all sorts of vengeance on the tortoise; but no one came, as the people and animals of the forest do not like to hear the leopard's voice.

In the morning, when the animals began to go about to get their food, the leopard called out to everyone he saw to come and untie him, but they all refused, as they knew that if they did so the leopard would most likely kill them at once and eat them. At last a bush rat came near and saw the leopard tied up to the tree and asked him what was the matter, so the leopard told him that he had been playing a game of 'tight' and 'loose' with the tortoise, and that he had tied him up and left him there to starve. The leopard then implored the bush rat to cut the ropes with his sharp teeth. The bush rat was very sorry for the leopard; but at the same time he knew that, if he let the leopard go, he would most likely be killed and eaten, so he hesitated, and said that he did not quite see his way to cutting the ropes. But this bush rat, being rather kind-hearted, and having had some experience of traps himself, could sympathise with the leopard in his uncomfortable position. He therefore thought for a time, and then hit upon a plan. He first started to dig a hole under the tree, quite regardless of the leopard's cries. When he had finished the hole he came out and cut one of the ropes, and immediately ran into his hole, and waited there to see what would happen; but although the leopard struggled frantically, he could not get loose, as the tortoise had tied him up so fast. After a time, when he saw that there was no danger, the bush rat crept out again and very carefully bit through another rope, and then retired to his hole as before. Again nothing happened, and he began to feel more confidence, so he bit several strands through one after the other until at last the leopard was free. The leopard, who was ravenous with hunger, instead of being grateful to the bush rat, directly he was free, made a dash at the bush rat with his big paw, but just missed him, as the bush rat had dived for his hole; but he was not quite quick enough to escape altogether, and the leopard's sharp claws scored his back and left marks which he carried to his grave.

Ever since then the bush rats have had white spots on their skins, which represent the marks of the leopard's claws.

How the Tortoise Overcame the Elephant and the Hippopotamus
(From southern Nigeria)

THE ELEPHANT AND THE HIPPOPOTAMUS always used to feed together, and were good friends. One day when they were both dining together, the tortoise appeared and said that although they were both big and strong, neither of them could pull him out of the water with a strong piece of tie-tie, and he offered the elephant ten thousand rods if he could draw him out of the river the next day.

The elephant, seeing that the tortoise was very small, said, "If I cannot draw you out of the water, I will give you twenty thousand rods." So on the following morning the tortoise got some very strong tie-tie and made it fast to his leg, and went down to the river. When he got there, as he knew the place well, he made the tie-tie fast round a big rock, and left the other end on the shore for the elephant to pull by, then went down to the bottom of the river and hid himself. The elephant then came down and started pulling, and after a time he smashed the rope.

Directly this happened, the tortoise undid the rope from the rock and came to the land, showing all people that the rope was still fast to his leg, but that the elephant had failed to pull him out. The elephant was thus forced to admit that the tortoise was the winner, and paid to him the twenty thousand rods, as agreed. The tortoise then took the rods home to his wife, and they lived together very happily.

After three months had passed, the tortoise, seeing that the money was greatly reduced, thought he would make some more by the same trick, so he went to the hippopotamus and made the same bet with him. The hippopotamus said, "I will make the bet, but I shall take the water and you shall take the land; I will then pull you into the water."

To this the tortoise agreed, so they went down to the river as before, and having got some strong tie-tie, the tortoise made it fast to the hippopotamus' hind leg, and told him to go into the water. Directly the hippo had turned his back and disappeared, the tortoise took the rope twice round a strong palm-tree which was growing near, and then hid himself at the foot of the tree.

When the hippo was tired of pulling, he came up puffing and blowing water into the air from his nostrils. Directly the tortoise saw him coming up, he unwound the rope, and walked down towards the hippopotamus, showing him the tie-tie round his leg. The hippo had to acknowledge that the tortoise was too strong for him, and reluctantly handed over the twenty thousand rods.

The elephant and the hippo then agreed that they would take the tortoise as their friend, as he was so very strong; but he was not really so strong as they thought, and had won because he was so cunning.

He then told them that he would like to live with both of them, but that, as he could not be in two places at the same time, he said that he would leave his son to live with the elephant on the land, and that he himself would live with the hippopotamus in the water.

This explains why there are both tortoises on the land and tortoises who live in the water. The water tortoise is always much the bigger of the two, as there is plenty of fish for him to eat in the river, whereas the land tortoise is often very short of food.

The Elephant and the Tortoise; or, Why Worms Are Blind and Why Elephant Has Small Eyes
(From southern Nigeria)

WHEN AMBO WAS KING of Calabar, the elephant was not only a very big animal, but he had eyes in proportion to his immense bulk. In those days men and animals were friends, and all mixed together quite freely. At regular intervals King Ambo used to give a feast, and the elephant used to eat more than anyone, although the hippopotamus used to do his best; however, not being as big as the elephant, although he was very fat, he was left a long way behind.

As the elephant ate so much at these feasts, the tortoise, who was small but very cunning, made up his mind to put a stop to the elephant eating more than a fair share of the food provided. He therefore placed some dry kernels and shrimps, of which the elephant was very fond, in his bag, and went to the elephant's house to make an afternoon call.

When the tortoise arrived the elephant told him to sit down, so he made himself comfortable, and, having shut one eye, took one palm kernel and a shrimp out of his bag, and commenced to eat them with much relish.

When the elephant saw the tortoise eating, he said, as he was always hungry himself, "You seem to have some good food there; what are you eating?"

The tortoise replied that the food was "sweet too much," but was rather painful to him, as he was eating one of his own eyeballs; and he lifted up his head, showing one eye closed.

The elephant then said, "If the food is so good, take out one of my eyes and give me the same food."

The tortoise, who was waiting for this, knowing how greedy the elephant was, had brought a sharp knife with him for that very purpose, and said to the elephant, "I cannot reach your eye, as you are so big."

The elephant then took the tortoise up in his trunk and lifted him up. As soon as he came near the elephant's eye, with one quick scoop of the sharp knife he had the elephant's right eye out. The elephant trumpeted with pain; but the tortoise gave him some of the dried kernels and shrimps, and they so pleased the elephant's palate that he soon forgot the pain.

Very soon the elephant said, "That food is so sweet, I must have some more"; but the tortoise told him that before he could have any the other eye must come out. To this the elephant agreed; so the tortoise quickly got his knife to work, and very soon the elephant's left eye was on the ground, thus leaving the elephant quite blind. The tortoise then slid down the elephant's trunk on to the ground and hid himself. The elephant then began to make a great noise, and started pulling trees down and doing much damage, calling out for the tortoise; but of course he never answered, and the elephant could not find him.

The next morning, when the elephant heard the people passing, he asked them what the time was, and the bush buck, who was nearest, shouted out, "The sun is now up, and I am going to market to get some yams and fresh leaves for my food."

Then the elephant perceived that the tortoise had deceived him, and began to ask all the passers-by to lend him a pair of eyes, as he could not see, but everyone refused, as they wanted their eyes themselves. At last the worm grovelled past, and seeing the big elephant, greeted him in his humble way. He was much surprised when the king of the forest returned his salutation, and very much flattered also.

The elephant said, "Look here, worm, I have mislaid my eyes. Will you lend me yours for a few days? I will return them next market day."

The worm was so flattered at being noticed by the elephant that he gladly consented, and took his eyes out – which, as everyone knows, were very small – and gave them to the elephant. When the elephant had put the worm's eyes into his own large eye-sockets, the flesh immediately closed round them so tightly that when the market day arrived it was impossible for the elephant to get them out again to return to the worm; and although the worm repeatedly made applications to the elephant to return his eyes, the elephant always pretended not to hear, and sometimes used to say in a very loud voice, "If there are any worms about, they had better get out of my way, as they are so small I cannot see them, and if I tread on them they will be squashed into a nasty mess."

Ever since then the worms have been blind, and for the same reason elephants have such small eyes, quite out of proportion to the size of their huge bodies.

The Affair of the Hippopotamus and the Tortoise; or, Why the Hippopotamus Lives in the Water
(From southern Nigeria)

MANY YEARS AGO the hippopotamus, whose name was Isantim, was one of the biggest kings on the land; he was second only to the elephant. The hippo had seven large fat wives, of whom he was very fond. Now and then he used to give a big feast to the people, but a curious thing was that, although everyone knew the hippo, no one, except his seven wives, knew his name.

At one of the feasts, just as the people were about to sit down, the hippo said, "You have come to feed at my table, but none of you know my name. If you cannot tell my name, you shall all of you go away without your dinner."

As they could not guess his name, they had to go away and leave all the good food and tombo behind them. But before they left, the tortoise stood up and asked the hippopotamus what he would do if he told him his name at the next feast? So the hippo replied that he would be so ashamed of himself, that he and his whole family would leave the land, and for the future would dwell in the water.

Now it was the custom for the hippo and his seven wives to go down every morning and evening to the river to wash and have a drink. Of this custom the tortoise was aware. The hippo used to walk first, and the seven wives followed. One day when they had gone down to the river to bathe, the tortoise made a small hole in the middle of the path, and then waited. When the hippo and his wives returned, two of the wives were some distance behind, so the tortoise came out from where he had been hiding, and half buried himself in the hole he had dug, leaving the greater part of his shell exposed. When the two hippo wives came along, the first one knocked her foot against the tortoise's shell, and immediately called out to her husband, "Oh! Isantim, my husband, I have hurt my foot." At this the tortoise was very glad, and went joyfully home, as he had found out the hippo's name.

When the next feast was given by the hippo, he made the same condition about his name; so the tortoise got up and said, "You promise you will not kill me if I tell you your name?" and the hippo promised. The tortoise then shouted as loud as he was able, "Your name is Isantim," at which a cheer went up from all the people, and then they sat down to their dinner.

When the feast was over, the hippo, with his seven wives, in accordance with his promise, went down to the river, and they have always lived in the water from that day till now; and although they come on shore to feed at night, you never find a hippo on the land in the daytime.

Why Lizard's Head Is Always Moving up and Down

(By Ojong Itaroga, of the Ekoi people, Nigeria and Cameroon)

Φ

IN THE OLD DAYS, when all the beasts could speak like men, Obassi Nsi married many wives. These were the daughters of nearly all animals on earth, and each creature who gave his daughter in marriage to Obassi received a very rich gift in exchange.

Now Tortoise also wanted a gift like the rest, but he had only sons and no daughter. He took a long time to think over the matter; at length he made a plan. He called two of his sons and told them that he was about to give them to Obassi as wives, so they must take care never to let anyone see their nakedness. After warning them in this way, he dressed them in very rich robes, like girls, and they set forth.

When Tortoise and his two seeming daughters reached the hall where Obassi was sitting, he stood forth and said:

"I am the best of all your friends, for the rest have given you each a wife, but I alone bring two."

Obassi thanked him, and gave him in return twice as great riches as he had given to the others. "Lord," said Tortoise, "there is one thing which I must tell you. No one must see my daughters' nakedness, else they will die."

"What a thing to say!" answered Obassi. "It would be death to any man to see one of my wives unclothed." "I spoke," said Tortoise, "of their fellow women." "Fear not," answered Obassi; "since you have told me this, there is no danger of such a thing."

On this Tortoise went away, rejoicing in his success, while Obassi handed over the two new wives to his head wife that she might look after them, never thinking that they were boys.

Not long after, their mistress found out the true state of the case. She went secretly to Obassi and told him that the two girls whom Tortoise had given him in marriage possessed the masculine nakedness.

Obassi questioned the woman very earnestly if she meant what she said, and when she assured him that it was true, he replied quietly:

"Do not speak of this any more, lest the two Tortoises should overhear and flee away to their father."

Obassi fixed a day on which to make known to all the trick which had been played upon him. He sent round to his fathers-in-law to tell them that he was about to give a great show, and that he expected all those who were invited to be present and in good time. By this invitation he meant to have Tortoise punished, and perhaps even killed, for his deceit.

The two sons of Tortoise suspected what was going on, so they sent for Lizard, and from her they borrowed the feminine nakedness. When, therefore, the day came round, and Obassi went very early in the morning to ascertain the fact that his two young wives were boys, he found them girls after all.

The guests came in great multitudes and sat down in companies, eager to see the wonders which Obassi had promised. The latter was very angry, and began scolding his head wife for lying to him, not knowing that all she had said was true. Then he went to the audience hall, and simply told the people that there would be no show, for his wife had disappointed him. So all departed with much discontent.

Three days later Lizard went to the boys to ask for the parts she had lent them, but they only asked her to take a seat and eat a few balls of fu-fu. Later they begged her to come again in a few days' time, when they would do as she asked.

Over and over again Lizard came, but each day she was put off in the same manner. At length one day she began to sing loudly, and her song was as follows:

> "Ared nkui, kumm 'me ndipp eyama
> (Ared Tortoise, give me secret parts mine.)
> Affion nkui, kumm 'me ndipp eyama
> (Affion Tortoise, give me secret parts mine.)
> 'Me nkpaw, 'me nkpaw, ka ndipp eyama
> I die, I die, for secret parts mine.
> Fenne, kpe nde mbitt, nde ka ndipp eyama
> Also, if I live life, I live for secret parts mine."

The people in the compound heard the singing, and ran to see who it was who could make such a song. Tortoise boys (now girls) begged Lizard to take a seat once more and eat a few fu-fu balls as usual. She sat down and began eating. One of them then said, "Let us each make fu-fu balls for the others to swallow," and all agreed to the fun. One of our well-known two then rolled a fine ball and secretly put some pricking fishbones within it, dipped it in the soup-pot, and put it in poor Lizard's mouth. The latter tried to swallow it, but it stuck in her throat, where the pin-like bones held it fast. Lizard lay on the ground voicelessly stretching her neck, and trying in vain to swallow the ball or eject it.

This is the cause why Lizards are seen to raise and let fall their heads. They are still trying to get rid of the fu-fu ball given them by the sons of Tortoise.

That is the reason why Tortoise's trick has never been discovered up to this day, and thus it is that Lizard lost her voice and her "Ndipp," and only gained in exchange the habit of lifting her head up and down.

How Tortoise Got the Cracks and Bumps on His Back
(By Effion Mkpat Okun of Niaji, of the Ekoi people, Nigeria and Cameroon)

ONCE NKUI (TORTOISE) was a great friend of Obassi Osaw. He went to visit Obassi and ate and drank in his house. Before he left he said, "Let us make a rule." Obassi asked, "How do you mean?" "I mean about the funeral 'play'," said Nkui. "Whichever of us shall die first, the other must kill an elephant for the 'customs'." To this Obassi agreed, but when his friend had left, he ordered his people to build a house without doors or windows. There was only a hole in the roof. Through this Obassi let himself down with all his chop and his loving wife. He said to his eldest son, "Please go and tell Tortoise that I am dead." This the son did, and Tortoise

started out to go to his friend's town. As he went along the road, he saw an Elephant feeding on some grass down by the water. Tortoise said:

"Lord, you are eating. They have sent to call me because my friend is dead. I am looking for someone who will be able to dance at the funeral. Will you go with me for the dancing? I think you could dance very finely indeed."

Next Tortoise got some pods of the Agara tree, which, when shaken, make a noise like little bells. These he made into anklets and tied them round the feet of Elephant. Then he said, "Try, Lord, and see how you can dance." Elephant danced, and Tortoise cried out, "In all the world there is no such dancer! The ceremonies will be held next month. I shall come along this road early in the morning and trust that I may see you, so that we may go together to the dancing."

Now during all this time Obassi was inside the house, but Tortoise was making a very strong rope all covered with the little bell-like pods. When the new moon shone, Nkui took the rope and went along the road as before. He called to Elephant, "Lord, Lord, it is time now."

Elephant heard and came. Tortoise took the anklets and tied them round the great feet. Next he took the rope and threw it round Elephant's neck, saying, "Come, Lord, I will lead you to the dance."

When the two reached Obassi's town all the people danced with joy at the sight of them. Tortoise tied Elephant to the Juju tree before the Egbo house. When he thought that his prey was safely tied, he went away.

Two small children ran out and said, "Ho! here is the Elephant which Nkui said he would kill for the burial of his friend. Ho! Elephant will be killed very soon."

When Elephant heard this he knew that he had been deceived. He was very angry, and strained at the rope till it broke. Then he ran round seeking Nkui, who fled before him into the bush. Elephant went round and round, but could not find whom he sought, because Tortoise had hidden himself in a very cunning place by the river. One day, as the latter sat in this new home, he cooked plantains, then peeled them and threw the skins into the water. They floated down stream till they came to the place where Elephant was walking along the bank. He picked them up with his trunk, and asked, "Where do you come from?" They answered, "We come from Nkui's place." So he begged them to guide him thither.

When Tortoise saw them coming, he called to his wife, "Turn me over, and grind medicine upon my breast. Should Elephant ask for me, say that I am not at home."

When Elephant arrived he saw the wife of Nkui grinding medicine and asked, "Where is your husband?" She replied, "I have been very ill for a long time, and do not know where he has gone."

Elephant looked fixedly at the stone, and then said, "If you do not mind, I think that I had better throw away that stone."

She answered, "Do you not hear that I am very ill, and am grinding medicine for my sickness. Certainly you must not touch my stone."

On that Elephant laughed and turned the stone over with his foot. He saw Nkui and knew him. He placed his foot upon him, pressed him into the earth and broke all his shell. Up till that time Tortoise had had a smooth skin, but it has since been broken and humpy because Elephant smashed it up in punishment for his deceit.

How Obassi Osaw Proved
the Wisdom of Tortoise
(By Anjong Ntui Animbun of Nsan, of the Ekoi people, Nigeria and Cameroon)

OBASSI OSAW married many wives. Among these was the daughter of Tortoise. She was so proud of her father that she annoyed Obassi by exclaiming, "Oh, my father, you have more sense than any other person!" whenever the least thing happened, even if she only knocked her foot or felt surprised.

Obassi determined to find out for himself if Tortoise was really so very wise. He therefore built a room without doors or windows. Into this he secretly let down eight persons, and sent to Tortoise to come at once and tell him what was within.

Tortoise sent back a message that he would certainly come next day, but in such a way that no one should see him enter, for he was surely the wisest of men, and none could know how he came. Obassi was still more displeased when he heard this.

Now the daughter went and told Tortoise that her husband was annoyed with her for constantly praising her father's wisdom. "Perhaps," said she, "it is to prove this that he has sent for you." Tortoise answered, "It is well."

Next morning Obassi sent other messengers to bid his father-in-law hasten, but, when the men arrived, Tortoise was nowhere to be found. His wife said that he had gone hunting, so the messengers had better not wait. They agreed to this, and set out once more. The woman ran after them with a parcel and said, "Will you please take this to my daughter?"

This the men promised, and gave the parcel to the girl, not knowing that it was Tortoise whom they carried. She bore the packet before Obassi, set it on the ground and unfastened the tie-tie, when out stepped – what? Tortoise himself.

Obassi was very much surprised, and bade the guest go and stay in his daughter's house till next morning. So they went off together.

At night, when all was quiet, Tortoise made a small hole in the wall of the room which Obassi had built. Then he took a stick and dipped it into some foul-smelling stuff. The men who were inside noticed the bad odour, and began calling to each other by name, asking its cause.

In this way Tortoise heard that there were eight men in the secret room, and also learned their names. He was very careful to fill up the little hole which he had made, and afterwards went back to bed.

Next morning a great company was gathered together to witness the shame of Tortoise when he should fail to answer the question of their Lord.

Obassi stood in the middle of the audience room and said very loudly that Tortoise must now tell him what was hidden in the windowless house, or suffer death if he could not do so.

Then Tortoise rose and said that there were eight men shut up within, and, to the surprise of all the people, he repeated their names, thus proving himself to be wiser than all his fellows, just as his daughter had said.

Obassi was so vexed that he ordered his men to seize Tortoise, sharpen a stick, and drive it through this overwise creature, so as to fasten him to the ground at a place where cross-roads meet. He also ordered that the beast should be fixed upright, so as to look at his judge on high. Obassi decreed further that, whenever a man wished to make him a sacrifice, Tortoise should be offered in this way. That is why we often see Tortoise impaled before Jujus, or at cross-roads.

Tortoise Covers His Ignorance
(From the Fang and Bulu peoples, Cameroon)

TORTOISE (KUDU) arose and went to the town of his father-in-law Leopard (Njĕ). Leopard sent him on an errand, saying, "Go, and cut for me utamba-mwa-Ivâtâ." (The fiber of a vine is used for making nets.)

Then he went. But, while he still remembered the object, he forgot the name of the kind of Vine that was used for that purpose. And he was ashamed to confess his ignorance. So, he came back to call the people of the town, and said, "Come ye and help me! I have enclosed Ihĕli (Gazelle) in a thicket."

The people came, and at once they made a circle around the spot. But when they closed in, they saw no beasts there.

Then Tortoise called out, "Let someone of you cut for me, utamba-mwa-Ivâtâ." (As if that was the only thing needed to catch the animal which he had said was there.)

Thereupon, his brother-in-law cut for him a vine which he brought to him, saying, "Here is an Ihenga vine which we use for making nets." Whereupon Tortoise exclaimed, "Is it possible that it was the Ihenga vine that I mistook?"

A Question as to Age
(From the Fang and Bulu peoples, Cameroon)

SHRIKE (ASANZE) was a blacksmith. So, all the Beasts went to the forge at his town. Each day, when they had finished at the anvil, they took all their tools and laid them on the ground (as pledges). Before they should go back to their towns, they would say to the Bird, "Show us which is the eldest, and then you give us the things, if you are able to decide our question."

He looked at and examined them; but he did not know, for they were all apparently of the same age; and they went away empty-handed, leaving their tools as a challenge. Every day it was that same way.

On another day, Tortoise (Kudu) being a friend of the Bird, started to go to work for him at the bellows. Also, he cooked three bundles of food; one of Civet (Njâbâ) with the entrails of a red Antelope; and one of Genet (Uhingi); and one of an Edubu-Snake. (Suited for different tastes and ages.) Then he blew at the bellows.

When the others were hungry at meal time, Tortoise took up the jomba-bundles; and he said, "Come ye! take up this jomba of Njâbâ with the entrails, and eat." (They were the old ones who chose to come and eat it.)

Again Tortoise said, "Come ye! take up the jomba of Uhingi." (They were the younger men who chose to pick it up and eat it.)

He then took up the jomba of the Snake. And he said, "Come ye! and take of the jomba of Edubu." (Those who took it were the youngest.)

After awhile they all finished their work at the bellows. They still left their tools lying on the ground, and came near to the Bird, and they said, as on other occasions, "Show us who is the eldest."

Then Tortoise at the request of the Bird, announced the decision, as if it was its own, "Ye who ate of the Njâbâ are the ones who are oldest; ye who ate of Uhingi are the ones who are younger men; and ye who ate of the Edubu are the ones who are the youngest."

So, they assented to the decision, and took away their belongings.

The Treachery of Tortoise
(From the Fang and Bulu peoples, Cameroon)

LEOPARD (Njĕˇ) married a wife. After awhile she was about to
become a mother. Boa (Mbâmâ) also married a wife; and, after
awhile, she also, was about to become a mother.

In a short time, like the drinking of a draught of water, the month passed,
both for Leopard's wife and for Boa's wife also. Then Boa's wife said, "It is
time for the birth!"

So she gave birth to a child. And she lay down on her mother's bed.
When they were about to cook food for her, she said, "I want to eat nothing
but Njĕ!"

The next day, the wife of Leopard said, "It is time for the birth!" And she
also gave birth to a child. Food was given to her. But she said, "I am wanting
only Mbâmâ!"

When told of his wife's wish, Boa said, "What shall I do? Where shall I
go? Where shall I find Mangwata?" (A nickname for Leopard.) Also, Leopard
said, in regard to his wife's wish, "Where shall I find Mbâmâ?" Then Leopard
went walking, on and on, and looking. He met with Manima-ma-Evosolo (a
nickname for Tortoise). Leopard asked him, "Can you catch me Mbâmâ?"
Manima said, "What's that?" And he laughed, Kyĕ! Kyĕ! Kyĕ; and said, "That
is as easy as play." Leopard said, "Chum, please do such a thing for me." And
Tortoise said, "Very good!"

When they separated, and Tortoise was about to go a little further on
ahead, at once he met with Boa. And Boa asked him, "Chum! Manima-ma-
Evosolo! Where have you come from?" Tortoise answered, "I have come,
going on an excursion." Boa asked to Tortoise, "But, could you catch me
Njĕ?" He replied, "That is a little thing." Then Boa begged him, "Please,
since my wife has born a child, she has not eaten anything. She says she
wants to eat only Njĕ."

Tortoise returned back at once to his village. He called to the people of
his village, saying, "Come ye! to make for me a pit." They at once went, and

dug a pit. When they had finished it, Tortoise went to Leopard, and said to him, "Come on!"

Leopard at once started on the journey (thinking he was going to get Boa). When they came to the place of the pit, Leopard fell suddenly into it headlong, volomu! He called to Tortoise, saying, "Chum! Where is Mbâmâ?" (Leopard did not understand that he was being deceived.)

Tortoise did not reply, but started off clear to the village of Boa. He said to Boa, "Come on!" Boa did not doubt at all that he was going to get Leopard. He started, and went with Tortoise towards the pit. When he was passing near the spot, Boa fell headlong into the pit, volumu! And Leopard exclaimed, "Ah! now, what is this?"

Tortoise only said to them, "You yourselves can kill each other."

A Chain of Circumstances
(From the Fang and Bulu peoples, Cameroon)

TORTOISE (KUDU) was a blacksmith, and allowed other people to use his bellows. Cockroach (Etanda) had a spear that was known of by all people and things. One day, he went to the smithy at the village of Tortoise. When he started to work the bellows, as he looked out in the street, he saw Chicken (Kuba) coming; and he said to Tortoise, "I'm afraid of Kuba, that he will catch me. What shall I do?" So Tortoise told him, "Go! and hide yourself off there in the grass." At once he hid himself.

Then arrived Chicken, and he, observing a spear lying on the ground, asked Tortoise, "Is not this Etanda's Spear?" Tortoise assented, "Yes, do you want him?" And Chicken said, "Yes, where is he?" So Tortoise said, "He hid himself in the grass on the ground yonder; catch him." Then Chicken went and caught Cockroach, and swallowed him.

When Chicken was about to go away to return to his place, Tortoise said to him, "Come back! work for me this fine bellows!" As Chicken, willing to return a favor, was about to stand at it, he looked around and saw Genet (Uhingi) coming in the street. Chicken said to Tortoise, "Alas! I'm afraid that Uhingi will see me, where shall I go?" So, Tortoise says, "Go! and hide!" Chicken did so. When Genet came, he, seeing the spear, asked, "Is it not so that this is Etanda's Spear?" Tortoise replied, "Yes." Genet asked him, "Where is Etanda?" He replied, "Chicken has swallowed him." Genet inquired, "And where is Chicken?" Tortoise showed him the place where Chicken was hidden. And Genet went and caught and ate Chicken.

When Genet was about to go, Tortoise called to him, "No! come! to work this fine bellows." Genet set to work; but, when he looked into the street, he hesitated; for, he saw Leopard (Njĕ) coming. Genet said to Tortoise, "I must go, lest Njĕ should see me!" Then Tortoise said, "Go! and hide in the grass." So, Genet hid himself in the grass.

Leopard, having arrived and wondering about the Spear, asked Tortoise, "Is it not so that this is the Spear of Etanda?" Tortoise answered, "Yes." Then Leopard asked, "Where is Etanda?" Tortoise replied, "Kuba has swallowed him." "And, where is Kuba?" Tortoise answered, "Uhingi has eaten him." Then Leopard asked, "Where then is Uhingi?" Tortoise asked, "Do you want him? Go and catch him! He is hidden yonder there." Then Leopard caught and killed Genet.

Leopard was going away, but Tortoise told him, "Wait! come! to work this fine bellows." When Leopard was about to comply, he looked around the street, and he saw a Human Being coming with a gun carried on his shoulder. Leopard exclaimed, "Kudu-O! I do not want to see a Man, let me go!" Then Tortoise said to him, "Go! and hide." Leopard did so.

When the Man had come, and he saw the Spear of Cockroach, he inquired, "Is it not so that this is Cockroach's wonderful Spear?" Tortoise answered, "Yes."

And the Man asked, "Where then is Cockroach?" Tortoise answered, "Kuba has swallowed him."

Man asked, "And where is Chicken?" Tortoise answered, "Uhingi has eaten him."

Man asked, "And where is Genet?" Tortoise answered, "Njĕ has killed him."

Man asked, "And where is Leopard?" Tortoise did not at once reply; and Man asked again, "Where is Leopard?" The Tortoise said, "Do you want him? Go! and catch him. He had hidden himself over there."

Then the Man went and shot Leopard,

Who had killed Genet,

Who had eaten Chicken,

Who had swallowed Cockroach,

Who owned the wonderful Spear,

At the smithy of Tortoise.

Other Animal Stories & Fables

ANIMAL CHARACTERS appeal to us. They are inherently engaging. Think of all those TV cartoons we've loved – as children and as grown-ups too. It's fun to find a lion or a wolf displaying weaknesses we associate with humans; it makes us see both animal and human in a new and intriguing light. And it's ironic to see a creature we see as 'dumb', and therefore innocent, as capable of crime (like a thieving deer); particularly poignant to see a blameless turtle suffer.

But it's also a good way for a story to spotlight certain faults or foibles without the need to develop a more 'rounded' psychology. We can focus on one attribute and forget the rest. Hence their suitability to stories that set out to make a point; to explanatory 'just-so' stories, for example. How the leopard got his spots; why the turtle thrashes with its forelegs: these curious quandaries can be amusingly accounted for. And, as we know from Aesop, they're absolutely perfect for use in fables, for setting out moral principles in the very simplest and clearest terms. West African mythology abounds in stories of both kinds..

The King's Magic Drum
(From southern Nigeria)

EFRIAM DUKE was an ancient king of Calabar. He was a peaceful man, and did not like war. He had a wonderful drum, the property of which, when it was beaten, was always to provide plenty of good food and drink. So whenever any country declared war against him, he used to call all his enemies together and beat his drum; then to the surprise of everyone, instead of fighting the people found tables spread with all sorts of dishes, fish, foo-foo, palm oil chop, soup, cooked yams and ocros, and plenty of palm wine for everybody. In this way he kept all the country quiet, and sent his enemies away with full stomachs, and in a happy and contented frame of mind. There was only one drawback to possessing the drum, and that was, if the owner of the drum walked over any stick on the road or stept over a fallen tree, all the food would immediately go bad, and three hundred Egbo men would appear with sticks and whips and beat the owner of the drum and all the invited guests very severely.

Efriam Duke was a rich man. He had many farms and hundreds of slaves, a large store of kernels on the beach, and many puncheons of palm oil. He also had fifty wives and many children. The wives were all fine women and healthy; they were also good mothers, and all of them had plenty of children, which was good for the king's house.

Every few months the king used to issue invitations to all his subjects to come to a big feast, even the wild animals were invited; the elephants, hippopotami, leopards, bush cows, and antelopes used to come, for in those days there was no trouble, as they were friendly with man, and when they were at the feast they did not kill one another. All the people and the animals as well were envious of the king's drum and wanted to possess it, but the king would not part with it.

One morning Ikwor Edem, one of the king's wives, took her little daughter down to the spring to wash her, as she was covered with yaws, which are bad sores all over the body. The tortoise happened to be up a palm tree, just over the spring, cutting nuts for his midday meal; and while he was cutting, one of the nuts fell to the ground, just in front of the child. The little girl, seeing the good food, cried for it, and the mother, not knowing any better, picked up the palm nut and gave it to her daughter. Directly the tortoise saw this he climbed down the tree, and asked the woman where his palm nut was. She replied that she had given it to her child to eat. Then the tortoise, who very much wanted the king's drum, thought he would make plenty palaver over this and force the king to give him the drum, so he said to the mother of the child –

"I am a poor man, and I climbed the tree to get food for myself and my family. Then you took my palm nut and gave it to your child. I shall tell the whole matter to the king, and see what he has to say when he hears that one of his wives has stolen my food," for this, as everyone knows, is a very serious crime according to native custom.

Ikwor Edem then said to the tortoise –

"I saw your palm nut lying on the ground, and thinking it had fallen from the tree, I gave it to my little girl to eat, but I did not steal it. My husband the king is a rich man, and if you have any complaint to make against me or my child, I will take you before him."

So when she had finished washing her daughter at the spring she took the tortoise to her husband, and told him what had taken place. The king then asked the tortoise what he would accept as compensation for the loss of his palm nut, and offered him money, cloth, kernels or palm oil, all of which things the tortoise refused one after the other.

The king then said to the tortoise, "What will you take? You may have anything you like."

And the tortoise immediately pointed to the king's drum, and said that it was the only thing he wanted.

In order to get rid of the tortoise the king said, "Very well, take the drum," but he never told the tortoise about the bad things that would happen to him if he stept over a fallen tree, or walked over a stick on the road.

The tortoise was very glad at this, and carried the drum home in triumph to his wife, and said, "I am now a rich man, and shall do no more work.

Whenever I want food, all I have to do is to beat this drum, and food will immediately be brought to me, and plenty to drink."

His wife and children were very pleased when they heard this, and asked the tortoise to get food at once, as they were all hungry. This the tortoise was only too pleased to do, as he wished to show off his newly acquired wealth, and was also rather hungry himself, so he beat the drum in the same way as he had seen the king do when he wanted something to eat, and immediately plenty of food appeared, so they all sat down and made a great feast. The tortoise did this for three days, and everything went well; all his children got fat, and had as much as they could possibly eat. He was therefore very proud of his drum, and in order to display his riches he sent invitations to the king and all the people and animals to come to a feast. When the people received their invitations they laughed, as they knew the tortoise was very poor, so very few attended the feast; but the king, knowing about the drum, came, and when the tortoise beat the drum, the food was brought as usual in great profusion, and all the people sat down and enjoyed their meal very much. They were much astonished that the poor tortoise should be able to entertain so many people, and told all their friends what fine dishes had been placed before them, and that they had never had a better dinner. The people who had not gone were very sorry when they heard this, as a good feast, at somebody else's expense, is not provided every day. After the feast all the people looked upon the tortoise as one of the richest men in the kingdom, and he was very much respected in consequence. No one, except the king, could understand how the poor tortoise could suddenly entertain so lavishly, but they all made up their minds that if the tortoise ever gave another feast, they would not refuse again.

When the tortoise had been in possession of the drum for a few weeks he became lazy and did no work, but went about the country boasting of his riches, and took to drinking too much. One day after he had been drinking a lot of palm wine at a distant farm, he started home carrying his drum; but having had too much to drink, he did not notice a stick in the path. He walked over the stick, and of course the Ju Ju was broken at once. But he did not know this, as nothing happened at the time, and eventually he arrived at his house very tired, and still not very well from having drunk too much. He threw the drum into a corner and went to sleep. When he woke up in the morning the tortoise began to feel hungry, and as his wife and children were calling out for food, he beat the drum; but instead of food being brought, the house was filled with Egbo men, who beat the tortoise, his wife and children, badly. At this the tortoise was very angry, and said to himself –

"I asked everyone to a feast, but only a few came, and they had plenty to eat and drink. Now, when I want food for myself and my family, the Egbos come and beat me. Well, I will let the other people share the same fate, as I do not see why I and my family should be beaten when I have given a feast to all people."

He therefore at once sent out invitations to all the men and animals to come to a big dinner the next day at three o'clock in the afternoon.

When the time arrived many people came, as they did not wish to lose the chance of a free meal a second time. Even the sick men, the lame, and the blind got their friends to lead them to the feast. When they had all arrived, with the exception of the king and his wives, who sent excuses, the tortoise beat his drum as usual, and then quickly hid himself under a bench, where he could not be seen. His wife and children he had sent away before the feast, as he knew what would surely happen. Directly he had beaten the drum three hundred Egbo men appeared with whips, and started flogging all the guests, who could not escape, as the doors had been fastened. The beating went on for two hours, and the people were so badly punished, that many of them had to be carried home on the backs of their friends. The leopard was the only one who escaped, as directly he saw the Egbo men arrive he knew that things were likely to be unpleasant, so he gave a big spring and jumped right out of the compound.

When the tortoise was satisfied with the beating the people had received he crept to the door and opened it. The people then ran away, and when the tortoise gave a certain tap on the drum all the Egbo men vanished. The people who had been beaten were so angry, and made so much palaver with the tortoise, that he made up his mind to return the drum to the king the next day. So in the morning the tortoise went to the king and brought the drum with him. He told the king that he was not satisfied with the drum, and wished to exchange it for something else; he did not mind so much what the king gave him so long as he got full value for the drum, and he was quite willing to accept a certain number of slaves, or a few farms, or their equivalent in cloth or rods.

The king, however, refused to do this; but as he was rather sorry for the tortoise, he said he would present him with a magic foo-foo tree, which would provide the tortoise and his family with food, provided he kept a certain condition. This the tortoise gladly consented to do. Now this foo-foo tree only bore fruit once a year, but every day it dropped foo-foo and soup on the ground. And the condition was, that the owner should gather sufficient food for the day, once, and not return again for more. The tortoise, when he had thanked the king for his generosity, went home to his wife and told her to bring her calabashes to the tree. She did so, and they gathered plenty of foo-foo and soup quite sufficient for the whole family for that day, and went back to their house very happy.

That night they all feasted and enjoyed themselves. But one of the sons, who was very greedy, thought to himself –

"I wonder where my father gets all this good food from? I must ask him."

So in the morning he said to his father –

"Tell me where do you get all this foo-foo and soup from?"

But his father refused to tell him, as his wife, who was a cunning woman, said –

"If we let our children know the secret of the foo-foo tree, some day when they are hungry, after we have got our daily supply, one of them may go to the tree and gather more, which will break the Ju Ju."

But the envious son, being determined to get plenty of food for himself, decided to track his father to the place where he obtained the food. This was rather difficult to do, as the tortoise always went out alone, and took the greatest care to prevent anyone following him. The boy, however, soon thought of a plan, and got a calabash with a long neck and a hole in the end. He filled the calabash with wood ashes, which he obtained from the fire, and then got a bag which his father always carried on his back when he went out to get food. In the bottom of the bag the boy then made a small hole, and inserted the calabash with the neck downwards, so that when his father walked to the foo-foo tree he would leave a small trail of wood ashes behind him. Then when his father, having slung his bag over his back as usual, set out to get the daily supply of food, his greedy son followed the trail of the wood ashes, taking great care to hide himself and not to let his father perceive that he was being followed. At last the tortoise arrived at the tree, and placed his calabashes on the ground and collected the food for the day, the boy watching him from a distance. When his father had finished and went home the boy also returned, and having had a good meal, said nothing to his parents, but went to bed. The next morning he got some of his brothers, and after his father had finished getting the daily supply, they went to the tree and collected much foo-foo and soup, and so broke the Ju Ju.

At daylight the tortoise went to the tree as usual, but he could not find it, as during the night the whole bush had grown up, and the foo-foo tree was hidden from sight. There was nothing to be seen but a dense mass of prickly tie-tie palm. Then the tortoise at once knew that someone had broken the Ju Ju, and had gathered foo-foo from the tree twice in the same day; so he returned very sadly to his house, and told his wife. He then called all his family together and told them what had happened, and asked them who had done this evil thing. They all denied having had anything to do with the tree, so the tortoise in despair brought all his family to the place where the foo-foo tree had been, but which was now all prickly tie-tie palm, and said –

"My dear wife and children, I have done all that I can for you, but you have broken my Ju Ju; you must therefore for the future live on the tie-tie palm."

So they made their home underneath the prickly tree, and from that day you will always find tortoises living under the prickly tie-tie palm, as they have nowhere else to go to for food.

The Ants And The Treasure
(From the Yoruba people, southern Nigeria)

THERE ONCE WAS a poor man who was very kind to animals and birds. However little he had, he always spared a few grains of corn, or a few beans, for his parrot, and he was in the habit of spreading on the ground every morning some titbits for the industrious ants, hoping that they would be satisfied with the corn and leave his few possessions untouched.

And for this the ants were grateful.

In the same village there lived a miser who had by crafty and dishonest means collected a large store of gold, which he kept securely tied up in the corner of a small hut. He sat outside this hut all day and all night, so that nobody could steal his treasure.

When he saw any bird, he threw a stone at it, and he crushed any ant which he found walking on the ground, for he detested every living creature and loved nothing but his gold.

As might be expected, the ants had no love for this miser, and when he had killed a great many of their number, they began to think how they might punish him for his cruelty.

"What a pity it is," said the King of the ants, "that our friend is a poor man, while our enemy is so rich!"

This gave the ants an idea. They decided to transfer the miser's treasure to the poor man's house. To do this they dug a great tunnel under the ground. One end of the tunnel was in the poor man's house, and the other end was in the hut of the miser.

On the night that the tunnel was completed, a great swarm of ants began carrying the miser's treasure into the poor man's house, and when morning came and the poor man saw the gold lying in heaps on the floor, he was overjoyed, thinking that the gods had sent him a reward for his years of humble toil.

He put all the gold in a corner of his hut and covered it up with native cloths.

Meanwhile the miser had discovered that his treasure was greatly decreased. He was alarmed and could not think how the gold could have disappeared, for he had kept watch all the time outside the hut.

The next night the ants again carried a great portion of the miser's gold down the tunnel, and again the poor man rejoiced and the miser was furious to discover his loss.

On the third night the ants laboured long and succeeded in removing all the rest of the treasure.

"The gods have indeed sent me much gold!" cried the poor man, as he put away his treasure.

But the miser called together his neighbours and related that in three consecutive nights his hard-won treasure had vanished away. He declared that nobody had entered the hut but himself, and therefore the gold must have been removed by witchcraft.

However, when the hut was searched, a hole was found in the ground, and they saw that this hole was the opening of a tunnel. It seemed clear that the treasure had been carried down the tunnel, and everyone began hunting for the other end of the tunnel. At last it was discovered in the poor man's hut! Under the native cloths in the corner they found the missing treasure.

The poor man protested in vain that he could not possibly have crept down such a small tunnel, and he declared that he had no notion how the gold had got into his but. But the rest said that be must have some charm by which he made himself very small and crept down the tunnel at night into the miser's hut.

For this offence they shut him up in a hut and tightly closed the entrance. On the next day he was to be burnt alive.

When the ants saw what had come of their plan to help him, they were sorely perplexed and wondered how they could save their poor friend from such a painful death

There seemed nothing for them to do but to eat up the whole of the hut where the prisoner was confined. This they accomplished after some hours, and the poor man was astonished to find himself standing in an open space. He ran away into the forest and never came back.

In the morning the people saw that the ants had been at work, for a few stumps of the hut remained. They said: "The gods have taken the punishment out of our hands! The ants have devoured both the hut and the prisoner!"

And only the ants knew that this was not true.

The Lord of the Bush
(From the Ekoi people, Nigeria and Cameroon)

Φ

IN THE BEGINNING OF THINGS, Nkimm (Python) and Njokk (Elephant) were Lords of the Bush. They disputed together as to which was the strongest. One said, "The bush belongs

to me." The other answered, "Nay, it is mine." Osian (the black ants) listened and said, "In seven days' time, let us all fight; then he who shall beat the others shall be called Lord of the Bush." The two great beasts laughed, because the ants are so small; but they agreed, and from that time the latter gathered together over every tree and rock. When the seventh day came they began to fight. First, they saw Iku. Him they surrounded and bit so badly that he ran to the river and was drowned. Next they sought out Nkimm, whom they found with his young ones. They came in such thousands that the great snake had to take his children and flee to the water, where they escaped. Next the ants pursued the monkeys, many of whom they killed, while the rest sprang up very high trees, calling out, "We leave the ground to you."

After this the Osian gathered themselves together in vast, numbers, and set out to fight with Njokk; but the latter only laughed. For several days they fought, but could not prevail, and at length sent a message to their king that the battle went against them, and that they would all be trampled to death beneath the great feet of their enemy if help were not sent.

Then the King of all the ants called together his people, even to the last one, and they came in such numbers that the whole earth was dark with them. Into Elephant's mouth they poured and into his eyes, his nose and his belly, till he could no longer stand against them, but fled to the water for refuge as the other beasts had done. When the bush creatures saw him fleeing they knew for true that the ants were lords of the bush. So they called a meeting and brought out a great chair. The King of the ants came and sat upon it, and all the animals stood before him, holding out their hands and saying:

"From to-day you are our lord. The land is yours, the bush is yours, and we will obey your orders."

During this time the monkeys were still amid the tree tops. The other beasts called to them and said, "Will you come down?" but they answered:

"No, we will make our homes in the branches." From that time onward the Ant King has been Lord of the Bush.

The Fisherman[1]
(From the Jabo people, Liberia)

SEA GULL, the fisherman, lived on the shore of the great ocean. Each day he waited until the tide went out, and then he found many small fish left in little pools along the water's edge.

One day the gull waited patiently for the tide to go down so that he could begin eating. But it seemed to him that the water didn't get lower at all but rose higher and higher. The gull was perplexed. "Formerly at this time of day the sea went down," he said. "Now it is coming up. I wonder what is the matter?"

He decided to consult some other people and make inquiries about the situation. So he flew to the village where the chickens lived. At the gate he met a rooster.

"One moment, my friend," the gull said. "I need your advice. When does the low tide of the ocean generally begin?"

The rooster answered, "Low tide? Just what do you mean by that? And what is this thing, ocean, that you are talking about?"

The gull had no time for explanations. He flew off, and after a while he met a duck swimming in a lake. He said, "One moment, friend. What time does the high tide end and the low tide begin?"

"What are you talking about?" the duck answered. "There is no high tide or low tide. The water here always remains the same."

"I am speaking of the ocean," the gull said. "I don't speak of this miserable little lake."

"Ocean? Whatever is that?" the duck asked.

"What kind of people are these?" the gull said. "They know nothing at all about important things." He flew on toward the bush country and came to a flock of rice birds feeding in a field.

---

1   From *The King's Drum and Other African Stories* by Harold Courlander. Copyright 1962, 1990 by Harold Courlander. Reprinted by permission of The Emma Courlander Trust.

"Friends," he said to them, "what time does the ocean tide go out?"

"Ocean tide go out?" they answered. "We don't know about such things. We are busy getting our rice before the farmer comes to drive us away. We have no time for this kind of conversation."

So the gull flew on. He came to one village, then another, asking he same question and getting no answer. Deep in the bush country, he met a mourning dove who sat in a tree crying over and over, "Neo-o-o balo-o-o! huuu! huuu! huuu!" The gull interrupted, saying, "Excuse me, friend. What time does the sea go down?"

The mourning dove answered: "Don't you see that I am mourning the death of my mother? Why do you bother me with questions at a time like this? Go find the pigeon; he is the one that knows the time of things."

And the gull flew on. Far in the bush country he found the pigeon. He said: "People around here are not helpful. When a question is asked, they known nothing of the answer. But you, you have been highly recommended. Tell me, when does the tide of the ocean fall? This is a matter of great importance, for I eat when the low tide leaves fish in the pools along the ocean's edge."

The pigeon replied: "You live at the ocean's edge, while I live here in the bush country. Isn't it strange that you, a seacoast dweller, come to me, a bush dweller who has never seen the sea, to ask what time the tide falls? Be-gone, you stupid creature. Go back where you came from. The gull should not ask the pigeon about affairs of the ocean."

It is said: "Every man should be the master of his own profession."

How the Leopard Got His Spots
(From Sierra Leone)

LONG AGO, Leopard and Fire were the best of friends. Every morning, without fail, Leopard made a special effort to visit his friend even though the journey took him quite a distance from his own home. It had never before bothered him that Fire did not

visit him in return, until the day his wife began to mock and tease him on the subject.

"He must be a very poor friend indeed," she jeered, "if he won't come and see you even once in your own house."

Day and night, Leopard was forced to listen to his wife taunt him, until finally he began to believe that his house was somehow unworthy of his friend.

"I will prove my wife wrong," he thought to himself, and set off before dawn on the following day to beg Fire to come and visit his home.

At first, Fire presented him with every possible excuse. He never liked to travel too far, he explained to Leopard. He always felt uncomfortable leaving his family behind. But Leopard pleaded and pleaded so that eventually Fire agreed to the visit on the condition that his friend construct a path of dry leaves leading from one house to the other.

As he walked homewards, Leopard gathered as many leaves as he could find and laid them in a long line between the two houses just as Fire had instructed him. He brought his wife the good news and immediately she began to prepare the finest food to welcome their guest.

When the meal was ready and the house sparkled as if it were new, the couple sat down to await the arrival of their friend. They had been seated only a moment when suddenly they felt a strong gust of wind and heard a loud crackling noise outside their front door. Leopard jumped up in alarm and pulled open the door, anxious to discover who could be making such a dreadful commotion. He was astonished to see Fire standing before him, crackling and sparking in a haze of intense heat, his body a mass of flames that leapt menacingly in every direction.

Soon the entire house had caught fire and the smell of burning skin filled the air. Leopard grabbed hold of his squealing wife and sprang, panic-stricken, through the window, rolling in the grass to put out the flames on his back.

The two lay there exhausted, grateful to be alive. But ever since that day, their bodies were covered all over with black spots where the fingers of Fire, their reluctant house-guest, had touched them.

How Leopard Got His Spots
(From the Yoruba people, southern Nigeria)

A T ONE TIME the Leopard was coloured like a lion, and he had no dark markings; but he was pursued by Akiti, the renowned hunter, and feared that he might be slain.

To avoid this he ate the roots of a certain magic plant, which had the effect of making him invulnerable to any of the hunter's weapons.

Soon afterwards Akiti saw him as he slipped through the dense undergrowth of the forest, but though he shot his poisoned arrows, Leopard escaped.

But where each arrow struck him, there appeared a dark mark, and now, though hunters still pursue him, he is rarely caught, but his body is covered with the marks of the arrows, so that as he goes among the trees he looks exactly like the mingling of the sun and shadow.

Another Story of Leopard's Spots

According to another story, Leopard once had a very dark skin. He was prowling one day in a beautiful compound, when he noticed a little hut in which a lady was taking her bath.

Round and round the hut Leopard walked, waiting for an opportunity to spring into the hut and seize his victim, for he was hungry.

But as he passed the opening of the hut, the lady saw him, and, uttering a scream of terror, she threw at him her loofah, which was full of soap.

"She flung it at him and he fled,
But to this day the Leopard still
Is flecked with soap from foot to head!"

The Leopard and the Ram
(From the Akan peoples, Ghana)

A RAM ONCE DECIDED to make a clearing in the woods and build himself a house. A leopard who lived near also made up his mind to do the very same thing.

Unknown to each other they both chose the same site. Ram came one day and worked at the clearing. Leopard arrived after Ram had gone and was much surprised to find some of his work already done. However, he continued what Ram had begun. Each was daily surprised at the progress made in his absence, but concluded that the fairies had been helping him. He gave them thanks and continued with his task.

Thus the matter went on – the two working alternately at the building and never seeing one another. At last the house was finished to the satisfaction of both.

The two prepared to take up their abode in the new home. To their great astonishment they met. Each told his tale, and after some friendly discussion, they decided to live together.

Both Leopard and Ram had sons. These two young animals played together while their parents hunted. The leopard was very much surprised to find that every evening his friend Ram brought home just as much meat or venison from the hunt as he himself did. He did not dare, however, to ask the other how he obtained it.

One day, before setting out to hunt, Leopard requested his son to find out, if possible, from young Ram, how his father managed to kill the animals. Accordingly while they were at play, little Leopard inquired how Father Ram, having neither claws nor sharp teeth, succeeded in catching and killing the beasts. Ram refused to tell unless young Leopard would promise to show his father's way also. The latter agreed. Accordingly they took two large pieces of plantain stem and set out into the woods.

Young Leopard then took one piece and placed it in position. Then, going first to the right, then to the left – bowing and standing on his hind legs and peeping at the stem just as his father did – he took aim, sprang toward the stem and tore it.

Young Ram then took the other piece and placed it in position. Wasting no time he went backward a little way, took aim, then ran swiftly forward- pushing his head against the stem and tearing it to pieces. When they had finished they swept the place clean and went home.

In the evening the leopard obtained all the information about the hunt from his son. The latter warned him that he must always be careful when he saw the ram go backward. He kept this in mind, and from that day watched the ram very closely.

Some time afterward it rained, making the floor of the house very slippery. The leopard called the ram, as usual, to dine with him. As he was coming, the ram slipped backward on the wet floor. The leopard, seeing this, thought the other was about to kill him. Calling to his son to follow, he sprang with all his might over the wall of the house and fled to the woods. The ram called him back, but he did not listen. From that time leopards have made their abode in the woods while rams have remained at home.

Why the Leopard Can Only Catch Prey on Its Left Side
(From the Akan peoples, Ghana)

AT ONE TIME leopards did not know how to catch animals for food. Knowing that the cat was very skilful in this way, Leopard one day went to Cat and asked very politely if she would teach him the art. Cat readily consented.

The first thing Leopard had to learn was to hide himself among the bushes by the roadside, so that he would not be seen by any animal passing by. Next, he must learn how to move noiselessly through the woods. He must never allow the animal he chased to know that he was following it. The third great principle was how to use his left paws and side in springing upon his prey.

Having taught him these three things, Cat requested him to go and practise them well. When he had learnt them thoroughly he could return to her and she would give him more lessons in hunting.

Leopard obeyed. At first he was very successful and obtained all the food he wanted. One day, however, he was unable to catch anything at all.

Being very hungry, he bethought himself what he could have for dinner. Suddenly he remembered that the cat had quite a large family. He went straight to her home and found her absent.

Never thinking of her kindness to him – Leopard only remembered that he was hungry – he ate all her kittens. Puss, on discovering this dreadful fact, was so angry that she refused to have anything more to do with the great creature.

Consequently the leopard has never been able to learn how to catch animals that pass him on the right side.

The Lion and the Wolf
(From the Akan peoples, Ghana)

A CERTAIN OLD LADY had a very fine flock of sheep. She had fed and cared for them so well that they became famous for their fatness. In time a wicked wolf heard of them and determined to eat them.

Night after night he stole up to the old dame's cottage and killed a sheep. The poor woman tried her best to save her animals from harm – but failed.

At last there was only one sheep left of all the flock. Their owner was very sad. She feared that it, too, would be taken away from her, in spite of all she could do. While she was grieving over the thought of this a lion came to her village.

Seeing her sad face, he asked the reason of it. She soon told him all about it. He thereupon offered to do his best to punish the wicked wolf. He himself went to the place where the sheep was generally kept – while the latter was removed to another place.

In the meantime the wolf was on his way to the cottage. As he came he met a fox. The fox was somewhat afraid of him and prepared to run away. The wolf, however, told him where he was going, and invited him to go too. The fox agreed and the two set off together. They arrived at the cottage and went straight to the place where the sheep generally slept. The wolf at once rushed upon the animal, while Fox waited a little behind. Just as Fox was deciding to enter and help Wolf there came a bright flash of lightning. By the light of it the fox could see that the wolf was attacking – not a sheep – but a lion. He hastily ran away, shouting as he went: "Look at his face! Look at his face!"

During the flash Wolf did look at the pretended sheep. To his dismay he found he had made a great mistake. At once he began to make humble apologies – but all in vain. Lion refused to listen to any of his explanations, and speedily put him to death.

Why There Are No More Lions in the Bush
(By Okun Asukwor of Ndebbji, of the Ekoi people, Nigeria and Cameroon)

A MAN NAMED ETIM married a wife. After a time she told him that a son was about to be born. He left home and went out hunting, but Nki (lion) sprang from out the bush and killed him.

The wife remained in charge of a brother of her late husband. When the babe was born, this man took care of both. One day when the boy was nearly grown up the uncle called to him, saying "My son." The lad answered, "Do not call me thus. I am no son of yours. My father was killed in the bush by Nki."

One day the boy went out and collected a great quantity of palm kernels. He took these to the white traders and exchanged them for guns. When he reached home, he went to the bush near the town and climbed up a tree. On this he made two seats, one high up and the other low down. He took his gun to the high place and left it there, while he went to call one of his sisters. Her he set in the lower place, with a small bell in her hand, and a horn with which to blow. He himself climbed up on high and lay in wait, and told his sister to ring the bell and blow the horn to call their enemy Nki.

It was day time. The girl rang the bell and blew the horn as her brother had bidden. After a while the lion heard, and sent a poisonous snake to go and spy and bring him back word.

When Snake came the boy said, "I am not looking for you, but for my enemy Nki. I could easily kill you with my matchet and would not need a gun." So Snake went back and reported what he had heard.

When he had gone, the girl again began to ring and blow the horn, and this time Lion sent Python to go and bring him back word.

When the boy saw Python he said, "You are big and long, yet I could cut you in pieces without a gun. I wait here for my enemy Nki."

Again the third time, the girl began to ring the bell and to blow, and this time Nki sent Flame to report to him; but the boy called, "I could quench you with water. Go back and tell Nki that I wait for him alone."

After this Nki himself came. "Who is it who keeps calling me?" he roared out.

The boy answered never a word, but raised his gun and fired, and Nki fell down dead. For a while the two children did not dare to come down from the tree, for fear that their enemy still lived, and would harm them. A Parrot flew by, and the boy said, "Will you go down and cut off a finger from Lion for me?"

Parrot answered, "He is a very fearful animal; therefore I must refuse."

Just then Hawk flew past. To him also the boy called, and asked the same question. Hawk replied, "Give me a matchet." When this had been given, he flew down and cut off the middle finger from Nki.

Then the boy came down and turned the dead lion round. From its breast he saw the head of his own dead father hanging. This he loosed and put it, together with the claw, in his hunting bag.

As the couple walked through the streets of their town, the boy cried out, "I have killed a lion to-day." The people said, "We do not believe it," but the lad opened his bag and pulled out his father's head, and the claw of the lion, so that they might know. All clapped their hands and shouted. The boy said:

"We will keep my father's funeral customs."

He buried the head and gave a great "play." After this some of the people whose relations had also been devoured by the lion went and found these heads too hanging to the breast of the dead beast.

Up to that time no one could go into the bush alone for fear of the lions. Since the boy killed their chief, however, they have gone far away and left our bush free.

The Tail of the Princess Elephant
(From the Akan peoples, Ghana)

THERE ONCE LIVED a woman who had three sons. These sons were very much attached to their mother and always tried to please her. She at last grew very old and feeble. The three sons began to think what they could do to give her great pleasure. The eldest promised that when she was dead he would cut a fine sepulchre in stone for her. The second said he would make a beautiful coffin. The youngest said, "I will go and get the tail of the princess elephant and put it in the coffin with her." This promise was by far the hardest one to keep.

Soon after this their mother died. The youngest son immediately set out on his search, not knowing in the least where he would be likely to find the tail. He travelled for three weeks, and at the end of that time he came to a little village. There he met an old woman, who seemed very much surprised to see him. She said no human creature had ever been there before. The boy told the tale of his search for the princess elephant. The old woman replied that this village was the home of all the elephants, and the princess slept there every night. But she warned him that if the animals saw him they would kill him. The young man begged her to hide him – which she did, in a great pile of wood.

She also told him that when the elephants were all asleep he must get up and go to the eastern corner. There he would find the princess. He must walk boldly over, cut off the tail and return in the same manner. If he were to walk stealthily, the elephants would waken and seize him.

The animals returned as it was growing dark. They said at once that they smelt a human being. The old woman assured them that they were mistaken. Their supper was ready, so they ate it and went to bed.

In the middle of the night the young man got up and walked boldly across to where the princess slept. He cut off the tail and returned as he had come. He then started for home, carrying the tail very carefully.

When daylight came the elephants awoke. One said he had dreamed that the princess's tail was stolen. The others beat him for thinking such a thing. A second said he also had had the dream, and he also was beaten. The wisest of the elephants then suggested that they might do well to go and see if the dream were true. This they did. They found the princess fast asleep and quite ignorant of the loss of her tail. They wakened her and all started off in chase of the young man.

They travelled so quickly that in a few hours they came in sight of him. He was afraid when he saw them coming and cried out to his favourite idol (which he always carried in his hair), "O my juju Depor! What shall I do?" The juju advised him to throw the branch of a tree over his shoulder. This he did and it immediately grew up into a huge tree, which blocked the path of the elephants. They stopped and began to eat up the tree – which took them some little time.

Then they continued their way again. Again the young man cried, "O my juju Depor! What shall I do?" "Throw that corn-cob behind you," answered the juju. The lad did so, and the corn-cob immediately grew into a large field of maize.

The elephants ate their way through the maize, but when they arrived at the other side they found that the boy had reached home. So they had to give up the chase and return to their village. The princess, however, refused to do so, saying, "I will return when I have punished this impudent fellow."

She thereupon changed herself into a very beautiful maiden, and taking a calabash cymbal in her hand approached the village. All the people came out to admire this lovely girl.

She had it proclaimed through the village that whoever succeeded in shooting an arrow at the cymbal should have her for a bride. The young men all tried and failed. An old man standing by said, "If only Kwesi – the cutter of the princess elephant's tail – were here, he could hit the cymbal." "Then Kwesi is the man I will marry," replied the maiden, "whether he hit the cymbal or not."

Kwesi was quickly fetched from the field where he was ploughing, and told of his good luck. He, however, was not at all delighted to hear of it, as he suspected the maiden of some trick.

However, he came and shot an arrow which struck the centre of the cymbal. The damsel and he were accordingly married. She was all the time preparing to punish him.

The night following their marriage she turned into an elephant, while Kwesi was asleep. She then prepared to kill him, but Kwesi awoke in time. He called, "O my juju Depor! Save me!" The juju turned him into a grass mat lying on the bed and the princess could not find him. She was most annoyed and next morning asked him where he had been all night. "While you were an elephant I was the mat you lay on," replied Kwesi. The damsel took all the mats from the bed and burned them.

Next night the princess again became an elephant and prepared to kill her husband. This time the juju changed him into a needle and his wife could not find him. She again asked him in the morning where he had been. Hearing that the juju had helped him again she determined to get hold of the idol and destroy it.

Next day Kwesi was going again to his farm to plough a field. He told his wife to bring him some food to the resting-place. This time she had fairly made up her mind that he should not escape. When he had had his food she said, "Now lay your head in my lap and sleep." Kwesi quite forgot that his juju was hidden in his hair and did as she bid. As soon as he was asleep she took the juju out of his hair and threw it into a great fire which she had prepared. Kwesi awoke to find her an elephant once more. In great fear he cried out, "O my juju Depor! What am I to do?"

All the answer he got, however, came from the flames. "I am burning, I am burning, I am burning." Kwesi called again for help and the juju replied, "Lift up your arms as if you were flying." He did so and turned into a hawk.

That is the reason why hawks are so often seen flying in the smoke of fires. They are looking for their lost juju.

Why the Sea-turtle When Caught Beats Its Breast with Its Forelegs
(From the Akan peoples, Ghana)

MANY CENTURIES AGO, the people of this earth were much troubled by floods. The sea used at times to overflow its usual boundaries and sweep across the low, sandy stretches of land which bordered it. Time and again this happened, many lives being lost at each flood. Mankind was very troubled to find an escape from this oft-repeated disaster. He could think of no way of avoiding it.

Fortunately for him the wise turtle came to his help. "Take my advice," said she, "and plant rows of palms along the sea-coast. They will bind the sand together and keep it from being washed so easily away." He did so, with great success. The roots of the palms kept the sand firmly in its place. When the time came again for the sea to overflow, it washed just to the line of trees and came no farther. Thus many lives were saved annually by the kind forethought of the turtle.

In return – one would think – mankind would protect and cherish this poor animal. But no! Each time a turtle comes to the seashore to lay her eggs among the sand, she is caught and killed for the sake of her flesh. It is the thought of the ingratitude of mankind to her, which makes her beat her breast with her forelegs when she is caught. She seems to be saying, "Ah! this is all the return I get for my kindness to you."

Ohia and the Thieving Deer
(From the Akan peoples, Ghana)

THERE ONCE LIVED upon the earth a poor man called Ohia, whose wife was named Awirehu. This unfortunate couple had suffered one trouble after another. No matter what they took in hand misfortune seemed to lie in wait for them. Nothing they did met with success. They became so poor that at last they could scarcely obtain a cloth with which to cover themselves.

Finally, Ohia thought of a plan which many of his neighbours had tried and found successful. He went to a wealthy farmer who lived near, and offered to hew down several of his palm-trees. He would then collect their sap to make palm wine. When this should be ready for the market, his wife would carry it there and sell it. The proceeds would then be divided equally between the farmer, Ohia, and Awirehu.

This proposal having been laid before the farmer, he proved quite willing to agree to it. Not only so, but he granted Ohia a supply of earthen pots in which to collect the sap, as the miserable man was far too poor to buy any.

In great delight Ohia and his wife set to work. They cut down the trees and prepared them – setting the pots underneath to catch the sap. Before cock-crow on market-day, Ohia set off, with a lighted torch, to collect the wine and prepare it for his wife to take into the town. She was almost ready to follow.

To his great distress, on arriving at the first tree, instead of finding his earthen pot filled with the sweet sap, he saw it lying in pieces on the ground – the wine all gone. He went on to the second and third trees – but there, and at all the others, too, the same thing had happened.

His wife, in high spirits and ready for market, joined him at this moment. She saw at once by his face that some misfortune had again befallen them. Sorrowfully, they examined the mischief, and agreed that some wicked person had stolen the wine and then broken the pots to hide the theft. Awirehu returned home in despair, but Ohia set to work once more. He fetched a second supply of pots and placed them all ready to catch the sap.

On his return next morning, he found that the same behaviour had been repeated. All his wine was again stolen and his pots in fragments. He had no resource but to go to the farmer and tell him of these fresh misfortunes. The farmer proved to be very kind and generous and gave orders that Ohia might have as many pots as he should require.

Once more the poor fellow returned to the palm-trees, and set his pots ready. This third attempt, however, met with no better result than the two previous. Ohia went home in despair. His wife was of the opinion that they should give up trying to overcome their evil fortunes. It was quite evident that they could never attain success. The husband, however, determined that, at least, he would find and punish the culprit, if that were possible.

Accordingly, he bravely set his pots in order for the last time. When night came, he remained on guard among the trees. Midnight passed and nothing happened, but toward two o'clock in the morning a dark form glided past him to the nearest palm-tree. A moment after he heard the sound of a breaking pot. He stole up to the form. On approaching it he found that the thief was a bush-deer, carrying on its head a large jar, into which it was pouring the wine from Ohia's pots. As it emptied them it threw them carelessly on the ground, breaking them in pieces.

Ohia ventured a little nearer, intending to seize the culprit. The latter, however, was, too quick for him and escaped, dropping his great pot on the ground as he ran. The deer was very fleet, but Ohia had fully determined to catch him – so followed. The chase continued over many miles until mid-day arrived, at which time they had reached the bottom of a high hill. The deer immediately began to climb, and Ohia – though almost tired out – still followed. Finally, the summit of the hill was reached, and there Ohia found himself in the midst of a great gathering of quadrupeds. The deer, panting, threw himself on the ground before King Tiger. (Footnote: Tiger in West African stories is a leopard.) His Majesty commanded that Ohia should be brought before him to be punished for this intrusion into such a serious meeting.

Ohia begged for a hearing before they condemned him. He wished to explain fully his presence there. King Tiger, after consulting with some of the other animals, agreed to listen to his tale. Thereupon Ohia began the story of his unfortunate life. He told how one trial after another had failed, and how, finally, he had thought of the palm wine. He described his feelings on discovering the first theft after all his labour. He related his second, third, and fourth attempts, with the result of each. He then went on to tell of his chase after the thief, and thus explained his presence at their conference.

The quadrupeds listened very attentively to the recital of Ohia's troubles. At the conclusion they unanimously agreed that the deer was the culprit and the man blameless. The former was accordingly sentenced to punishment, while the latter received an apology in the name of the entire conference. King Tiger, it appeared, had each morning given Deer a large sum of money wherewith to purchase palm wine for the whole assembly. The deer had stolen the wine and kept the money.

To make up to Ohia for his losses, King Tiger offered him, as a gift, the power of understanding the conversation of all animals. This, said he, would speedily make Ohia a rich man. But he attached one condition to the gift. Ohia must never – on pain of instant death – tell any one about his wonderful power.

The poor man, much delighted, set off for home. When it was reached, he lost no time in setting to work at his palm-trees again. From that day his troubles seemed over. His wine was never interfered with and he and Awirehu became more and more prosperous and happy.

One morning, while he was bathing in a pool quite close to his house, he heard a hen and her chickens talking together in his garden. He listened, and distinctly heard a chicken tell Mother Hen about three jars of gold buried in Ohia's garden. The hen bade the chicken be careful, lest her master should see her scraping near the gold, and so discover it.

Ohia pretended to take no notice of what they were saying, and went away. Presently, when Mother Hen and her brood had gone, he came back and commenced digging in that part of the garden. To his great joy, he soon found three large jars of gold. They contained enough money to keep him in comfort all his life. He was careful, however, not to mention his treasure to any one but his wife. He hid it safely inside his house.

Soon he and Awirehu had become one of the richest couples in the neighbourhood, and owned quite a large amount of property. Ohia thought he could afford now to keep a second wife, so he married again. Unfortunately, the new wife did not at all resemble Awirehu. The latter had always been a good, kind, honest woman. The new wife was of a very jealous and selfish disposition. In addition to this she was lame, and continually imagined that people were making fun of her defect. She took the idea into her head that Ohia and Awirehu – when together – were in the habit of laughing at her. Nothing was further from their thoughts, but she refused to believe so. Whenever she saw them together she would stand and listen outside the door to hear what they were saying. Of course, she never succeeded in hearing anything about herself.

At last, one evening, Ohia and Awirehu had gone to bed. The latter was fast asleep when Ohia heard a conversation which amused him very much. A couple of mice in one corner of the room were arranging to go to the larder to get some food, as soon as their master – who was watching them – was asleep. Ohia, thinking this was a good joke, laughed outright. His lame wife heard him, and rushed into the room. She thereupon accused him of making fun of her again to Awirehu. The astonished husband, of course, denied this, but to no purpose. The jealous woman insisted that, if he were laughing at an innocent joke, he would at once tell it to her. This Ohia could not do, without breaking his promise to King Tiger. His refusal fully confirmed the lame woman's suspicions and she did not rest till she had laid the whole matter before the chief. He, being an intimate friend of Ohia, tried to persuade him to reveal the joke and set the matter at rest. Ohia naturally was most unwilling to do anything of the sort. The persistent woman gave the chief no peace till he summoned her husband to answer her charge before the assembly.

Finding no way of escape from the difficulty, Ohia prepared for death. He first called all his friends and relatives to a great feast, and bade them farewell. Then he put his affairs in order – bequeathed all his gold to the faithful Awirehu, and his property to his son and servants. When he had finished, he went to the Assembly Place where the people of the neighbourhood were gathered together.

He first took leave of the chief, and then commenced his tale. He related the story of his many misfortunes – of his adventure with the deer, and of his promise to King Tiger. Finally, he explained the cause of his laughter which had annoyed his wife. In so speaking he fell dead, as the Tiger had warned him.

He was buried amid great mourning, for every one had liked and respected him. The jealous woman who had caused her husband's death was seized and burnt as a witch. Her ashes were then scattered to the four winds of heaven, and it is owing to this unfortunate fact that jealousy and selfishness are so widespread through the world, where before they scarcely existed.

King Chameleon and the Animals
(From the Akan peoples, Ghana)

Ϙ

IN THE OLDEN DAYS all the animals of the world lived together in friendship. They had no one to rule over them and judge them. In consequence, many very wicked deeds were constantly being done, as no one needed to fear any punishment.

At last they all met together to discuss this bad state of affairs, and, as a result, they decided to choose a king. The great difficulty was how to choose him.

Lion was the first animal suggested. But all opposed him because, they said, he was too fierce. Wolf was next named – but the sheep and goats refused to have him because he was their foe. They knew they would have bad treatment if he were chosen.

As it was impossible to please every one by choice, they decided in another way. Two miles away was a great stool, placed under a very ancient tree which they believed to be the abode of some of their gods. They would have a great race. The animal which reached and sat down first on the stool should be chosen king.

The day of the race arrived. All animals, great and small, prepared to take part in it. The signal being given, they started off. The hare – being a very fine runner – speedily outdistanced the others. He reached the stool quite five hundred yards ahead of the next animal. You may judge of his annoyance when, just as he was going to sit down, a voice came from the stool saying, "Take care, Mr. Hare, take care. I was here first." This was the chameleon. He, being able to change his colour to suit his surroundings, had seized Mr.

Hare's tail just as the race began. Having made his colour match the hare's, no one had noticed him. He had held on very tightly, and when the hare turned round to take his seat Chameleon dropped off and landed on the stool.

The hare saw how he had been tricked and was very angry. The other animals, however, arrived before he could harm the chameleon. According to the agreement they had made, they had no choice but to make Chameleon king.

But none of the animals were satisfied with the choice. So as soon as the meeting was over, all scattered in every direction and left Chameleon quite alone.

He was so ashamed that he went and made his home at the top of a very high tree on a mountain. In the dead of night you may hear him calling his attendants to come and stay with him. But he is left quite alone. "A king without subjects is no king."

Why Tigers Never Attack Men Unless They Are Provoked
(From the Akan peoples, Ghana)

A MAN, hunting one day in the forest, met a tiger. At first each was afraid of the other; but after some talking they became quite friendly. They agreed to live together for a little time. First the man would live with the tiger in his forest home for two weeks. Then the tiger would come and live in the man's home.

The tiger behaved so well to the man during his visit that the man felt he had never been so well treated in all his life. Then came the time for the tiger to return home with the man. As they were going the tiger was somewhat afraid. He asked the man if he really thought he would be safe. "What if your friends do not like my face and kill me?" he asked. "You need fear nothing," said his host; "no one will touch you while I am there." The tiger therefore came to the man's house and stayed with him three weeks.

He had brought his male cub with him, and the young tiger became very friendly with the man's son.

Some months later the man's father died. When Tiger heard of his friend's great loss, he and his cub set out at once to see and condole with him. They brought a large sum of money to help the man.

As Tiger was going home again two of the man's friends lay in hiding for him and shot him. Fortunately he was not killed, but he was very much grieved lest these men had shot him at his friend's wish. He determined to find out if the man had known anything at all about the shot.

Accordingly he went to the place in the forest where he had first met his friend. There he lay down as if he were dead, after telling his cub to watch and see what would happen.

By and by the man came along. When he saw the tiger lying, as he thought, dead, he was terribly troubled. He began to cry and mourn for his friend, and sat there all night long with Tiger's cub, to watch that no harm should befall the body.

When morning came and Tiger was quite assured that his friend had had nothing at all to do with the shot, he was very glad. He got up, then, to the man's great astonishment, and explained why he had pretended to be dead.

"Go home," said Tiger, "and remember me always. In future for your sake I will never touch a man unless he first meddles with me."

The Story About a Beautiful Maiden, and How the Hartebeest Got the Marks Under Its Eyes like Teardrops
(From the Hausa people, southern Niger and northern Nigeria)

THIS IS A STORY about an alliance. A chief begat a beautiful daughter; she had no equal in the town. And he said, "He who hoes on the day the people come together and whose area hoed surpasses every one else's he marries the chief's daughter."

So on the day the chief calls his neighbours to hoe (gayaa), "Let the suitors come and hoe for me. But he who hoes and surpasses every one else, to him a wife."

Now of a truth the chameleon had heard about this for a long time past, and he came along. He was eating hoeing medicine. Now when the day of the hoeing came round the chameleon was at home. He did not come out until those hoeing were at work and were far away; then the chameleon came. He struck one blow on the ground with the hoe, then he climbed on the hoe and sat down, and the hoe started to hoe, and fairly flew until it had done as much as the hoers. It passed them, and reached the boundary of the furrow.

The chameleon got off, sat down, and rested, and later on the other hoers got to where he was. Then the chief would not consent, but now said he who ran and passed every one, he should marry his daughter. Then the hartebeest said he surpassed every one in running. So they had a race. But the chameleon turned into a needle; he leaped and stuck fast to the tail of the hartebeest, and the hartebeest ran until he passed every one, until he came to the entrance of the house of the chief. He passed it.

Then the chameleon let go the hartebeest's tail; of a truth the chameleon had seen the maiden. So he embraced her, and when the hartebeest came along he met the chameleon embracing the girl. Thereupon the hartebeest began to shed tears, and that was the origin of what you see like tears in a hartebeest's eyes. From that day he has wept and not dried his tears.

How Pythons Lost Hands and Feet
(From the Ekoi people, Nigeria and Cameroon)

THERE WAS ONCE a Python, whose wife was about to bear him a child. One day, in coming through the bush, he saw some ripe Aju fruits, and plucked them, as he thought, "Perhaps my wife would like these."

The woman ate them with great delight, and from that day on, kept begging her husband to bring her some more. He went out to the bush to search, but could not find any. She, however, threatened that unless more were brought to her, she would break her pregnancy.

In those days Pythons had hands and feet like men, and could walk upright. When therefore he found no fruits in the bush with which to satisfy his wife's desire, Python went to the farm of a man, where an Aju tree stood, and each day plucked some of the fruit.

Now the owner of the tree had a son named Monn-akat-chang-obbaw-chang (Child-feet-not-hands-not), because he had neither hands nor feet. One day he complained to his father that someone was stealing their Aju, and begged that he should be carried to the foot of the tree, so that he might watch for the thief. To this the father consented.

When Nkimm (Python) came next day, he found the tree guarded by a wonderful boy without hands or feet. So soon as the latter saw the snake he called, "Are you the person who steals my father's Aju?" Nkimm denied his guilt, and said that this was the first time he had seen the tree, but begged the boy to give him a few of the fruits for his sick wife.

Akat Chang replied that he would do so with pleasure, had he but hands and feet with which to climb the tree, but, since he had not, this was impossible, as he could not allow any stranger to pluck his father's fruits.

Python offered to take off his own hands and feet and lend them to the boy, that he might be able to climb. This was done and the limbs bound on, after which the boy quickly went up into the tree, and threw down as many of the fruits as the visitor could carry away. He then came down again and returned the limbs to their owner, who thanked him and left with his load. When he reached his house he gave the Aju to his wife, who ate them with great delight.

Before it grew dark, the father of Akat Chang came to the tree to carry the boy home for the night. His son related how he had spent the time with the Aju thief, and enjoyed the advantage of using the latter's hands and feet.

Two days afterwards, Nkimm's wife had finished all the Aju, so told her husband that he must fetch her some more, again threatening to break her pregnancy if he did not do as she asked. So Python was obliged to set out once more for his well-known tree. There again he met his friend, the boy, who had been told by his mother to ask the thief to fix on the hands and feet very firmly. She bade him then climb into the tree, and stay there until his father came.

Once more Python took off his feet and hands and bound them strongly to the boy's body as the latter asked him to do. What a loss to Nkimm!

Off went the boy up the tree, and did not cease from climbing till he reached the topmost branch. Then he began to sing:

> "*Sini sini mokkaw. Sine sine mokkaw*
> *Oro obba*
> *Nta abe Aju, monn akat akpim.*
> *(Lord plant Aju, child feet not get)*
> *Oro obba*
> *Nkimm afonn akat, akaw anam Aju.*
> *(Python has feet, take buy (with) Aju fruit).*
> *Oro obba*
> *Sini sini mokkaw. Sine sine mokkaw.*
> *Oro obba.*"

(The narrator repeated the song very carefully as it had been taught him by his grandfather, but he had no idea of the meaning of the refrain. The latter appears to have some similarity to the Efut language.)

When the parents heard the singing, they ran towards their son. In his hands the father bore a great spear. When Nkimm saw this, he rushed off for his life in the opposite direction, throwing himself along the ground in the only way possible to him.

Since then, no man has been born without hands or feet and no Python or other snake with them.

Had it not been for this act of Monn-Akat-Chang, snakes would have continued to be footed animals instead of creepers, and man would sometimes have been born without feet or hands.

Why Snake Has Neither Hands nor Feet
(By Itambo Asong of Oban, of the Ekoi people, Nigeria and Cameroon)

OBASSI NSI once made a farm. In it he put three animals, Mfong (cow), Mbui (goat), and Nyaw (snake). Cow and Goat were the gardeners, while Snake was ordered to collect the fruits and take them to the house of Obassi.

Before leaving them to their work, Obassi said, "Of all the fruits of this farm you may not eat. Even should any plantains or other fruits fall down, you must not touch them."

One day some strangers came from a far town to visit Obassi; whereon the latter sent Snake to his farm to bring back a supply of food for them. At that time Snake had hands and feet just like all other creatures. The first day he went quickly and brought back a plentiful supply, but the second day, when he went again, Cow asked, "Why does our master want so many plantains?" Snake said, "He is feeding the strangers who have come to stay with him."

Goat said, "I do not quite understand. Do you mean that our master eats none of all these good things, but only gives them to strangers?" The three of them disputed the question, and it was late when Snake got back with his load. Obassi was angry and beat him because he was so long on the way.

Next time Snake was sent to the farm he said to Cow and Goat:

"I do not see why we should die of hunger while all the food is devoured by strangers. Why should not we ourselves enjoy the fruits of our labours?"

To this the others agreed, and Cow sent Goat to cut plantains. They were ripe, and when Cow divided them out, Goat said to him:

"You are the head man in the farm. You should eat first." On this Cow began to eat, and cried out, "Oh, very sweet plantains!" Then both the others joined him in eating.

Snake went and got yams. He came back and said to the others, "Do not tell anyone what I have done, for if my master heard, he would do something to me."

On his return, Obassi was more vexed than before. He said, "Why did you stay away so long? You already knew that there were strangers in the house."

Next day again Obassi sent the Snake, but this time he bade one of his daughters, named Afion Obassi, follow secretly, that she might learn why Snake stayed so long in the farm.

When Afion arrived, she found Cow and Goat eating. She said, "Who told you to eat the fruits in my father's farm?" They answered, "It was Snake who told us we might eat."

After the girl returned home, she told her father what she bad seen. Obassi therefore sent for the three animals. When they stood before him he asked, "How is it that you ate the fruit in my farm, which I had forbidden you to touch?" They answered, "It was Snake who taught us to eat."

Obassi said, "Each of you must suffer for disobeying my orders." To Cow he said, "From now onward, when men pick plantains, they will keep the good part for themselves and throw only the rind to you." That is the reason why we always see Cow eating plantain skins. To Goat he said, "When people prepare their yams, the peelings only shall be your portion." That is why we see Goat eating up the yam parings.

Obassi seized Snake, pressed him and pulled off his hands and feet. That is the reason why he no longer has these, like other animals.

Why Frog and Snake Never Play Together
(From the Ekoi people, Nigeria and Cameroon)

FROG HAD A SON. Snake also had a son. Both children went out to play in the bush. They said, "We feel hungry; let us go home." When they arrived at home, each of them went to his mother's house. Mrs. Frog asked her son, "Where have you been this morning?" He said, "I was in the bush playing with Snake-child." His mother said, "Don't you know that the Snake family are bad people? They have poison."

Also, when the little Snake went home, his mother asked, "Who was your playmate?" Snake-child said, "Frog was my playmate." Mrs. Snake said, "What foolishness is this to come and tell me you feel hungry! Don't you know that it is the custom of our house to eat frogs? Next time you play with him, catch him and eat him."

Snake-child therefore went to call Frog to play with him again, but the latter refused. Snake-child then said:

"Evidently your mother has given you instructions. My mother also has given me instructions."

From that day Frog and Snake never played together again.

Why the Bat Is Ashamed to Be Seen in the Daytime
(From southern Nigeria)

THERE WAS ONCE an old mother sheep who had seven lambs, and one day the bat, who was about to make a visit to his father-in-law who lived a long day's march away, went to the old sheep and asked her to lend him one of her young lambs to carry his load for him. At first the mother sheep refused, but as the young lamb was anxious to travel and see something of the world, and begged to be allowed to go, at last she reluctantly consented.

So in the morning at daylight the bat and the lamb set off together, the lamb carrying the bat's drinking-horn. When they reached half-way, the bat told the lamb to leave the horn underneath a bamboo tree. Directly he arrived at the house, he sent the lamb back to get the horn. When the lamb had gone the bat's father-in-law brought him food, and the bat ate it all, leaving nothing for the lamb. When the lamb returned, the bat said to him, "Hullo! you have arrived at last I see, but you are too late for food; it is all finished." He then sent the lamb back to the tree with the horn, and when the lamb returned again it was late, and he went supperless to bed. The next day, just before it was time for food, the bat sent the lamb off again for the drinking-horn, and when the food arrived the bat, who was very greedy, ate it all up a second time. This mean behaviour on the part of the bat went on for four days, until at last the lamb became quite thin and weak. The bat decided to return home the next day, and it was all the lamb could do to carry his load. When he got home to his mother the lamb complained bitterly of the treatment he had received from the bat, and was baa-ing all night, complaining of pains in his inside. The old mother sheep, who was very fond of her children, determined to be revenged on the bat for the cruel way he had starved her lamb; she therefore decided to consult the tortoise, who, although very poor, was considered by all people to be the wisest of all animals. When the old sheep had told the whole story to the tortoise, he considered for some time, and then told the sheep that she might leave the matter entirely to him, and he would take ample revenge on the bat for his cruel treatment of her son.

Very soon after this the bat thought he would again go and see his father-in-law, so he went to the mother sheep again and asked her for one of her sons to carry his load as before. The tortoise, who happened to be present, told the bat that he was going in that direction, and would cheerfully carry his load for him. They set out on their journey the following day, and when they arrived at the half-way halting-place the bat pursued the same tactics that he had on the previous occasion. He told the tortoise to hide his drinking-horn under the same tree as the lamb had hidden it before; this the tortoise did, but when the bat was not looking he picked up the drinking-horn again and hid it in his bag. When they arrived at the house the tortoise hung the horn up out of sight in the back yard, and then sat down in the house. Just before it was time for food the bat sent the tortoise to get the drinking-horn, and the tortoise went outside into the yard, and waited until he heard that the beating of the boiled yams into foo-foo had finished; he then went into the house and gave the drinking-horn to the bat, who was so surprised and angry, that when the food was passed he refused to eat any of it, so the tortoise ate it all; this went on for four days, until at last the bat became as thin as the poor little lamb had been on the previous occasion.

At last the bat could stand the pains of his inside no longer, and secretly told his mother-in-law to bring him food when the tortoise was not looking. He said, "I am now going to sleep for a little, but you can wake me up when the food is ready." The tortoise, who had been listening all the time, being hidden in a corner out of sight, waited until the bat was fast asleep, and then carried him very gently into the next room and placed him on his own bed; he then very softly and quietly took off the bat's cloth and covered himself in it, and lay down where the bat had been; very soon the bat's mother-in-law brought the food and placed it next to where the bat was supposed to be sleeping, and having pulled his cloth to wake him, went away. The tortoise then got up and ate all the food; when he had finished he carried the bat back again, and took some of the palm oil and foo-foo and placed it inside the bat's lips while he was asleep; then the tortoise went to sleep himself. In the morning when he woke up the bat was more hungry than ever, and in a very bad temper, so he sought out his mother-in-law and started scolding her, and asked her why she had not brought his food as he had told her to do. She replied she had brought his food, and that he had eaten it; but this the bat denied, and accused the tortoise of having eaten the food. The woman then said she would call the people in and they should decide the matter; but the tortoise slipped out first and told the people that the best way to find out who had eaten the food was to make both the bat and himself rinse their mouths out with clean water into a basin. This they decided to do, so the tortoise got his tooth-stick which he always used, and having cleaned his teeth properly, washed his mouth out, and returned to the house.

When all the people had arrived the woman told them how the bat had abused her, and as he still maintained stoutly that he had had no food for five days, the people said that both he and the tortoise should wash their mouths out with clean water into two clean calabashes; this was done, and at once it could clearly be seen that the bat had been eating, as there were distinct traces of the palm oil and foo-foo which the tortoise had put inside his lips floating on the water. When the people saw this they decided against the bat, and he was so ashamed that he ran away then and there, and has ever since always hidden himself in the bush during the daytime, so that no one could see him, and only comes out at night to get his food.

The next day the tortoise returned to the mother sheep and told her what he had done, and that the bat was forever disgraced. The old sheep praised him very much, and told all her friends, in consequence of which the reputation of the tortoise for wisdom was greatly increased throughout the whole country.

The Woman, the Ape and the Child
(From southern Nigeria)

OKUN ARCHIBONG was one of King Archibong's slaves, and lived on a farm near Calabar. He was a hunter, and used to kill bush buck and other kinds of antelopes and many monkeys. The skins he used to dry in the sun, and when they were properly cured, he used to sell them in the market; the monkey skins were used for making drums, and the antelope skins were used for sitting mats. The flesh, after it had been well smoked over a wood fire, he also sold, but he did not make much money.

Okun Archibong married a slave woman of Duke's house named Nkoyo. He paid a small dowry to the Dukes, took his wife home to his farm, and in the dry season time she had a son. About four months after the birth of the child Nkoyo took him to the farm while her husband was absent hunting. She placed the little boy under a shady tree and went about her work, which was clearing the ground for the yams which would be planted about two months before the rains. Every day while the mother was working a big ape used to come from the forest and play with the little boy; he used to hold him in his arms and carry him up a tree, and when Nkoyo had finished her work, he used to bring the baby back to her. There was a hunter named Edem Effiong who had for a long time been in love with Nkoyo, and had made advances to her, but she would have nothing to do with him, as she was very fond of her husband. When she had her little child Effiong Edem was very jealous, and meeting her one day on the farm without her baby, he said: "Where is your baby?" And she replied that a big ape had taken it up a tree and was looking after it for her. When Effiong Edem saw that the ape was a big one, he made up his mind to tell Nkoyo's husband. The very next day he told Okun Archibong that he had seen his wife in the forest with a big ape. At first Okun would not believe this, but the hunter told him to come with him and he could see it with his own eyes. Okun Archibong therefore made up his mind to kill the ape. The next day he went with the other hunter to the farm and saw the ape up a tree playing with his son, so he took very careful aim and shot the ape, but it was not quite killed. It was so angry, and its strength was so great, that it tore the child limb from limb and threw it to the ground. This so enraged Okun Archibong that seeing his wife standing near he shot her also. He then ran home and told King Archibong what had taken place. This king was very brave and fond of fighting, so as he knew that King Duke would be certain to make war upon him, he immediately called in all his fighting men. When he was quite prepared he sent a messenger to tell King Duke what had happened. Duke was very angry, and sent the messenger back to King Archibong to say that he must send the hunter to him, so that he could kill him in any way he pleased. This Archibong refused to do, and said he would rather fight. Duke then got his men together, and both sides met and fought in the market square. Thirty men were killed of Duke's men, and twenty were killed on Archibong's side; there were also many wounded. On the whole King Archibong had the best of the fighting, and drove King Duke back. When the fighting was at its hottest the other chiefs sent out all the Egbo men with drums and stopped the fight, and the next day the palaver was tried in Egbo house. King Archibong was found guilty, and was ordered to pay six thousand rods to King Duke. He refused to pay this amount to Duke, and said he would rather go on fighting, but he did not mind paying the six thousand rods to the town, as the Egbos had decided the case. They were about to commence fighting again when the whole country rose up and said they would not have any more fighting, as Archibong said to Duke that the woman's death was not really the fault of his slave Okun Archibong, but of Effiong Edem, who made the false report. When Duke heard this he agreed to leave the whole matter to the chiefs to decide, and Effiong Edem was called to take his place on the stone. He was tried and found guilty, and two Egbos came out armed with cutting whips and gave him two hundred lashes on his bare back, and then cut off his head and sent it to Duke, who placed it before his Ju Ju. From that time to the present all apes and monkeys have been frightened of human beings; and even of little children. The Egbos also passed a law that a chief should not allow one of his men slaves to marry a woman slave of another house, as it would probably lead to fighting.

Candor
(From the Fang and Bulu peoples, Cameroon)

GORILLA (NGIYA), among all Beasts, was derided and jeered at by them. They called him "Broken-face." So, he spoke to Ingenda of the Monkey Tribe, and ordered it, "Just examine for me this face of mine; whether it is really so, you tell me."

The monkey was afraid to refuse, and afraid also to tell the truth. So it ascended a tree; and, as it went, it plucked the fruits. It said to Gorilla, "I must first eat before answering your question; I feel hungry." (As an excuse to give itself time to escape.)

So Ingenda went; and, by the time it had eaten two of the fruits, it was near the tree-top. Then it called to Gorilla "Look here! with your face turned upward." So the Gorilla looked, with its face upward. And Ingenda, being in a safe place, acknowledged, "It is really so, really so."

Gorilla was angry; but was helpless to revenge itself on Ingenda for its candid statement; for, he had no way by which to catch him. And Ingenda went off, leaping as it went from tree-top to tree-top.

A Lesson in Evolution
(From the Fang and Bulu peoples, Cameroon)

SHREW (UNYUNGE) and Lemur (Po) were neighbors in the town of Beasts. At that time, the Animals did not possess fire. Lemur said to Shrew, "Go! and take for us fire from the town of Mankind." Shrew consented, but said, "If I go, do not look, while I am gone, toward any other place except the path on which I go. Do not even wink. Watch for me."

So Shrew went, and came to a Town of Men; and found that the people had all emigrated from that town. Yet, he went on, and on, seeking for fire; and for a long time found none. But, as he continued moving forward from house to house, he at last found a very little fire on a hearth. He began blowing it; and kept on blowing, and blowing; for, the fire did not soon ignite into a flame. He continued so long at this that his mouth extended forward permanently, with the blowing.

Then he went back, and found Lemur faithfully watching with his eyes standing very wide open. Shrew asked him, "What has made your eyes so big?" In return, Lemur asked him, "What has so lengthened your mouth to a snout?"

Why Nki (Small Dormouse) Lives in the Tops of Palm Trees
(From the Ekoi people, Nigeria and Cameroon)

A NEW PIECE OF LAND had been cleared by the people of a certain town. Next morning, when they went thither to work, they found the place befouled. Inquiry was made, but the offender was not to be found. The head chief therefore gave a gun to Ise and set him to watch.

When night fell, Ejaw (Civet) crept out of the bush, and began to befoul the place as before. Ise took aim and shot him, then ran and told the people what he had done.

At daybreak they all went forth and brought in the body. They cut up the flesh, and asked Ise to dry it in the smoke of the fire that they might feast upon it next day. Ise did as he was bidden, and, when he had laid the pieces in order upon the drying shelf, sat down to watch by the hearth.

Now Nki loved fresh meat, and thought of a way by which he alone might feast upon the kill. He took a great jar of palm wine, and went to visit Ise. The latter was very thirsty, so he drank a deep draught and then lay down and fell asleep. While he slept Nki stole all the meat, then, when dawn broke, before the theft could be discovered, this treacherous animal took a drum and stood in the open space before the Egbo house playing:

> *"Ofu awche, kpa kun edingi ane aba.*
> *Day breaks, now we may know each other.*
> *Mbana nyamm aba kare nyamm.*
> *Drier of meat come give meat."*

Ise awoke and found all the flesh gone, so he cried out:

"A thief has taken all the meat which was given me to guard. Take my flesh instead that the town may feast."

On this the people said, "It is just," so they killed Ise and gave his body to Etuk (Bay Duiker), that it might be smoked before the fire.

Nki did as before, stole the meat, and at daybreak beat upon the summoning drum. So Etuk lost his life as Ise had done, and his flesh was entrusted to Nkongam (Yellow-backed Duiker).

On him Nki played the same trick, with the result that he also was slain, and his body given in charge to Ngumi (Boar). This latter also fell a victim to Nki in exactly the same manner as the other beasts, and this time Mbaw (Large Dormouse) was chosen to smoke the meat.

Now the latter is a very cunning animal, and no sooner had he reached his house than he laid the flesh upon the drying shelf, and spread over it great lumps of rubber. Next he piled high the fire, so that the rubber grew soft, and sat down to wait for the thief.

After a while Nki appeared as before, but Mbaw only pretended to drink the palm wine, and poured it away little by little when his visitor was not looking. At length he too lay down as if overcome by sleep.

Nki called, "Mbaw, Mbaw, are you awake?" but the latter did not answer.

The thief thought that all was now safe, so he rose up softly, and laid his hand upon the meat. At once the rubber caught him and held him fast. Nki was angry and cried, "Let go of me, whoever you are, or I will punch your head." Still the rubber held fast. Then Nki drove his own head against the place where his hand was held, thinking to force back his enemy, but the rubber caught his hair and held that also. In vain he struggled and fought, threatening his unseen foe all the while. Rubber answered nothing, but only held the tighter.

At dawn Mbaw went out and beat upon the summoning drum, "Day breaks now, we may know each other; drier of meat come and give meat."

The people came together, and found the thief caught fast. They debated as to how he could best be punished for the deaths of all those beasts who had died through his fault.

While they talked together, each proposing some more cruel fate than the other, Nki began to wring his hands and to weep. With each new suggestion he heartily agreed, adding always, "Yes, yes, kill me in any of these ways, only do not fix spears in the ground, and throw me up so that I may fall upon their points."

The people were so angry that they shouted, "Since he dreads this death above all others, it is by this that he shall die." They got spears, and fixed them firmly in the earth, points upward. Then they freed Nki from the rubber which had held him till now, and placed him before the spears. Six of the strongest men advanced to seize him and fling him into the air, but to the surprise of everyone, he himself gave a great leap, and sprang up a palm tree which stood near.

At once the people got axes, and cut down the tree, but before it fell, Nki sprang to another. Then they said:

"If we follow this man, we shall ruin all the palm trees. It is better to leave him alone."

That is why Nki always stays in the tops of palm trees. Up to that time he had lived on earth like all other animals, but since he caused the death of so many creatures, no one will be his friend, and he cannot come back to dwell among them any more.

The Voices of Birds
(From the Yoruba people, southern Nigeria)

A MAGICIAN ONCE PASSED through a grove in the forest where a great many brown birds fluttered from tree to tree and filled the air with songs. For a long time he sat and listened, enraptured by their beautiful melodies, but in the end he became very jealous, for he himself could not sing.

At last he felt that he must by some means or other possess the voices of these singing birds, so he called them all together and said:

"It grieves me that the gods have given you all such poor, ugly brown feathers. How happy you would be if you were brilliantly coloured with red, blue, orange, and green!"

And the birds agreed that it was a great pity to be so ugly.

The magician then suggested that by means of his charms he could give them all beautiful feathers in exchange for their voices – which were, after all, of very little use to them, since nobody came into the grove to hear them.

The birds thought over his words, and desired very much the beauty he promised them. So they foolishly agreed to give him their voices, which the magician placed all together in a large calabash. He then used his charms to turn the dull brown feathers of the birds into orange and green and red, and they were very pleased.

The magician hurried away, and as soon as he came to a deserted place he opened the calabash and swallowed its contents. From that day he had an exceedingly sweet voice, and people came from far and near to listen to his songs.

But the birds were satisfied with their bright feathers. And this is why the most beautiful birds are quite unable to sing.

Why Bush Fowl (Ikpai) Always Calls up the Dawn
(By Ndum Agurimon of Nsan, of the Ekoi people, Nigeria and Cameroon)

A MAN ONCE WENT into the bush with his wife to collect palm nuts. He saw a palm with ripe clusters upon it, and climbed up to get them. While he was trying to cut through the stems, a black fly named Njinn-I-Nyakk began to buzz round him, dash into his eyes, against his nose, and all over his face. He raised his hand to drive it away, and as he did so the knife fell from his

grasp. "Run, run," he called to his wife, who was just beneath the tree, for he feared that it might fall upon her. It was the time of the woman's seventh month, but she sprang aside so quickly that she was out of the way before the knife reached the ground. In her haste she jumped over a serpent called Nkimm. This startled him so that he dived down a brown rat's hole, and begged for a drink of water. Rat handed him a calabash full, and he emptied it at one draught.

Rat was so frightened at her visitor that she sprang past him out of the hole and ran up a tree, where she sat trembling. The place she had chosen was near Nkundak's (Greater Plantain-eater) nest. No sooner did the latter see her than she raised a war cry. This startled a monkey named Nyak-I-Mbuk (Black Monkey), who sallied out ready for a fight. In his haste to meet his enemy, Nyak sprang on to a ripe fruit of the tree called Ntun. This fell from its stalk on to the back of an elephant who was passing beneath. The latter rushed away so furiously, that he tore down, and carried off a flowering creeper called Mfinn, which caught round his neck.

The Mfinn in turn pulled over an ant heap, which fell on to Bush-fowl's nest, and completely destroyed her eggs.

Bush-fowl was so sad because of her loss, that she sat brooding over the crushed eggs, and forgot to call the dawn. For two days therefore the whole world was dark.

All the beasts wondered what could be the reason of this continued night, and at length Obassi summoned them before him to inquire into the matter.

When all were present Obassi asked Bush-fowl why it was now forty-eight hours since she had called for light. Then she stood foi-th and answered:

"My eggs were broken by Ekughi Nke (ant hill), which was pulled over by Mfinn, which was dragged down by Elephant, who was knocked by Ntun fruit, which was plucked by Monkey, who was challenged by Nkundak, who was startled by Rat, who was frightened by Serpent, who had been jumped over by a sick woman, who had been made to run by the fall of a knife, which had been dropped by her husband, who had been teased by a black fly. Through vexation, therefore, at the loss of my eggs, I refused to call the day."

Each thing and every beast was asked in turn to give the reason for the damage it had done, and each in turn gave the same long answer, till it came to the turn of Black Fly, who was the first cause of all the mischief. He, instead of answering properly, as the others had done, only said "Buzz, buzz." So Obassi commanded him to remain speechless for evermore, and to do nothing but buzz about and be present wherever a foul thing lies. To Bush-fowl he also gave judgment that she should call on the instant for the long-delayed dawn, and never again refuse to do so, whether her eggs were destroyed or not.

Were it not that Obassi had given strict orders to Bush-fowl, it might easily happen that one day or another she would again refuse to call, and then we should unawaredly enter on a long night, which might perhaps last for a week or more.

Concerning the Hawk and the Owl
(From southern Nigeria)

IN THE OLDEN DAYS when Effiong was king of Calabar, it was customary at that time for rulers to give big feasts, to which all the subjects and all the birds of the air and animals of the forest, also the fish and other things that lived in the water, were invited. All the people, birds, animals, and fish, were under the king, and had to obey him. His favourite messenger was the hawk, as he could travel so quickly.

The hawk served the king faithfully for several years, and when he wanted to retire, he asked what the king proposed to do for him, as very soon he would be too old to work anymore. So the king told the hawk to bring any living creature, bird or animal, to him, and he would allow the hawk for the future to live on that particular species without any trouble. The hawk then flew over a lot of country, and went from forest to forest, until at last he found a young owl which had tumbled out of its nest. This the hawk brought to the king, who told him that for the future he might eat owls. The hawk then carried the owlet away, and told his friends what the king had said.

One of the wisest of them said, "Tell me when you seized the young owlet, what did the parents say?" And the hawk replied that the father and mother owls kept quite quiet, and never said anything. The hawk's friend then advised him to return the owlet to his parents, as he could never tell what the owls would do to him in the night-time, and as they had made no noise, they were no doubt plotting in their minds some deep and cruel revenge.

The next day the hawk carried the owlet back to his parents and left him near the nest. He then flew about, trying to find some other bird which would do as his food; but as all the birds had heard that the hawk had seized the owlet, they hid themselves, and would not come out when the hawk was near. He therefore could not catch any birds.

As he was flying home he saw a lot of fowls near a house, basking in the sun and scratching in the dust. There were also several small chickens running about and chasing insects, or picking up anything they could find to eat, with the old hen following them and clucking and calling to them from time to time. When the hawk saw the chickens, he made up his mind that he would take one, so he swooped down and caught the smallest in his strong claws. Immediately he had seized the chicken the cocks began to make a great noise, and the hen ran after him and tried to make him drop her child, calling loudly, with her feathers fluffed out and making dashes at him. But he carried it off, and all the fowls and chickens at once ran screaming into the houses, some taking shelter under bushes and others trying to hide themselves in the long grass. He then carried the chicken to the king, telling him that he had returned the owlet to his parents, as he did not want him for food; so the king told the hawk that for the future he could always feed on chickens.

The hawk then took the chicken home, and his friend who dropped in to see him, asked him what the parents of the chicken had done when they saw their child taken away; so the hawk said –

"They all made a lot of noise, and the old hen chased me, but although there was a great disturbance amongst the fowls, nothing happened."

His friend then said as the fowls had made much palaver, he was quite safe to kill and eat the chickens, as the people who made plenty of noise in the daytime would go to sleep at night and not disturb him, or do him any injury; the only people to be afraid of were those who when they were injured, kept quite silent; you might be certain then that they were plotting mischief, and would do harm in the night-time.

The Nsasak Bird and the Odudu Bird
(From southern Nigeria)

A LONG TIME AGO, in the days of King Adam of Calabar, the king wanted to know if there was any animal or bird which was capable of enduring hunger for a long period. When he found one the king said he would make him a chief of his tribe.

The Nsasak bird is very small, having a shining breast of green and red; he also has blue and yellow feathers and red round the neck, and his chief food consists of ripe palm nuts. The Odudu bird, on the other hand, is much larger, about the size of a magpie, with plenty of feathers, but a very thin body; he has a long tail, and his colouring is black and brown with a cream-coloured breast. He lives chiefly on grasshoppers, and is also very fond of crickets, which make a noise at night.

Both the Nsasak bird and the Odudu were great friends, and used to live together. They both made up their minds that they would go before the king and try to be made chiefs, but the Odudu bird was quite confident that he would win, as he was so much bigger than the Nsasak bird. He therefore offered to starve for seven days.

The king then told them both to build houses which he would inspect, and then he would have them fastened up, and the one who could remain the longest without eating would be made the chief.

They both then built their houses, but the Nsasak bird, who was very cunning, thought that he could not possibly live for seven days without eating anything. He therefore made a tiny hole in the wall (being very small himself), which he covered up so that the king would not notice it on his inspection. The king then came and looked carefully over both houses, but failed to detect the little hole in the Nsasak bird's house, as it had been hidden so carefully. He therefore declared that both houses were safe, and then ordered the two birds to go inside their respective houses, and the doors were carefully fastened on the outside.

Every morning at dawn the Nsasak bird used to escape through the small opening he had left high up in the wall, and fly away a long distance and enjoy himself all day, taking care, however, that none of the people on the farms should see him. Then when the sun went down he would fly back to his little house and creep through the hole in the wall, closing it carefully after him. When he was safely inside he would call out to his friend the Odudu and ask him if he felt hungry, and told him that he must bear it well if he wanted to win, as he, the Nsasak bird, was very fit, and could go on for a long time.

For several days this went on, the voice of the Odudu bird growing weaker and weaker every night, until at last he could no longer reply. Then the little bird knew that his friend must be dead. He was very sorry, but could not report the matter, as he was supposed to be confined inside his house.

When the seven days had expired the king came and had both the doors of the houses opened. The Nsasak bird at once flew out, and, perching on a branch of a tree which grew near, sang most merrily; but the Odudu bird was found to be quite dead, and there was very little left of him, as the ants had eaten most of his body, leaving only the feathers and bones on the floor.

The king therefore at once appointed the Nsasak bird to be the head chief of all the small birds, and in the Ibibio country even to the present time the small boys who have bows and arrows are presented with a prize, which sometimes takes the shape of a female goat, if they manage to shoot a Nsasak bird, as the Nsasak bird is the king of the small birds, and most difficult to shoot on account of his wiliness and his small size.

The Election of the King Bird
(From southern Nigeria)

OLD TOWN, CALABAR, once had a king called Essiya, who, like most of the Calabar kings in the olden days, was rich and powerful; but although he was so wealthy, he did not possess many slaves. He therefore used to call upon the animals and birds to help his people with their work. In order to get the work done quickly and well, he determined to appoint head chiefs of all the different species. The elephant he appointed king of the beasts of the forest, and the hippopotamus king of the water animals, until at last it came to the turn of the birds to have their king elected.

Essiya thought for some time which would be the best way to make a good choice, but could not make up his mind, as there were so many different birds who all considered they had claims. There was the hawk with his swift flight, and of hawks there were several species. There were the herons to be considered, and the big spur-winged geese, the hornbill or toucan tribe, and the game birds, such as guinea fowl, the partridge, and the bustards. Then again, of course, there were all the big crane tribe, who walked about the sandbanks in the dry season, but who disappeared when the river rose, and the big black-and-white fishing eagles. When the king thought of the plover tribe, the sea-birds, including the pelicans, the doves, and the numerous shy birds who live in the forest, all of whom sent in claims, he got so confused, that he decided to have a trial by ordeal of combat, and sent word round the whole country for all the birds to meet the next day and fight it out between themselves, and that the winner should be known as the king bird ever afterwards.

The following morning many thousands of birds came, and there was much screeching and flapping of wings. The hawk tribe soon drove all the small birds away, and harassed the big waders so much, that they very shortly disappeared, followed by the geese, who made much noise, and winged away in a straight line, as if they were playing "Follow my leader." The big forest birds who liked to lead a secluded life very soon got tired of all the noise and bustle, and after a few croaks and other weird noises went home. The game birds had no chance and hid in the bush, so that very soon the only birds left were the hawks and the big black-and-white fishing eagle, who was perched on a tree calmly watching everything. The scavenger hawks were too gorged and lazy to take much interest in the proceedings, and were quietly ignored by the fighting tribe, who were very busy circling and swooping on one another, with much whistling going on. Higher and higher they went, until they disappeared out of sight. Then a few would return to earth, some of them badly torn and with many feathers missing.

At last the fishing eagle said –

"When you have quite finished with this foolishness please tell me, and if any of you fancy yourselves at all, come to me, and I will settle your chances of being elected head chief once and for all;" but when they saw his terrible beak and cruel claws, knowing his great strength and ferocity, they stopped fighting between themselves, and acknowledged the fishing eagle to be their master.

Essiya then declared that Ituen, which was the name of the fishing eagle, was the head chief of all the birds, and should thenceforward be known as the king bird.

From that time to the present day, whenever the young men of the country go to fight they always wear three of the long black-and-white feathers of the king bird in their hair, one on each side and one in the middle, as they are believed to impart much courage and skill to the wearer; and if a young man is not possessed of any of these feathers when he goes out to fight, he is looked upon as a very small boy indeed.

Which is the Better Hunter, an Eagle or a Leopard?
(From the Fang and Bulu peoples, Cameroon)

EAGLE (MBELA) and Leopard (Njě) had a discussion about obtaining prey. Eagle said, "I am the one who can surpass you in preying." Leopard said, "Not so! Is it not I?"

Then Eagle said, "Wait; see whether you are the one to surpass me in preying." Thereupon he descended from above, seized a child of Leopard, and flew up with it to his nest.

Leopard exclaimed, "Alas! what shall I do?" And he went, and went, walking about, coming to one place, and going to another, wishing to fly in order to go to the rescue of his child. He could not fly, for want of wings; therefore it was the other one who flew up and away.

So it was that the eagle proved that he surpassed the leopard in seeking prey.

Parrot Standing on One Leg
(From the Fang and Bulu peoples, Cameroon)

ELEPHANT (NJÂKU) built his own town; and Parrot (Koho) built also his. Then the children of Parrot went a-hunting every day; and when they came back, the town had wild meat in abundance, hida! hida!

One day Elephant announced, "I must go on an excursion to the town of Chum Koho."

He arrived there and found him, with that fashion of his, of standing with one leg bent up under his feathers hidden. His friend Elephant asked him, "Chum! what have you done to your leg?" He answered him (falsely), "My children have gone with it a-hunting." Elephant being astonished said, "On your oath?" He replied, "Truly!"

Then Elephant said, "I came to see you, only to see. I'm going back." The other said, "Yes; very good."

Elephant returned to his town, and said to his children, "Arrange the nets today; tomorrow for a hunt!"

The next day, the children made ready. And he, ashamed that a small Bird should do a greater act than himself said, "Take ye a saw, and cut off my leg." His children did not hesitate at his command, as they were accustomed to implicit obedience. So, they cut it off; and they carried with them, as he directed, the leg, on their hunt.

When they were gone, to their father Elephant came Death (Iwedo), saying, "I have arrived!" People of the town cried for help, "Come ye! Njâku is not well!" But, the children were beyond hearing, being still away at the hunt. During their absence, Elephant died. When they arrived, they found their father a corpse.

People wondered, saying, "What is this? Since we were born, we have not heard this, that hunting is carried on with the legs of one who remains behind in the town." When others, coming to the funeral, from other towns, asked the children, "Who was the person who counseled you such advice as that?" they said, "Himself it was who told us; he said to us 'Cut.' So we cut."

Then, on farther investigation, the people said, "The blame belongs to Koho," so, they called Parrot to account. But, Parrot said, "It is not mine. I did not tell him to cut off his leg." So, the charge was dismissed. And the burial proceeded.

A Question of Right of Inheritance
(From the Fang and Bulu peoples, Cameroon)

PARROT (KOHO) and Sparrow (Utati-Mboka) argued about their right to inherit the property that a Man had left. The Sparrow said, "The Man and I lived all our days in the same town. If he moved, I also moved. Our interests were similar. At whatever place he went to live, there also I stood in the street."

The Parrot spoke, and based his claim on the ground that he was the original cause of the Man's wealth. He said, "I was born in the tree-tops; then the Man came and took me, to live with him.

"When my tail began to grow, he and his people took my feathers; With which they made a handsome head-dress; Which they sold for very many goods; With which they bought a wife; And that woman bore daughters; Who, for much money, were sold into marriages; And their children also bore other children; Wherefore, for that reason, it is that I say that I caused for them all these women, and was the foundation of all this wealth."

This was what Parrot declared.

So, the people decided, "Koho is the source of those things." And he was allowed to inherit.

An Oath, With a Mental Reservation
(From the Fang and Bulu peoples, Cameroon)

DOVE (IBEMBE) was building in a tree-trunk by a river, because it preferred to walk on the ground. And Crocodile (Ngando) just then emerged from the river to the bank, and lay on his log where he usually rested.

They two said, "Let us eat a Medicine-charm."

So, Dove agreed, and swore, saying, "I say to you that, when anything at all shall happen openly, if I do not tell it to you, then may this Medicine find me out and kill me." Crocodile also uttered his oath, "When whatever thing shall come out from the river onto the ground, if I do not tell it to you, this Medicine must find me out and kill me!"

When they had finished their Covenant, Crocodile returned to his hollow in the ground by the river. Dove also arose, and went away, walking to his place. Then he and Leopard (Njĕ) suddenly met, on the path.

Leopard asked, "Are you able to see Ngando for me? I want to eat it." Dove answered, "Ah! would that you and I were living in one place with an Agreement!" Leopard replied, "Come then! let us, I and you, eat a Medicine."

So Leopard began. He said as his oath: "Anything at all that shall come to my place where I dwell, if I be there, and it wants to get hold of you, if I tell it not to you, let this Medicine find and certainly kill me!" Dove also with his oath, said, "If I see Ngando, and I do not tell you, let this Medicine find me and certainly kill me!"

So, they made their promise; then they separated; and each one went to his own village.

Thus Dove and Leopard ate their kind of "Medicine," after Dove and Crocodile had already eaten theirs.

Then, one day, Crocodile came out from the river. Dove at once began to tell Leopard, saying, "He has emerged from the river and is about to settle on the log!" So, Leopard began slowly to come, and watching Crocodile, as he came. When he was near, in his advance, Dove spoke, telling Crocodile, and said, "Your watcher! Your watcher is coming! Do not approach here!"

Thereat, Crocodile slipped back into the water.

The next time that Dove and Leopard met, Leopard demanded, "What is this you have done to me? You swore to me this: 'If I see Crocodile I will tell you; and you must come catch him.' Now, as soon as you saw me, you turned around, and told Crocodile, 'Fall into the River!' You have mocked me!"

And Leopard grew very angry.

(And so, because Dove "abused" Leopard, that is, deceived him, the dove no longer builds its nest on the ground, through fear of leopards.)

Human Stories
& Parables

MOST OF THE WORLD'S mythologies are fairly accommodating when it comes to animal characters. Heroes hear birds talking; receive protection from wild beasts. That's not really so surprising: such stories originate in what for most of us in the modern world is a long-ago age when we didn't live in cities but saw animals about us every day. We invested in them more as well, living comparatively 'close to nature' (as the cliché has it). A lot was riding on the success of a hunt or harvest; the health of a herd.

It's nevertheless striking just how many animal characters there are in West African myth. And how that contextualizes tales of men and women. Frequently these show a sort of psychological depth and moral complexity we couldn't hope to find in animal protagonists, however subtly delineated. For the most part, though, they're exemplary as well. Like the animals, these characters tend to illustrate an axiom or make a point. Many of these stories are frankly fables. But they're invariably vividly-realized and enormously entertaining: not just morally instructive but a real treat.

The King of Sedo[2]
(From the Wolof people, Senegal)

IN THE TOWN OF SEDO, it is said, there was a King named Sabar. Sabar's armies were powerful. They conquered many towns, and many people paid tribute to him. If a neighbouring Chief passed through Sedo, he came to Sabar's house, touched his forehead to the ground, and presented gifts to the King. As the King grew old, he grew proud. His word was law in Sedo. And if his word was heard in other places, it was law there too. Sabar said to himself, "I am indeed great, for who is there to contradict me? And who is my master?"

There came to Sedo one day a minstrel, and he was called on to entertain the King. He sang a song of praise to Sabar and to Sabar's ancestors. He danced. And then he sang:

> *"The dog is great among dogs,*
> *Yet he serves man.*
> *The woman is great among women,*
> *Yet she waits upon her children.*
> *The hunter is great among hunters,*
> *Yet he serves the village.*
> *Minstrels are great among minstrels,*
> *Yet they sing for the King and his slaves."*

When the song was finished, Sabar said to the minstrel, "What is the meaning of this song?"

The minstrel replied, "The meaning is that all men serve, whatever their station."

---

2   From *The King's Drum and Other African Stories* by Harold Courlander. Copyright 1962, 1990 by Harold Courlander. Reprinted by permission of The Emma Courlander Trust.

And Sabar said to him, "Not all men. The King of Sedo does not serve. It is others who serve him."

The minstrel was silent, and Sabar asked, "Is this not the truth?"

The minstrel answered, "Who am I to say the King of Sedo speaks what is not true?"

At this moment a wandering holy man came through the crowd and asked for some food. The minstrel said to the King. "Allow me to give this unfortunate man a little of the food which you have not eaten."

Sabar said, "Give it, and let us get on with the discussion."

The minstrel said, "Here is my harp until I have finished feeding him." He placed his harp in the King's hands, took a little food from the King's bowl, and gave it to the holy man. Then he came back and stood before Sabar.

"O King of Sedo," he said, "you have spoken what I could not say, for who contradicts a king? You have said that all men serve the King of Sedo and that he does not serve. Yet you have given a wandering holy man food from your bowl, and you have held the harp for a mere minstrel while he reserved another. How then can one say a king does not serve? It is said, 'The head and the body must serve each other.'"

And the minstrel picked up his harp from the hands of the King and sang"

> *"The soldier is great among soldiers,*
> *Yet he serves the clan.*
> *The King is great among kings,*
> *Yet he serves his people."*

Three Fast Men[3]
(From the Mende people, Ivory Coast)

THREE YOUNG MEN went out to their fields to harvest millet. It began to rain. One of the men carried a basket of millet on his head. The earth was wet form the rain, and the man slipped. His foot skidded from the city of Bamako to the town of Kati. The basket of millet on his head began to fall. The man reached into a house as he slid by and picked up a knife. He cut the tall reed grass that grew along the path, wove a mat out of it, and laid it on the ground beneath him. Spilling from the falling basket, the millet fell upon the mat. The man arose, shook the millet from the mat back into the basket, and said: "If I had not had the presence of mind to make a mat and put it beneath me, I would have lost my grain."

The second young man had forty chickens in fifteen baskets, and on the way to his millet field he took the chickens from the baskets to let them feed. Suddenly a hawk swooped down, its talons ready to seize one of the chickens. The man ran swiftly among his chickens, picked them up, put each one in its proper basket, covered the baskets, and caught the swooping hawk by its talons. He said, "What do you think you are doing – trying to steal my chickens?"

The third young man and the first young man went hunting together. The first man shot an arrow at an antelope. The other man leaped forward at the same instant, caught the antelope, killed it, skinned it, cut up the meat, stretched the skin out to dry, and placed the meat in his knapsack. Then he reached out his hand and caught the first man's arrow as it arrived. He said, "What do you think you are doing – trying to shoot holes in my knapsack?"

---

3   From *The King's Drum and Other African Stories* by Harold Courlander. Copyright 1962, 1990 by Harold Courlander. Reprinted by permission of The Emma Courlander Trust.

Morning Sunrise
(From the Akan peoples, Ghana)

A MAN in one of the villages had a very beautiful daughter. She was so lovely that people called her "Morning Sunrise." Every young man who saw her wanted to marry her. Three, in particular, were very anxious to have her for their wife. Her father found it difficult to decide among them. He determined to find out by a trick which of the three was most worthy of her.

He bade her lie down on her bed as if she were dead. He then sent the report of her death to each of the three lovers, asking them to come and help him with her funeral.

The messenger came first to "Wise Man." When he heard the message, he exclaimed, "What can this man mean? The girl is not my wife. I certainly will not pay any money for her funeral."

The messenger came next to the second man. His name was "Wit." The latter at once said, "Oh dear, no! I shall not pay any money for her funeral expenses. Her father did not even let me know she was ill." So he refused to go.

"Thinker," the third young man – when he received the message – at once got ready to start. "Certainly I must go and mourn for Morning Sunrise," said he. "Had she lived, surely she would have been my wife." So he took money with him and set out for her home.

When he reached it her father called out, "Morning Sunrise, Morning Sunrise. Come here. This is your true husband."

That very day the betrothal took place, and soon after the wedding followed. "Thinker" and his beautiful wife lived very happily together.

Adzanumee and Her Mother
(From the Akan peoples, Ghana)

THERE ONCE LIVED a woman who had one great desire. She longed to have a daughter – but alas! she was childless. She could never feel happy, because of this unfulfilled wish. Even in the midst of a feast the thought would be in her mind – "Ah! if only I had a daughter to share this with me!"

One day she was gathering yams in the field, and it chanced that she pulled out one which was very straight and well shaped. "Ah!" she thought to herself, "if only this fine yam were a daughter, how happy I should be!" To her astonishment the yam answered, "If I were to become your daughter, would you promise never to reproach me with having been a yam?" She eagerly gave her promise, and at once the yam changed into a beautiful, well-made girl. The woman was overjoyed and was very kind to the girl. She named her Adzanumee. The latter was exceedingly useful to her mother. She would make the bread, gather the yams, and sell them at the market-place.

She had been detained, one day, longer than usual. Her mother became impatient at her non-appearance and angrily said, "Where can Adzanumee be? She does not deserve that beautiful name. She is only a yam."

A bird singing near by heard the mother's words and immediately flew off to the tree under which Adzanumee sat. There he began to sing:

"Adzanumee! Adzanumee!
Your mother is unkind – she says you are only a yam,
You do not deserve your name!
Adzanumee! Adzanumee!"

The girl heard him and returned home weeping. When the woman saw her she said, "My daughter, my daughter! What is the matter?" Adzanumee replied:

"O my mother! my mother!
You have reproached me with being a yam.
You said I did not deserve my name.
O my mother! my mother!"

With these words she made her way toward the yam-field. Her mother, filled with fear, followed her, wailing:

"Nay, Adzanumee! Adzanumee!
Do not believe it – do not believe it.
You are my daughter, my dear daughter
Adzanumee!"

But she was too late. Her daughter, still singing her sad little song, quickly changed back into a yam. When the woman arrived at the field there lay the yam on the ground, and nothing she could do or say would give her back the daughter she had desired so earnestly and treated so inconsiderately.

Honourable Minu
(From the Akan peoples, Ghana)

IT HAPPENED ONE DAY that a poor Akim-man had to travel from his own little village to Accra – one of the big towns on the coast. This man could only speak the language of his own village – which was not understood by the men of the town. As he approached Accra he met a great herd of cows. He was surprised at the number of them, and wondered to whom they could belong. Seeing a man with them he asked him, "To whom do these cows belong?" The man did not know the language of the Akim-man, so he replied, "Minu" (I do not understand). The traveller, however, thought that Minu was the name of the owner of the cows and exclaimed, "Mr. Minu must be very rich."

He then entered the town. Very soon he saw a fine large building, and wondered to whom it might belong. The man he asked could not understand his question, so he also answered, "Minu." "Dear me! What a rich fellow Mr. Minu must be!" cried the Akim-man.

Coming to a still finer building with beautiful gardens round it, he again asked the owner's name. Again came the answer, "Minu." "How wealthy Mr. Minu is!" said our wondering traveller.

Next he came to the beach. There he saw a magnificent steamer being loaded in the harbour. He was surprised at the great cargo which was being put on board and inquired of a bystander, "To whom does this fine vessel belong?"

"Minu," replied the man. "To the Honourable Minu also! He is the richest man I ever heard of!" cried the Akim-man.

Having finished his business, the Akim-man set out for home. As he passed down one of the streets of the town he met men carrying a coffin, and followed by a long procession, all dressed in black. He asked the name of the dead person, and received the usual reply, "Minu." "Poor Mr. Minu!" cried the Akim-man. "So he has had to leave all his wealth and beautiful houses and die just as a poor person would do! Well, well – in future I will be content with my tiny house and little money." And the Akim-man went home quite pleased to his own hut.

Kwofi and the Gods
(From the Akan peoples, Ghana)

KWOFI WAS THE ELDEST son of a farmer who had two wives. Kwofi's mother had no other children. When the boy was three years old his mother died. Kwofi was given to his stepmother to mind. After this she had many children. Kwofi, of course, was the eldest of all.

When he was about ten years old his father also died. Kwofi had now no relative but his stepmother, for whom he had to work.

As he grew older, she saw how much more clever and handsome he was than her own children, and grew very jealous of him. He was such a good hunter that day after day he came home laden with meat or with fish.

Every day she treated him in the same way. She cooked the meat, then portioned it out. She gave to each a large helping, but when it came to Kwofi's turn she would say, "Oh, my son Kwofi, there is none left for you! You must go to the field and get some ripe paw-paw." Kwofi never complained. Never once did he taste any of the meat he had hunted. At every meal the others were served, but there was never enough for him.

One evening, when the usual thing had happened, Kwofi was preparing to go to the field to fetch some paw-paw for his supper. All at once one of the gods appeared in the village, carrying a great bag over his shoulder. He summoned all the villagers together with these words: "Oh, my villagers, I come with a bag of death for you!"

Thereupon he began to distribute the contents of his bag among them. When he came to Kwofi he said: "Oh, my son Kwofi, there was never sufficient meat for you, neither is there any death."

As he said these words every one in the village died except Kwofi. He was left to reign there in peace, which he did very happily.

Maku Mawu and Maku Fia; or "I Will Die God's Death" and "I Will Die the King's Death"
(From the Akan peoples, Ghana)

ONCE UPON A TIME there were two men who were such great friends that they were almost always together. If one was seen the other was sure to be near. They had given one another special names, which were to be used only by themselves. One name, Maku Mawu, meant, "I will die God's death," and the other, Maku Fia, "I will die the King's death."

By and by, however, the other villagers heard these names and gradually every one got into the habit of calling the two friends by the nicknames in preference to the real ones. Finally, the King of the country heard of them and wished to see the men who had chosen such strange titles. He sent for them to Court, and they came together. He was much pleased with the one who had chosen the name of "Maku Fia," but he was annoyed at the other man's choice and sought a chance of punishing him.

When he had talked to them a little while, he invited both to a great feast which he was to give in three days' time. As they went away he gave a fine large yam to Maku Mawu and only a small round stone to his own favourite. The latter felt somewhat aggrieved at getting only a stone, while his friend got such a fine yam. Very soon he said, "Oh, dear! I do not think it is any use carrying this stone home. How I wish it were a yam! Then I could cook it for dinner." Maku Mawu being very generous – immediately replied, "Then change with me, for I am quite tired of carrying my great yam." They exchanged, and each went off to his own home. Maku Fia cut up his yam and cooked it. Maku Mawu broke his stone in half and found inside some beautiful ornaments which the King had hidden there. He thought that he would play a trick on the King, so told nobody what had been in the stone.

On the third day they dressed to go to the King's feast. Maku Mawu put on all the beautiful ornaments out of the stone. Maku Fia dressed himself just as usual.

When they reached the palace the King was amazed to see the wrong man wearing his ornaments, and determined to punish him more effectually next time. He asked Maku Fia what he had done with the stone, and the man told him he had exchanged it for his friend's yam.

At first the King could not think of any way to punish Maku Mawu, as, of course, the latter had not done anything wrong. He soon had an idea, however. He pretended to be very pleased with the poor man and presented him with a beautiful ring from his own finger. He then made him promise to come back in seven days and show the ring to the King again, to let the latter see that it was not lost. If by any chance he could not produce the ring – he would lose his head. This the King did, meaning to get hold of the ring in some way and so get the young man killed.

Maku Mawu saw what the King's design was, so determined to hide the ring. He made a small hole in the wall of his room, put the ring in it, and carefully plastered over the place again. No one could see that the wall had been touched.

After two days the King sent for the wife of Maku Mawu and asked her to find the ring. He promised her a large sum of money for it not telling her, of course, what would happen to her husband if the ring were lost. The woman went home and searched diligently but found nothing. Next day she tried again with no better success. Then she asked her husband what he had done with it. He innocently told her it was in the wall. Next day, when he was absent, she searched so carefully that at last she found it.

Delighted, she ran off to the King's palace and gave the ring to him. She got the promised money and returned home, never dreaming that she had really sold her husband's life.

On the sixth day the King sent a message to Maku Mawu, telling him to prepare for the next day. The poor man bethought himself of the ring and went to look if it were still safe. To his despair the hole was empty. He asked his wife and his neighbours. All denied having seen it. He made up his mind that he must die.

In the meantime the King had laid the ring in one of the dishes in his palace and promptly forgot about it. When the seventh morning had arrived he sent messengers far and wide, to summon the people to come and see a man punished for disobeying the King's orders. Then he commanded his servants to set the palace in order, and to take the dishes out of his room and wash them.

The careless servants – never looking to see if the dishes were empty or not took them all to a pool near by. Among them was the dish containing the ring. Of course, when the dish was being washed, out fell the ring into the water – without being noticed by the servants.

The palace being all in readiness, the King went to fetch the ring. It was nowhere to be found and he was obliged to go to the Assembly without it.

When every one was ready the poor man, Maku Mawu, was called to come forward and show the ring. He walked boldly up to the King and knelt down before him, saying. "The ring is lost and I am prepared to die. Only grant me a few hours to put my house in order." At first the king was unwilling to grant even that small favour, but finally he said, "Very well, you may have four hours. Then you must return here and be beheaded before the people."

The innocent man returned to his home and put everything in order. Then, feeling hungry, he thought, "I may as well have some food before I die. I will go and catch a fish in the pool."

He accordingly took his fish-net and bait, and started off to the very pool where the King's dishes had been washed. Very soon he caught a fine large fish. Cutting it open, to clean it, his delight may be imagined at finding the lost ring inside it.

At once he ran off to the palace crying: "I have found the ring! I have found the ring!" When the people heard him, they all shouted in joy: "He named himself rightly 'Maku Mawu,' for see – the death God has chosen for him, that only will he die." So the King had no excuse to harm him, and he went free.

The Robber and the Old Man
(From the Akan peoples, Ghana)

IN A BIG TOWN lived a very rich gentleman. The fame of his wealth soon spread. A clever thief heard of it and determined to have some for himself.

He managed to hide himself in a dark corner of the gentleman's room – while the latter was counting his bags of money. As soon as the old gentleman left the room to fetch something, the thief caught up two of the bags and escaped.

The owner was astonished, on his return a few minutes later, to find two bags short. He could find no trace of the thief.

Next morning, however, he chanced to meet the robber just outside the house. The dishonest man looked so confused that the rich man at once suspected he was the thief. He could not, however, prove it, so took the case before the judge.

The thief was much alarmed when he heard this. He sought a man in the village and asked his advice. The wise man undertook to help him – if he would promise to pay him half the money when he got off. This the robber at once said he would do.

The old man then advised him to go home and dress in rags. He must ruffle his hair and beard and behave as if he were mad. If any one asked a question he must answer "Moo."

The thief did so. To every question asked by the judge he said, "Moo, moo." The judge at last grew angry and dismissed the court. The thief went home in great glee.

Next day, the wise man came to him for his half of the stolen money. But he could get no answer but "Moo" from the thief, and at last, in despair, he had to go home without a penny. The ungrateful robber kept everything for himself. The wise man regretted very much that he had saved the thief from his just punishment but it was now too late.

The Ungrateful Man
(From the Akan peoples, Ghana)

A HUNTER, who was terribly poor, was one day walking through the forest in search of food. Coming to a deep hole, he found there a leopard, a serpent, a rat, and a man. These had all fallen into the trap and were unable to get out again. Seeing the hunter, they begged him to help them out of the hole.

At first he did not wish to release any but the man. The leopard, he said, had often stolen his cattle and eaten them. The serpent very frequently bit men and caused their death. The rat did no good to any one. He saw no use in setting them free.

However, these animals pleaded so hard for life that at last he helped them out of the pit. Each, in turn, promised to reward him for his kindness – except the man. He, saying he was very poor, was taken home by the kind-hearted hunter and allowed to stay with him.

A short time after, Serpent came to the hunter and gave him a very powerful antidote for snake-poison. "Keep it carefully," said Serpent. "You will find it very useful one day. When you are using it, be sure to ask for the blood of a traitor to mix with it." The hunter, having thanked Serpent very much, took great care of the powder and always carried it about with him.

The leopard also showed his gratitude by killing animals for the hunter and supplying him with food for many weeks.

Then, one day, the rat came to him and gave him a large bundle. "These," said he, "are some native cloths, gold dust, and ivory. They will make you rich." The hunter thanked the rat very heartily and took the bundle into his cottage.

After this the hunter was able to live in great comfort. He built himself a fine new house and supplied it with everything needful. The man whom he had taken out of the pit still lived with him.

This man, however, was of a very envious disposition. He was not at all pleased at his host's good fortune, and only waited an opportunity to do him some harm. He very soon had a chance.

A proclamation was sounded throughout the country to say that some robbers had broken into the King's palace and stolen his jewels and many other valuables. The ungrateful man instantly hurried to the King and asked what the reward would be if he pointed out the thief. The King promised to give him half of the things which had been stolen. The wicked fellow thereupon falsely accused his host of the theft, although he knew quite well that he was innocent.

The honest hunter was immediately thrown into prison. He was then brought into Court and requested to show how he had become so rich. He told them, faithfully, the source of his income, but no one believed him. He was condemned to die the following day at noon.

Next morning, while preparations were being made for his execution, word was brought to the prison that the King's eldest son had been bitten by a serpent and was dying. Any one who could cure him was begged to come and do so.

The hunter immediately thought of the powder which his serpent friend had given him, and asked to be allowed to use it. At first they were unwilling to let him try, but finally he received permission. The King asked him if there were anything he needed for it and he replied, "A traitor's blood to mix it with." His Majesty immediately pointed out the wicked fellow who had accused the hunter and said: There stands the worst traitor for he gave up the kind host who had saved his life." The man was at once beheaded and the powder was mixed as the serpent had commanded. As soon as it was applied to the prince's wound the young man was cured. In great delight, the King loaded the hunter with honours and sent him happily home.

The Omanhene Who Liked Riddles
(From the Akan peoples, Ghana)

THE OMANHENE is the chief of a village. A certain Omanhene had three sons, who were very anxious to see the world. They went to their father and asked permission to travel. This permission he readily gave.

It was the turn of the eldest to go first. He was provided with a servant and with all he could possibly require for the journey.

After travelling for some time he came to a town where lived an Omanhene who loved riddles. Being a stranger the traveller was, according to custom, brought by the people before the chief.

The latter explained to him that they had certain laws in their village. One law was that every stranger must best the Omanhene in answering riddles or he would be beheaded. He must be prepared to begin the contest the following morning.

Next day he came to the Assembly Place, and found the Omanhene there with all his attendants. The Omanhene asked many riddles. As the young man was unable to answer any of them, he was judged to have failed and was beheaded.

After some time the second son of the Omanhene started on his travels. By a strange chance he arrived at the same town where his brother had died. He also was asked many riddles, and failed to answer them. Accordingly he too was put to death.

By and by the third brother announced his intention of travelling. His mother did all in her power to persuade him to stay at home. It was quite in vain.

She was sure that if he also reached the town where his brothers had died, the same thing would happen to him. Rather than allow this, she thought she would prefer him to die on the way.

She prepared for him a food called cankey – which she filled with poison. Having packed it away in his bag, he set off. Very soon he began to feel hungry. Knowing, however, that his mother had not wished him to leave home, and therefore might have put some poison in the food, he thought he would test it before eating it himself. Seeing a vulture near by, he threw it half the cake.

The bird ate the cankey, and immediately fell dead by the roadside. Three panthers came along and began to eat the vulture. They also fell dead.

The young man cut off some of the flesh of the panthers and roasted it. He then packed it carefully away in his bundle.

A little farther on he was attacked by seven highway robbers. They wanted to kill him at once. He told them that he had some good roast meat in his bundle and invited them to eat with him first. They agreed and divided up the food into eight parts.

While they were eating the young man carefully hid his portion. Soon all the seven robbers fell ill and died. The young man then went on his way.

At last he reached the town where his brothers had died. Like them, he was summoned to the Assembly Place to answer the riddles of the Omanhene. For two days the contest proved equal. At the end of that time, the young man said, "I have only one riddle left. If you are able to answer that, you may put me to death." He then gave this riddle to the Omanhene:

Half kills one –
One kills three –
Three kills seven.

The ruler failed to answer it that evening, so it was postponed till the next day.

During the night the Omanhene disguised himself and went to the house where the stranger was staying. There he found the young man asleep in the hall.

Imagining that the man before him was the stranger's servant, and never dreaming-that it was the stranger himself, he roused the sleeper and promised him a large reward if he would give him the solution to the riddle.

The young man replied that he would tell the answer if the Omanhene would bring him the costume which he always wore at the Assembly.

The ruler was only too pleased to go and fetch it for him. When the young man had the garments quite safely, he explained the riddle fully to the crafty, Omanhene. He said that as they were leaving home, the mother of his master made him cankey. In order to find out if the cankey were good, they gave half to a vulture. The latter died. Three panthers which tasted the vulture also died. A little of the panther's roasted flesh killed seven robbers.

The Omanhene was delighted to have found out the answer. He warned the supposed servant not to tell his master what had happened.

In the morning all the villagers assembled together again. The Omanhene proudly gave the answer to the riddle as if he himself had found it out. But the young man asked him to produce his ceremonial dress, which he ought to be wearing in Assembly. This, of course, he was unable to do, as the young man had hidden it carefully away.

The stranger then told what had happened in the night, and how the ruler had got the answer to the riddle by cheating.

The Assembly declared that the Omanhene had failed to find out the riddle and must die. Accordingly he was beheaded – and the young man was appointed Omanhene in his place.

Farmer Mybrow and the Fairies
(From the Akan peoples, Ghana)

FARMER MYBROW was one day looking about for a suitable piece of land to convert into a field. He wished to grow corn and yams. He discovered a fine spot, close to a great forest – which latter was the home of some fairies. He set to work at once to prepare the field.

Having sharpened his great knife, he began to cut down the bushes. No sooner had he touched one than he heard a voice say, "Who is there, cutting down the bushes?" Mybrow was too much astonished to answer. The question was repeated. This time the farmer realized that it must be one of the fairies, and so replied, "I am Mybrow, come to prepare a field." Fortunately for him the fairies were in great good humour. He heard one say, "Let us all help Farmer Mybrow to cut down the bushes." The rest agreed. To Mybrow's great delight, the bushes were all rapidly cut down with very little trouble on his part. He returned home, exceedingly well pleased with his day's work, having resolved to keep the field a secret even from his wife.

Early in January, when it was time to burn the dry bush, he set off to his field, one afternoon, with the means of making a fire. Hoping to have the fairies' assistance once more, he intentionally struck the trunk of a tree as he passed. Immediately came the question, "Who is there, striking the stumps?" He promptly replied, "I am Mybrow, come to burn down the bush." Accordingly, the dried bushes were all burned down, and the field left clear in less time that it takes to tell it.

Next day the same thing happened. Mybrow came to chop up the stumps for firewood and clear the field for digging. In a very short time his faggots and firewood were piled ready, while the field was bare.

So it went on. The field was divided into two parts – one for maize and one for yams. In all the preparations – digging, sowing, planting – the fairies gave great assistance. Still, the farmer had managed to keep the whereabouts of his field a secret from his wife and neighbours.

The soil having been so carefully prepared, the crops promised exceedingly well. Mybrow visited them from time to time, and congratulated himself on the splendid harvest he would have.

One day, while maize and yams were still in their green and milky state, Mybrow's wife came to him. She wished to know where his field lay, that she might go and fetch some of the firewood from it. At first he refused to tell her. Being very persistent, however, she finally succeeded in obtaining the information – but on one condition. She must not answer any question that should be asked her. This she readily promised, and set off for the field.

When she arrived there she was utterly amazed at the wealth of the corn and yam. She had never seen such magnificent crops. The maize looked most tempting – being still in the milky state – so she plucked an ear. While doing so she heard a voice say, "Who is there, breaking the corn?" "Who dares ask me such a question?" she replied angrily – quite forgetting her husband's command. Going to the field of yams she plucked one of them also. "Who is there, picking the yams?" came the question again. "It is I, Mybrow's wife. This is my husband's field and I have a right to pick." Out came the fairies. "Let us all help Mybrow's wife to pluck her corn and yams," said they. Before the frightened woman could say a word, the fairies had all set to work with a will, and the corn and yams lay useless on the ground. Being all green and unripe, the harvest was now utterly spoiled. The farmer's wife wept bitterly, but to no purpose. She returned slowly home, not knowing what to say to her husband about such a terrible catastrophe. She decided to keep silence about the matter.

Accordingly, next day the poor man set off gleefully to his field to see how his fine crops were going on. His anger and dismay may be imagined when he saw his field a complete ruin. All his work and foresight had been absolutely ruined through his wife's forgetfulness of her promise.

A Story About an Orphan, Showing that "He Who Sows Evil, It Comes Forth in His Own Garden"

(From the Hausa people, southern Niger and northern Nigeria)

THIS IS THE STORY ABOUT ORPHANS. A certain man had wives, two in number. He died and left them. One among the wives fell ill. She saw she was near to death, so she said to the second wife, "Now you have seen this illness will not leave me. There is my daughter, I have left her as a trust to you; for the sake of Allah and the prophets look after her well for me."

So the woman died and was buried, and they were left with her child. Now always they were showing her cruelty, until one day a sickness took hold of the maiden. She was lying down. Her stepmother said, "Get up, and go to the stream."

The maid got up, she was groaning, she lifted a small calabash, and took the road. She went to the stream and drew water; she took it back and said, "Mother, lift the calabash down for me." But her step-mother said, "Do you not see I am pounding? Not now, when I have finished."

She finished husking the grain, she was winnowing, the maiden was standing by. The maiden said, "Mother, lift down the calabash for me." But her step-mother said, "Do you not see I am winnowing? Not now, when I have finished."

The maiden stood by till she had finished, until she had washed; she paid no attention to the maiden. The maiden said, "Mother, help me down with the water-pot." She said, "Do you not see I am pouring grain into the mortar? Not now, but when I have finished pounding." The maiden kept standing by till she finished pounding; she re-pounded, she winnowed, she finished, the maiden was still standing.

The maiden said, "Mother, help me down," but she said, "Do you not see I am putting porridge in the pot? When I have finished." The maiden kept standing by till the step-mother had finished putting the porridge in the pot. The maiden said, "Mother, help me down," but she said, "If I come to help you down the porridge will get burned; wait till the porridge boils." The porridge boiled, she took it out of the water, then she pounded it, squeezed it, and finished.

She did not say anything to the maid, till the wind came like a whirlwind; it lifted the maiden and went off with her and she was not seen. The wind took her to the forest (bush), there was no one but she alone. She was roaming in the forest till she saw a grass hut. Then she went up to it. She peeped in, and met a thigh-bone and a dog inside.

Then she drew back, but the thigh-bone said, "Us! us!", and the dog said, "He says you are to come back." The maiden came back, and the thigh-bone said, "Us! us!", and the dog said, "He says you are to enter." The maiden entered the hut, and bowed down and prostrated herself, and the thighbone said, "Us! us!", and the dog said, "He says, Can you cook food?" And the maiden said, "Yes."

So they gave her rice, one grain, and said she was to cook it. She picked up the single grain of rice. She did not grumble, she put it in the mortar and pounded, and when she had finished pounding, the rice filled the mortar. She dry pounded the rice and finished, and poured it from a height to let the wind blow away the chaff (*sheke*).

She went to the stream and washed it; she brought it back home, she set the pot on the fire, she poured in the rice and in a short time the rice filled the pot. Then the thigh-bone said, "Us! us!", and the dog said, "He says are you able to make soup?" The maiden said, "Yes, I can." The thighbone said, "Us! us!", so the dog got up and went to a small refuse heap, and scraped up an old bone, and gave it to the maiden. She received it and put it in the pot.

When a little while had passed, the meat filled the pot. When the meat was ready, she poured in salt and spice (*daudawa*), and she put in all kinds of soup spices. When the soup was ready she took the pot off the fire, she served out the food and divided it up. Ten helpings she set aside for the thigh-bone, for the dog she set aside nine helpings, and she set out for herself two.

They ate and were filled. So it is, because of this, if a stranger has come to you, honour him, give him food to eat. Meanwhile you study his nature, you see if it is bad or good. To return to the story. They went to sleep. At dawn the thigh-bone said, "Us! us!", and the dog said to the maiden, "He says, Can you make '*fura*' cakes?" She said, "Yes." The thigh-bone said, "Us! us!" Then the dog got up and came and lifted one grain of corn; he brought it and gave her. She received it and put it in the mortar; she poured in water, she lifted the pestle, she was pounding; as she pounded, the corn became much.

She took it out, she winnowed, she took it to the water, she washed it, she returned, she pounded, she took it out, she winnowed, she returned, and poured it in again. She pounded it very finely, she took it out, rolled it into cakes, and put it in the pot until it boiled. She took it off the fire, set it down, poured it into the mortar, pounded, took it out, rolled it up into balls, and gave to the thigh-bone three balls, to the dog she gave two.

When it was dawn the thigh-bone said, "Us! us!", and the dog said, "He says, Are you going home?" She said, "I will go, but I do not know the way."

Then the thigh-bone said, "Us! us!", and the dog rose up; he went and brought slaves, beautiful ones, he brought cattle and sheep, horses and fowls, camels and war-horses, and ostriches, and robes, everything in the world, the dog brought and gave to the maiden.

He said, "There they are, the thigh-bone says I must give you them; you will make them the provision for your journey. And he says he gives you leave to set out, and go to your home." But the maiden said, "I do not know the way." So the dog told the thigh-bone, and the thigh-bone said, "Us! Us!" And the dog said, "He says let us set out, and I must show you the way." So the dog passed on in front, the maiden mounted a camel, the camel was led.

They were going along. The dog brought them till they reached close to her home. The dog turned back, but she herself sent into the town; she said, let the chief be told it was she who was come. The chief said, "Let them go and meet her." They went and met her. They drew up at the chief's doorway, the chief gave them permission to alight, they alighted, She took out one tenth and gave the chief. She stayed there until the chief said he wished her in marriage. They were married. She also, that step-mother of hers, (her late father's second wife) was envious, so she told her own daughter to go to the stream to draw water for her. But the little girl said, "Mother, I am not going."

But the mother lifted a reed and drove her, and she went to the stream by compulsion. Now the girl went to the stream, drew water, and took it home. She came across her mother as she was pounding; she said, "Mother, help me down with the pot." But her mother said, "I am pounding, wait till I have finished." She finished pounding, and the girl said, "Mother, help me down." But she answered, "I am about to winnow, wait till I have finished." She finished winnowing and the girl said, "Mother, help me down with the pot." She replied, "I am just going to pound-when I have finished." When she had finished pounding then she sought the girl low and high; she did not see her, the wind has had lifted her and taken her to the bush.

It cast her there, she was roaming in the forest, when she saw a grass hut. She went and peeped in the hut, and she saw a thigh-bone and a dog. Then she drew back, and the thigh-bone said, "Us! Us!" The dog said, "He says you are to come." So she came and said, "Here I am." The thigh-bone said,

"Us! us!" The dog said, "He says you are to sit down." So she sat down, and said, "Mercy on us, a thighbone that talks. What sort of a thing is Us! us?" But they gave no answer.

A short time after the thigh-bone said, "Us! us!" Then the dog said, "He says, Can you cook food?" And she said, "Ah, it's a bad year when the partridge has seen them planting out the young trees (instead of sowing, when it could eat the seed). A thigh-bone, too, even it has an interpreter. I am able, you, I suppose, have the grain, when you are asking if people can cook food."

They gave no answer, but the dog got up; he lifted one single grain of rice and gave her. "What's this?" she said, "to-day I am about to see how one single grain of rice makes food." The dog replied, "As for you, make it thus." She lifted the rice and put it in the mortar, she was pounding, and after a little while the rice became much. She dry pounded it, took it out, poured it out so as to blow away the chaff, poured on water, cooked it.

By the time she had finished cooking it the rice filled the pot. She was amazed. The dog lifted up a year-old bone, brought it, and gave her. Then she said, "What am I to do with it, this is a year-old bone?" The dog replied, "As for you, make it thus." She said, "Are you supposed to be conjurers? I warn you; it is not my business that wizards should eat me." The dog remained silent; not a thing did he say.

She washed the bone and put it in the pot, and in a short time the pot was full of meat. The girl was amazed, but she stirred the food, she took it out and set the soup down. She put aside for the thigh-bone three helpings, for the dog two. But the dog was angry because he saw her share was large, theirs very small, and he said, "What's this?" When he would have said, "Haba," he could only say, "Hab hab," because he had not told the thigh-bone first before he spoke.

Formerly the dog was a minister at court and used to talk like a person, when on this day he got in a temper in front of the king, he condemned him to say "Hab! hab!" if he rose up to quarrel. And the moral of this is, a youth must not lose his temper in the presence of an elder.

Now they had eaten their food and slept. At dawn the thigh-bone said, "Us! us!" Then the dog was not able to speak, but he went and brought blind men, and lepers, and blind horses, and lame asses, and sheep, robes and trousers were brought to her, and the dog showed her the way. He brought her to near her home and turned back.

But the thigh-bone drove him away, so he came back very quickly and joined them, and followed them until they reached the house. That is the first time the dog came to the house, formerly he was in the bush. Well, to continue, when they had got near the house, then the girl sent one leper from among her retinue. He sat on a blind horse and his message was to tell the chief she has come. The chief allowed her to be met.

The chief made the galadima and many people to go and meet them. When they reached the open space in front of the chief's house, then a stink filled the town. Then the chief said they were to be taken far back to a' distance behind the town. They were led behind the town, far away they were to make their houses. When the mother of this maiden saw all this, then she became black of heart, and died.

That was the first appearance of wickedness, which is not a beautiful thing. Whoever commits a sin against another it comes back on himself, as a certain learned man sung, may Allah dispense mercy on him, he says, "Whosoever sows evil it comes forth in his own garden. That is true without a doubt, have you heard?"

A Story About Miss Salt, Miss Pepper, Etc.
(From the Hausa people, southern Niger and northern Nigeria)

THIS STORY IS ABOUT Salt, and Daudawa (sauce), and Nari (spice), and Onion-leaves, and Pepper, and Daudawar-batso (a sauce). A story, a story! Let it go, let it come.

Salt, and Daudawa, and Ground-nut, and Onion-leaves, and Pepper, and Daudawar-batso heard a report of a certain youth, by name Daskandarini. Now he was a beautiful youth, the son of the evil spirit.

They all rose up, and turned into beautiful maidens, and they set off. As they (Salt, Onion-leaves, etc.) were going along, Daudawar-batso followed them.

They drove her off, telling her she stank. But she crouched down until they had gone on. She kept following them behind, until they reached a certain stream. There they came across an old woman; she was bathing. She said they must rub down her back for her, but this one said, "May Allah save me that I should lift my hand to touch an old woman's back." And the old woman did not say anything more.

They passed on, and soon Daudawar-batso came, and met her washing. She greeted her, and she answered and said, "Maiden, where are you going?" She replied, "I am going to where a certain youth is." And the old woman said, "Rub my back for me!" She said, "All right." She stopped, and rubbed her back well for her. The old woman said, "May Allah bless you." And she said, "This youth to whom you are all going to, have you known his name?" She said, "No, we do not know his name."

Then the old woman said, "He is my son, his name is Daskandarini, but you must not tell them." Then she ceased. She was following them far behind till they got to the place where the boy was. They were about to enter, but he said, "Go back, and enter one at a time." They said, "It is well," and returned. And then Salt came forward, and was about to enter, "little girl, go back." She turned back. So Daudawa came forward.

When she was about to enter, she was asked, "Who are you?" She said, "It is I." "Who are you? What is your name?" "My name is Daudawa, who makes the soup sweet." And he said, "What is my name?" She said, "I do not know your name, little boy, I do not know your name." He said, "Turn back, little girl, turn back." She turned back, and sat down.

Then Nari (spice) rose up and came forward, and she was about to enter when she was asked, "Who is this little girl? Who is this?" She said, "It is I who greet you, little boy, it is I who greet you." "What is your name, little girl, what is your name?" "My name is Nari, who makes the soup savoury." "I have heard your name, little girl, I have heard your name. Speak my name." She said, "I do not know your name, little boy, I do not know your name." "Turn back, little girl, turn back." So she turned back, and sat down.

Then Onion-leaves rose and came up, and she stuck her head into the room and was asked, "Who is this little girl, who is this?" "It is I who salute you, little boy, it is I who salute you." "What is your name, little girl, what is your name?" "My name is Onion-leaves, who makes the soup smell nicely." He said, "I have heard your name, little girl. What is my name?" She said, "I do not know your name, little boy, I do not know your name." "Turn back, little girl, turn back." So she turned back.

Now Pepper came along; she said, "Your pardon, little boy, your pardon." She was asked who was there. She said, "It is I, Pepper, little boy, it is I, Pepper, who make the soup hot." "I have heard your name, little girl, I have heard your name. Tell me my name, little girl, tell me my name." "I do not know your name, little boy, I do not know your name." He said, "Turn back, little maid, turn back."

There was only left Daudawar-batso, and they said, "Are not you coming?" She said, "Can I enter the house where such good people as you have gone, and been driven away? Would not they the sooner drive me out who stink?" They said, "Rise up and go." So she got up and went. He asked her, "Who is there, little girl, who is there?" And she said, "It is I who am greeting you, little boy, it is I who am greeting you." "What is your name, little girl, what is your name?" "My name is Batso, little boy, my name is Batso, which makes the soup smell." He said, "I have heard your name, little girl, I have heard your name. There remains my name to be told." She said, "Daskandarini, little boy, Daskandarini." And he said, "Enter."

A rug was spread for her, clothes were given to her, and slippers of gold; and then of these who had driven her away one said, "I will always sweep for you"; another, "I will pound for you."

Another said, "I will see about drawing water for you"; and another, "I will pound the ingredients of the soup"; and another, "I will stir the food." They all became her handmaids.

And the moral of all this is, if you see a man is poor do not despise him; you do not know but that some day he may be better than you.

The Gaawoo-Tree and the Maiden, and the First Person Who Ever Went Mad

(From the Hausa people, southern Niger and northern Nigeria)

THIS STORY IS ABOUT a 'gawo'-tree and a maiden. There was a certain man, by name, Doctor Umaru, the husband of Ladi. He possessed two wives, one called Mowa, one called Baura. They both had children, girls. The one called Mowa, always, if she has swept, then she used to give the sweepings to her daughter, and she took them to where the gawo-tree was and threw them away.

Now the gawo-tree had some growth on it that looked like a person's navel, and if this maiden took the sweepings there she used to touch it and say, "The gawo-tree with the navel." And it was always so she used to do. One day she went, and threw out the sweepings, and then touched the mark.

But the gawo-tree pulled himself out of the ground and followed her, and was saying, "Of a morning it's, The gawo-tree with the navel; of an evening it's, The gawo-tree with the navel." Then the maiden ran away, and the gawo-tree followed her. She came and met some people sowing, and they said, "You, maiden, what is the matter?" She said, "Something is following me."

And they said, "Sit down here till it comes. We will take the sowing implements, and beat him and kill him." They waited a little and then the gawo-tree came along. He was saying, "In the morning it's, The gawo-tree with the navel; in the evening it's, The gawo-tree with the navel." Thereupon the sowers said, "Maiden, go further on."

And the maiden ran on. She came and met some people hoeing, and they said, "Maiden, what is the matter?" And she said, "Something is following me." And they said, "Stand here, let him come. Can we not then lift our hoes, and hit him, and kill him?" They waited a little while, then the gawo-tree came towards them; he was saying, "In the morning it's, The gawo-tree with the navel; in the evening it's, The gawo-tree with the navel; to-day you see the gawo-tree with the navel." And they said, "Maiden, pass on."

So she passed on, and went and met some people ploughing. They were ploughing, and they said, "You, maiden, what is the matter?" She replied, "Something is following me." And they said, "Sit down here till he comes." In a little while, then the gawo-tree came up; he was saying, "In the morning it's, The gawo-tree with the navel; in the evening it's, The gawo-tree with the navel. To-day you see the gawo-tree with the navel." Thereupon they said, "Maiden, pass on."

So the maiden ran on. Then she came and met a lizard; he was weaving and was saying, "Kiryan, not kiryan, throw to the right, throw to the left of the shuttle." And he said, "You, maiden, where are you going that you are running so?" She said, "Something is pursuing me." He said, "Wait here till it comes." The maiden nestled close up to the lizard, who was saying, "Kiryan not kiryan, a cast to the right, a cast to the left," until the gawo-tree came up.

He was saying, "In the morning it's, The gawo-tree with the navel, in the evening it's, The gawo-tree with the navel; to-day you see the gawo-tree with the navel." And the maiden said, "See, there he is coming." And the lizard said, "Let him come, but if he has come, and I separate you from him, are you going to marry me?" She said, "Yes." Now the gawo-tree came up.

He said, "Where is the thing I gave you to keep for me?" The lizard said, "What did you give me?" The gawo-tree replied, "The maiden who is behind you." The lizard said, "This maid is stronger than you." And the gawo-tree said, "Lizard, you are forward." But the lizard replied, "Ah! A man is like the little red peppers, not till you have tasted them do you know how hot they are."

Then the gawo-tree got angry. He seized hold of the lizard. He swallowed him, but he came out of the gawo-tree's eyes. Then he caught him again and swallowed him, but he came out at his ears. Then he caught him again and swallowed him, but he came out of his breast. Then he caught him again and swallowed him, but the lizard came out at his navel.

And the gawo-tree fell down and died. And the lizard said, "Rise up, and I shall accompany you home." So she rose up. They went to her home. The lizard stood at the entrance to the door of the house, but she entered into the house and went about her affairs. They asked her, "Where did you go to?" She did not make any answer.

Then her father came out, and met a man sitting at the door of the house. And he said, "Greetings. Are you well?" He replied, "I and the maiden have come, and so on, and so, and so, and so (relating all that happened), we did with her." And her father said, "Oh, she did not talk about it." And he entered the house, and told the women. Then they said, "How is it you came and did not say anything about it?" And she said, "May Allah save me from marrying a lizard."

Then her father went aside, and called Baura, and said, "Will you not give me your daughter, to make a present to the lizard?" And she said, "As for that, O learned one, do I possess a daughter? No, you are a master of your own property. Call her and speak with her." Then the Doctor called the maiden, and said, "I wish to take you away and make a present of you. I have told your mother, and she said I must call you and tell you." She replied, "O learned father, no, it is not my mother who possesses me, it is you, you possess me. Be it a dog or a wild beast, take me and give to him. That is all I have to say."

And her father said, "May Allah bless you." Then he came and told the lizard, in reality he was a chief's son. Then he went home and told his father, and his father said, "Indeed!" And he gave him ten slaves, ten female slaves, ten cattle, and everything imaginable, ten of each, and took them to his future wife's father's. Then he gave her clothes, and they came and were married, and he took away his bride.

Now the lizard's father had a certain slave, by name Albarka, a leper, and he went to their house, and said he was in love with that one, whom they had given to the lizard and who had refused him. But her mother said to her, "What will you do with a leper?" But her daughter said, "I love him, he is the son of a chief, in disguise." So they said she was to be given to him. They were married and all the ceremonies performed, even up to taking her to her husband's home; it was in the fields.

And the pair did not see any one, till one day the lizard, who had been given the daughter of Baura for a wife, said he was going for a walk round the farms. He mounted his horse amid clapping and sounds of joy. They came and he said, "Is Albarka at home?" Then Albarka came out and saw him, then he ran back in haste to the house and said, "Bring out water for my master's son." But the wife said, "Your master?" He replied, "Yes." "You are infleed a slave?" He said, "Yes." Now she was pounding, then she put down the pestle. She was with child. Then she entered the bush.

That was the first person who became mad.

Oluronbi
(From the Yoruba people, southern Nigeria)

IN A CERTAIN VILLAGE no children had been born for many years, and the people were greatly distressed. At last all the women of the village went together into the forest, to the magic tree, the Iroko, and implored the spirit of the tree to help them.

The Iroko-man asked what gifts they would bring if he consented to help them, and the women eagerly promised him corn, yams, fruit, goats, and sheep; but Oluronbi, the young wife of a wood-carver, promised to bring her first child.

In due course children came to the village, and the most beautiful of all the children was the one born to Oluronbi. She and her husband so greatly loved their child that they could not consent to give it up to the Iroko-man.

The other women took their promised gifts of corn, yams, fruit, goats, and sheep; but Oluronbi took nothing to propitiate the tree.

Alas! one day as Oluronbi passed through the forest, the Iroko-man seized her and changed her into a small brown bird, which sat on the branches of the tree and plaintively sang:

"One promised a sheep, One promised a goat, One promised fruit, But Oluronbi promised her child."

When the wood-carver heard the bird's song, he realized what had happened, and tried to find some means of regaining his wife.

After thinking for many days, he began to carve a large wooden doll, like a real child in size and appearance, and with a small gold chain round its neck. Covering it with a beautiful native cloth, he laid it at the foot of the tree. The Iroko-man thought that this was Oluronbi's child, so he transformed the little bird once more into a woman and snatched up the child into the branches.

Oluronbi joyfully returned home, and was careful never to stray into the forest again.

The Twin Brothers
(From the Yoruba people, southern Nigeria)

A CERTAIN YORUBA KING, Ajaka, had a favourite wife of whom he was very fond; but, alas for his hopes! she gave birth to twins.

At that time it was the universal custom to destroy twins immediately at birth, and the mother with them. But the King had not the heart to put this cruel law into execution, and he secretly charged one of his nobles to conduct the royal mother and her babes to a remote place where they might live in safety.

Here the twin brothers grew to manhood, and loved one another greatly. They were inseparable, and neither of them had any pleasure except in the company of the other. When one brother began to speak, the other completed his phrase, so harmonious were their thoughts and inclinations.

Their mother, before she died, informed them of their royal birth, and from this moment they spent the time vainly regretting their exile, and wishing that the law of the country had made it possible for them to reign.

At last they received the news that the King their father was dead, leaving no heir, and it seemed to the brothers that one of them ought to go to the capital and claim the throne. But which?

To settle this point they decided to cast stones, and the one who made the longer throw should claim the throne, and afterwards send for his brother to share in his splendour.

The lot fell on the younger of the twins, and he set off to the capital, announced himself as the Olofin's son, and soon became King with the consent of all the people. As soon as possible he sent for his brother, who henceforth lived with him in the palace and was treated with honour and distinction.

But alas! jealousy began to overcome his brotherly affection, and one day as he walked with the King by the side of the river, he pushed his brother suddenly into the water, where he was drowned.

He then gave out in the palace that his brother was weary of kingship, and had left the country, desiring him to reign in his stead.

The King had certainly disappeared, and as no suspicion fell on the twin brother, he was made King and so realized his secret ambition.

Some time later, happening to pass by the very spot where his brother had been drowned, he saw a fish rise to the surface of the water and begin to sing:

> *"Your brother lies here,*
> *Your brother lies here."*

The King was very much afraid. He took up a sharp stone and killed the fish.

But another day when he passed the spot, attended by his nobles and shielded by the royal umbrella made of the skins of rare animals, the river itself rose into waves and sang:

> *"Your brother lies here,*
> *Your brother lies here."*

In astonishment the courtiers stopped to listen. Their suspicions were aroused, and when they looked into the water they found the body of the King.

Thus the secret of his disappearance was disclosed, and the wicked brother was rejected in horror by his people. At this disgrace he took poison and so died.

Ole and the Ants
(From the Yoruba people, southern Nigeria)

THERE WAS A CERTAIN lazy and disagreeable man whom everyone called "Ole," or "Lazy one." He liked to profit by the work of others, and was also very inquisitive about other people's affairs.

Once he saw that the ants had begun building a pillar in the compound of his house. But though the ants destroyed all the plants in the compound, and stripped all the trees, Ole would not trouble to kill them, or to break down their pillar.

Instead, he thought to himself: "When the ants have made this pillar very high, I will sit on the top of it, and then I shall be able to see all that my neighbours are doing without leaving my compound."

This thought pleased him, and he was glad that the ants swarmed in his compound. Each day the pillar grew higher, and at last the ants ceased their building and began again elsewhere. Ole then climbed up on to the pillar and spent the whole day observing the doings of his neighbours, and laughing at their activity.

> *"Here sit I like a great Chief,*
> *And I see all things!"*

sang Ole.

But while he sat on the pillar, the ants began to demolish his house and all that it contained, and in a short time there was nothing left of all his food and possessions.

Ole thus became the laughing-stock of the village, and everyone who saw him cried: "Ku ijoko!" or "Greetings to you on your sitting!"

Soon afterwards he died, and it is not known to this day whether he died of shame or of laziness.

The Secret of the Fishing-Baskets
(From the Yoruba people, southern Nigeria)

ACROSS A CERTAIN RIVER a poor fisherman set a row of stakes, and on each stake was fastened a basket in which he hoped to trap the fishes as they swam down the river.

But his luck was very bad, and every evening, as he went from basket to basket in his canoe, he was disappointed to find that no fishes, or only a few very small ones, had been caught.

This made him very sad, and he was forced to live frugally.

One day he found a stranger lying asleep on the river-bank. Instead of killing the stranger, the fisherman spoke kindly to him, and invited him to share his evening meal.

The stranger appeared very pleased and ate and drank, but spoke no word at all. The fisherman thought: "He speaks another language."

Quite suddenly the stranger vanished, and only the remains of the meal convinced the fisherman that he had not been dreaming.

The next evening when he went to empty his baskets, he was astonished to find them overflowing with fish. He could not account for his good fortune, and his surprise was even greater when the same thing occurred the next day. On the third day the baskets were again quite full, and when the fisherman came to the last basket he saw that it contained a single monstrous fish.

"Do you not know me?" said the fish.

"Indeed no, Mr. Fish. I have never seen you before!" declared the fisherman, nearly upsetting the canoe in his astonishment.

"Have you forgotten the stranger whom you treated so courteously?" went on the fish. "It was I, and I am the King of the fishes. I am grateful for your kindness and intend to reward you."

Then the fish jumped into the river with a great splash. But ever afterwards the fishing-baskets were full every evening, and the fisherman became rich and prosperous.

The Ten Goldsmiths
(From the Yoruba people, southern Nigeria)

Ф

A GOLDSMITH in a small village had ten sons, to all of whom he taught his trade. In time they became skilful craftsmen, and when the old man was dying he called the ten around him and

addressed them thus: "My sons, in this small village there is certainly not enough work for ten goldsmiths. I have therefore decided that the most skilful of you shall remain here in my place, while the rest must go out into the world and seek their fortunes elsewhere."

At this all the sons exclaimed that the plan was good, but who was to say which of them was the most skilful? The old man smiled and answered:

"I have thought of this also. I shall allow you all a month in which to make some article of gold, and at the end of that time I will judge which has been most skilfully executed."

The ten sons immediately set to work to fashion some article, and all displayed great industry during the allotted space of time. At the end of the month they came to their father, as he lay dying on the ground, and placed before him the articles they had made.

One had made a chain of fine gold, every link of which was the perfect shape of an elephant; another had made a knife, beautifully ornamented; another a little casket; another a ring representing serpents twisted together, with shining scales; another a water-pot of pleasing shape; and so on.

The old man smiled with pleasure to see what the industry of his sons had accomplished, but when he counted the articles before him, he found there were only nine. When he found that one of his sons had produced nothing, he was angered, especially when this proved to be the eldest son, whom he had secretly thought to be more skilful than his brothers. After bitterly reproaching this son, whose name was Ayo, for his laziness, the father prepared to give his decision on the work of the other brothers; but Ayo suddenly stepped forward and begged him to wait for another hour before making his choice.

"Meanwhile, Father," said he, "let us sit round the fire all together for the last time, parching corn and telling stories."

This was how the family spent their time in the rainy season, and all gladly consented.

As they seated themselves upon the ground, the father took up a full ripe ear of corn which lay near him. What was his astonishment when he tried to pick the grains to discover that it was made of gold!

For this was what Ayo had made, and he had prepared a little trick to test the perfection of his work. So skilfully was it executed that all had been deceived, thinking it a real ear of corn, and on this account the father and nine brothers all agreed that Ayo's work was certainly the best.

Thus Ayo took his father's place, and the rest set out in different directions to seek their fortune.

The Slave Girl Who Tried to Kill Her Mistress
(From southern Nigeria)

✠

A MAN CALLED AKPAN, who was a native of Oku, a town in the Ibibio country, admired a girl called Emme very much, who lived at Ibibio, and wished to marry her, as she was the finest girl in her company. It was the custom in those days for the parents to demand such a large amount for their daughters as dowry, that if after they were married they failed to get on with their husbands, as they could not redeem themselves, they were sold as slaves. Akpan paid a very large sum as dowry for Emme, and she was put in the fatting-house until the proper time arrived for her to marry.

Akpan told the parents that when their daughter was ready they must send her over to him. This they promised to do. Emme's father was a rich man, and after seven years had elapsed, and it became time for her to go to her husband, he saw a very fine girl, who had also just come out of the fatting-house, and whom the parents wished to sell as a slave. Emme's father therefore bought her, and gave her to his daughter as her handmaiden.

The next day Emme's little sister, being very anxious to go with her, obtained the consent of her mother, and they started off together, the slave girl carrying a large bundle containing clothes and presents from Emme's father. Akpan's house was a long day's march from where they lived. When they arrived just outside the town they came to a spring, where the people used to get their drinking water from, but no one was allowed to bathe there. Emme, however, knew nothing about this. They took off their clothes to wash close to the spring, and where there was a deep hole which led to the

240

Water Ju Ju's house. The slave girl knew of this Ju Ju, and thought if she could get her mistress to bathe, she would be taken by the Ju Ju, and she would then be able to take her place and marry Akpan. So they went down to bathe, and when they were close to the water the slave girl pushed her mistress in, and she at once disappeared. The little girl then began to cry, but the slave girl said, "If you cry any more I will kill you at once, and throw your body into the hole after your sister." And she told the child that she must never mention what had happened to anyone, and particularly not to Akpan, as she was going to represent her sister and marry him, and that if she ever told anyone what she had seen, she would be killed at once. She then made the little girl carry her load to Akpan's house.

When they arrived, Akpan was very much disappointed at the slave girl's appearance, as she was not nearly as pretty and fine as he had expected her to be; but as he had not seen Emme for seven years, he had no suspicion that the girl was not really Emme, for whom he had paid such a large dowry. He then called all his company together to play and feast, and when they arrived they were much astonished, and said, "Is this the fine woman for whom you paid so much dowry, and whom you told us so much about?" And Akpan could not answer them.

The slave girl was then for some time very cruel to Emme's little sister, and wanted her to die, so that her position would be more secure with her husband. She beat the little girl every day, and always made her carry the largest water pot to the spring; she also made the child place her finger in the fire to use as firewood. When the time came for food, the slave girl went to the fire and got a burning piece of wood and burned the child all over the body with it. When Akpan asked her why she treated the child so badly, she replied that she was a slave that her father had bought for her. When the little girl took the heavy water pot to the river to fill it there was no one to lift it up for her, so that she could not get it on to her head; she therefore had to remain a long time at the spring, and at last began calling for her sister Emme to come and help her.

When Emme heard her little sister crying for her, she begged the Water Ju Ju to allow her to go and help her, so he told her she might go, but that she must return to him again immediately. When the little girl saw her sister she did not want to leave her, and asked to be allowed to go into the hole with her. She then told Emme how very badly she had been treated by the slave girl, and her elder sister told her to have patience and wait, that a day of vengeance would arrive sooner or later. The little girl went back to Akpan's house with a glad heart as she had seen her sister, but when she got to the house, the slave girl said, "Why have you been so long getting the water?" and then took another stick from the fire and burnt the little girl again very badly, and starved her for the rest of the day.

This went on for some time, until, one day, when the child went to the river for water, after all the people had gone, she cried out for her sister as usual, but she did not come for a long time, as there was a hunter from Akpan's town hidden near watching the hole, and the Water Ju Ju told Emme that she must not go; but, as the little girl went on crying bitterly, Emme at last persuaded the Ju Ju to let her go, promising to return quickly. When she emerged from the water, she looked very beautiful with the rays of the setting sun shining on her glistening body. She helped her little sister with her water pot, and then disappeared into the hole again.

The hunter was amazed at what he had seen, and when he returned, he told Akpan what a beautiful woman had come out of the water and had helped the little girl with her water pot. He also told Akpan that he was convinced that the girl he had seen at the spring was his proper wife, Emme, and that the Water Ju Ju must have taken her.

Akpan then made up his mind to go out and watch and see what happened, so, in the early morning the hunter came for him, and they both went down to the river, and hid in the forest near the water-hole.

When Akpan saw Emme come out of the water, he recognised her at once, and went home and considered how he should get her out of the power of the Water Ju Ju. He was advised by some of his friends to go to an old woman, who frequently made sacrifices to the Water Ju Ju, and consult her as to what was the best thing to do.

When he went to her, she told him to bring her one white slave, one white goat, one piece of white cloth, one white chicken, and a basket of eggs. Then, when the great Ju Ju day arrived, she would take them to the Water Ju Ju, and make a sacrifice of them on his behalf. The day after the sacrifice was made, the Water Ju Ju would return the girl to her, and she would bring her to Akpan.

Akpan then bought the slave, and took all the other things to the old woman, and, when the day of the sacrifice arrived, he went with his friend the hunter and witnessed the old woman make the sacrifice. The slave was bound up and led to the hole, then the old woman called to the Water Ju Ju and cut the slave's throat with a sharp knife and pushed him into the hole. She then did the same to the goat and chicken, and also threw the eggs and cloth in on top of them.

After this had been done, they all returned to their homes. The next morning at dawn the old woman went to the hole, and found Emme standing at the side of the spring, so she told her that she was her friend, and was going to take her to her husband. She then took Emme back to her own home, and hid her in her room, and sent word to Akpan to come to her house, and to take great care that the slave woman knew nothing about the matter.

So Akpan left the house secretly by the back door, and arrived at the old woman's house without meeting anybody.

When Emme saw Akpan, she asked for her little sister, so he sent his friend, the hunter, for her to the spring, and he met her carrying her water pot to get the morning supply of water for the house, and brought her to the old woman's house with him.

When Emme had embraced her sister, she told her to return to the house and do something to annoy the slave woman, and then she was to run as fast as she could back to the old woman's house, where, no doubt, the slave girl would follow her, and would meet them all inside the house, and see Emme, who she believed she had killed.

The little girl did as she was told, and, directly she got into the house, she called out to the slave woman: "Do you know that you are a wicked woman, and have treated me very badly? I know you are only my sister's slave, and you will be properly punished." She then ran as hard as she could to the old woman's house. Directly the slave woman heard what the little girl said, she was quite mad with rage, and seized a burning stick from the fire, and ran after the child; but the little one got to the house first, and ran inside, the slave woman following close upon her heels with the burning stick in her hand.

Then Emme came out and confronted the slave woman, and she at once recognised her mistress, whom she thought she had killed, so she stood quite still.

Then they all went back to Akpan's house, and when they arrived there, Akpan asked the slave woman what she meant by pretending that she was Emme, and why she had tried to kill her. But, seeing she was found out, the slave woman had nothing to say.

Many people were then called to a play to celebrate the recovery of Akpan's wife, and when they had all come, he told them what the slave woman had done.

After this, Emme treated the slave girl in the same way as she had treated her little sister. She made her put her fingers in the fire, and burnt her with sticks. She also made her beat foo-foo with her head in a hollowed-out tree, and after a time she was tied up to a tree and starved to death.

Ever since that time, when a man marries a girl, he is always present when she comes out of the fatting-house and takes her home himself, so that such evil things as happened to Emme and her sister may not occur again.

The Fate of Essido and His Evil Companions
(From southern Nigeria)

CHIEF OBORRI LIVED at a town called Adiagor, which is on the right bank of the Calabar River. He was a wealthy chief, and belonged to the Egbo Society. He had many large canoes, and plenty of slaves to paddle them. These canoes he used to fill up with new yams – each canoe being under one head slave and containing eight paddles; the canoes were capable of holding three puncheons of palm oil, and cost eight hundred rods each. When they were full, about ten of them used to start off together and paddle to Rio del Rey. They went through creeks all the way, which run through mangrove swamps, with palm oil trees here and there.

Sometimes in the tornado season it was very dangerous crossing the creeks, as the canoes were so heavily laden, having only a few inches above the water, that quite a small wave would fill the canoe and cause it to sink to the bottom. Although most of the boys could swim, it often happened that some of them were lost, as there are many large alligators in these waters. After four days' hard paddling they would arrive at Rio del Rey, where they had very little difficulty in exchanging their new yams for bags of dried shrimps and sticks with smoked fish on them.

Chief Oborri had two sons, named Eyo I. and Essido. Their mother having died when they were babies, the children were brought up by their father. As they grew up, they developed entirely different characters. The eldest was very hard-working and led a solitary life; but the younger son was fond of gaiety and was very lazy, in fact, he spent most of his time in the neighbouring towns playing and dancing. When the two boys arrived at the respective ages of eighteen and twenty their father died, and they were left to look after themselves. According to native custom, the elder son, Eyo I., was entitled to the whole of his father's estate; but being very fond of his younger brother, he gave him a large number of rods and some land with a house. Immediately Essido became possessed of the money he became wilder than ever, gave big feasts to his companions, and always had his house full of women, upon whom he spent large sums. Although the amount his brother had given him on his father's death was very large, in the course of a few years Essido had spent it all. He then sold his house and effects, and spent the proceeds on feasting.

While he had been living this gay and unprofitable life, Eyo I. had been working harder than ever at his father's old trade, and had made many trips to Rio del Rey himself. Almost every week he had canoes laden with yams going down river and returning after about twelve days with shrimps and fish, which Eyo I. himself disposed of in the neighbouring markets, and he very rapidly became a rich man. At intervals he remonstrated with Essido on his extravagance, but his warnings had no effect; if anything, his brother became worse. At last the time arrived when all his money was spent, so Essido went to his brother and asked him to lend him two thousand rods, but Eyo refused, and told Essido that he would not help him in any way to continue his present life of debauchery, but that if he liked to work on the farm and trade, he would give him a fair share of the profits. This Essido indignantly refused, and went back to the town and consulted some of the very few friends he had left as to what was the best thing to do.

The men he spoke to were thoroughly bad men, and had been living upon Essido for a long time. They suggested to him that he should go round the town and borrow money from the people he had entertained, and then they would run away to Akpabryos town, which was about four days' march from Calabar. This Essido did, and managed to borrow a lot of money, although many people refused to lend him anything. Then at night he set off with his evil companions, who carried his money, as they had not been able to borrow any themselves, being so well known. When they arrived at Akpabryos town they found many beautiful women and graceful dancers. They then started the same life again, until after a few weeks most of the money had gone. They then met and consulted together how to get more money, and advised Essido to return to his rich brother, pretending that he was going to work and give up his old life; he should then get poison from a man they knew of, and place it in his brother's food, so that he would die, and then Essido would become possessed of all his brother's wealth, and they would be able to live in the same way as they had formerly. Essido, who had sunk very low, agreed to this plan, and they left Akpabryos town the next morning. After marching for two days, they arrived at a small hut in the bush where a man who was an expert poisoner lived, called Okponesip. He was the head Ju Ju man of the country, and when they had bribed him with eight hundred rods he swore them to secrecy, and gave Essido a small parcel containing a deadly poison which he said would kill his brother in three months. All he had to do was to place the poison in his brother's food.

When Essido returned to his brother's house he pretended to be very sorry for his former mode of living, and said that for the future he was going to work. Eyo I. was very glad when he heard this, and at once asked his brother in, and gave him new clothes and plenty to eat.

In the evening, when supper was being prepared, Essido went into the kitchen, pretending he wanted to get a light from the fire for his pipe. The cook being absent and no one about, he put the poison in the soup, and then returned to the living-room. He then asked for some tombo, which was brought, and when he had finished it, he said he did not want any supper, and went to sleep. His brother, Eyo I., had supper by himself and consumed all the soup. In a week's time he began to feel very ill, and as the days passed he became worse, so he sent for his Ju Ju man.

When Essido saw him coming, he quietly left the house; but the Ju Ju man, by casting lots, very soon discovered that it was Essido who had given poison to his brother. When he told Eyo I. this, he would not believe it, and sent him away. However, when Essido returned, his elder brother told him what the Ju Ju man had said, but that he did not believe him for one moment, and had sent him away. Essido was much relieved when he heard this, but as he was anxious that no suspicion of the crime should be attached to him, he went to the Household Ju Ju, and having first sworn that he had never administered poison to his brother, he drank out of the pot.

Three months after he had taken the poison Eyo I. died, much to the grief of everyone who knew him, as he was much respected, not only on account of his great wealth, but because he was also an upright and honest man, who never did harm to anyone.

Essido kept his brother's funeral according to the usual custom, and there was much playing and dancing, which was kept up for a long time. Then Essido paid off his old creditors in order to make himself popular, and kept open house, entertaining most lavishly, and spending his money in many foolish ways. All the bad women about collected at his house, and his old evil companions went on as they had done before.

Things got so bad that none of the respectable people would have anything to do with him, and at last the chiefs of the country, seeing the way Essido was squandering his late brother's estate, assembled together, and eventually came to the conclusion that he was a witch man, and had poisoned his brother in order to acquire his position. The chiefs, who were all friends of the late Eyo, and who were very sorry at the death, as they knew that if he had lived he would have become a great and powerful chief, made up their minds to give Essido the Ekpawor Ju Ju, which is a very strong medicine, and gets into men's heads, so that when they have drunk it they are compelled to speak the truth, and if they have done wrong they die very shortly. Essido was then told to dress himself and attend the meeting at the palaver house, and when he arrived the chiefs charged him with having killed his brother by witchcraft. Essido denied having done so, but the chiefs told him that if he were innocent he must prove it by drinking the bowl of Ekpawor medicine which was placed before him. As he could not refuse to drink, he drank the bowl off in great fear and trembling, and very soon the Ju Ju having got hold of him, he confessed that he had poisoned his brother, but that his friends had advised him to do so. About two hours after drinking the Ekpawor, Essido died in great pain.

The friends were then brought to the meeting and tied up to posts, and questioned as to the part they had taken in the death of Eyo. As they were too frightened to answer, the chiefs told them that they knew from Essido that they had induced him to poison his brother. They were then taken to the place where Eyo was buried, the grave having been dug open, and their heads were cut off and fell into the grave, and their bodies were thrown in after them as a sacrifice for the wrong they had done. The grave was then filled up again.

Ever since that time, whenever anyone is suspected of being a witch, he is tried by the Ekpawor Ju Ju.

The Treasure House in the Bush
(By Ojong Akpan of Mfamosing, of the Ekoi people, Nigeria and Cameroon)

OBASSI OSAW had two sons. The name of the first was Oro, and of the second Agbo. When their father died, Oro took all the property, while Agbo remained in the sky as a poor washerman. One day the latter said to his wife, "There is no food either for you or me. I must go into the bush and hunt, that we may not die of hunger." He went along a road which brought him down to earth, and led him at length to a part of the bush where a house was standing by itself. He wondered whose it might be, and crept round behind some bushes to watch unseen.

Soon some white people came through the bush close to where the hunter was hidden. He saw them open the door, carry forth a great treasure, and then lock up again.

When they had gone, Agbo crept out from his hiding place, found a way to enter the house, and took from it as much treasure as he could carry. This he bore off to the sky. When his wife saw what he had brought she said, "Where did you get all this?" He answered, "From a house in the bush where white people keep it."

Some days later the hunter went down again, and once more brought back a great load of treasure. When he had secured as much as he wanted, he went to his elder brother and said:

"Please lend me a basket; I wish to measure my money."

Oro did as he was asked, but one of his wives thought, "I should like to know how this poor man can suddenly have become rich." She followed Agbo, and, when they reached his house, offered to help him measure the money.

It took seven days to measure, and, when at last all was ended, the woman went back and told her husband how rich his brother had grown. On learning this Oro went straight to the latter's house and said, "Open the door and let me see what you have got."

Agbo replied, "Why should I show it? I am but a very small man compared to you." His wife however said, "Open the door and let him see." So at length it was opened.

When Oro saw what was stored within he asked, "Where did you get all this?" Agbo replied, "It came from the Treasure House of the white people, which I found in the bush." Then the elder brother began to beg the younger to show him the place, and the latter said, "To-morrow I will not go; but if you will come for me the day after, we will set out." This they did, and when they reached the house, entered and carried off a load.

Another day Oro said, "I want to go again;" but Agbo replied, "You must go alone. I will go no more." This time, therefore, the elder brother set off by himself. When he reached the Treasure House, he crept in by the way his brother had made; but instead of quickly gathering together some of the treasure, he saw rich robes lying in a heap on one side, and began trying them on. One after another he tried, and each seemed to him more gorgeous than the last. While he was still robing himself, the owners came in. They bound him, cut him in pieces and laid the fragments on the threshold.

When night came, Agbo grew anxious because his brother did not return. All night he waited, and, when day dawned, set out by the way which Oro had taken. On and on he went till he came to the house in the bush. There, oh, terrible sight! he found the fragments of his brother's body lying before the door. He collected every bit, and carried them sadly away. After a while he sought out a tailor and said, "Here is the body of a man who got cut to pieces in the bush. Can you sew it together again? If you will do this for me I will pay you richly." The tailor answered, "I will try what I can do."

When the owner of the treasure returned and found all the pieces gone he was very angry. He thought, "Who can have carried away the dead man's body, and what can have been done with it?" In his turn he also went to the tailor and asked, "Has anyone brought you pieces to mend?" The tailor replied, "Yes, a man named Agbo brought some."

The owner asked, "Who is Agbo? I do not know him." One of his servants answered, "I know who he is, and can find out all about him."

One day therefore this boy sought out Agbo and said, "I want to be your friend."

Agbo was willing, and cooked chop for his guest, but his son said, "My father, do not be friends with this boy, for he will go and tell his master all that you have done, and then they will come and kill you."

The servant went back to earth and told everything. In the night time he came again with some white paint, and painted all the posts of Agbo's house. After this he returned and told his master, "The place where the man lives who has wronged you will be easy to find, for I have marked it with white paint. In the morning, therefore, you can go with a large following and kill him, with all who dwell in his compound." Now a bright moon had been shining while the servant worked, and the son of Agbo had seen what was done. So he also got white paint and ran hastily round and painted all the houses in the town in the same way.

When the white man came early in the morning with a great following, he found the whole town painted alike, so he could not find the house which he sought, and was forced to return home without doing anything. He blamed his servant because the latter had failed to keep his promise, but the boy said:

"If you will lend me some of your war men, you shall not only be avenged of your enemy, but recover all that he has stolen." To this the master agreed, and called together some of his bravest fighters. The boy collected a lot of empty casks. These they rolled along till they neared the entrance to Agbo's town. There the servant said to twelve of the war men who were strong above their fellows, "I beg that you will now get into the casks." When they had entered and the covers were replaced, the others rolled them along till they came to Agbo's door.

Then the boy called out, "Agbo, Agbo. I am your friend, come back with a great gift. See, here are many puncheons of palm oil."

Agbo was very pleased, but his son said, "I think that there are men hidden in those casks." The father answered, "How can you be so suspicious? There is nothing but oil." After that he made a great feast for his friend, and, when night came, prepared a bed for him in a room near to his own.

When all was quiet, the son got up and boiled much water. First he took a sharp knife and cut the throat of his father's guest. Next he went, very softly, to the casks, and made a small hole in each. Through this he poured in the boiling water till all were nearly full.

Next morning when Agbo came out of his room he called to his friend, but no answer came. He went to the side of the bed and found him lying with his throat cut. When he saw this he gave a great cry and called:

"Who has killed my friend?" His son answered, "It is I."

On this Agbo caught the boy, chained him, and dragged him before the Judge, and there accused him of having killed their guest.

The Judge asked, "Is it true that you have done this thing?" and the boy answered "Yes." Then he asked, "Why did you do it?" and he answered, "To save my father's life, for his friend tried to kill him."

Then the son told of the casks which had been brought to the house with soldiers inside. The Judge sent to fetch them, and when they were brought it was found to be even as the boy had said, for the boiling water had killed all the men.

The Judge said to Agbo, "I cannot blame your son, for he has saved your life." So they decided to send the lad away free with rich gifts.

When home was reached, Agbo let his son into the place where his treasure was kept, and said to him, "The half of this I give to you now. When I die, all that I have will be yours, for you have been a good son and have saved my life. Fathers should take care of their sons, and sons should always help fathers."

Further he gave the lad seven slaves.

Why a Murderer Must Die
(From the Ekoi people, Nigeria and Cameroon)

THERE WAS ONCE a woman named Ukpong Ma, who had only one daughter. Just before it was time to put the girl into the fatting-house the mother died.

One day the husband, whose name was Uponnsoraw, set out for market. On his way he passed through a neighbouring town, where he saw a beautiful woman, and persuaded her to return with him as his wife.

When the couple reached the man's house, his daughter came out to salute them, and the new wife saw that in a little while her step-daughter would be more beautiful than she. So she hated the girl, and thought how she might destroy her.

One day, therefore, when the husband went out to hunt, the new wife called to her step-child and said, "Take the great water-pot, and go to the far river for water. Do not bring home any from the streams near by."

So soon as the girl had set out, the new wife killed a goat, ate the best part of the meat herself, and hid what was left over.

As the girl came back from the river it began to grow dark. Rain fell and she felt cold. When she reached home she went to the fireside to warm herself. Some water fell down on her, and she said to the new wife, "Where does it come from?" and the latter answered, "The roof leaks."

When Uponnsoraw came back from the hunt, he could not see the goat, so he called to his daughter and asked where it was. She answered, "Your new wife sent me to the river for water. I have only just come back, and do not know what has been happening at home."

At this the cruel step-mother came out of her room and said, "Let us practise the charm to find who has stolen the goat."

They sent for the Diviner, and he came with a very long rope and said, "We will go down to the river where the girl filled the jar."

Now the new wife was a great witch, so she secretly made a strong charm. Then, when they came to the river and threw the rope across, she stood on the brink and called, "If I have stolen the goat may the rope break and let me fall into the river. If I am guiltless may I walk over safely."

She put her foot upon the rope, but the charm held, and she crossed without mishap.

The young girl stood by the river-side and said the same words. Then she walked on the rope as far as mid-stream. There the charm which the witch had made caused it to break, and the girl fell into the water. A great crocodile came up to the surface and caught her as she fell. Then all the people said, "She it was who stole the goat." Only her father said, "My daughter never stole anything. I must find out the reason of her death."

A palm tree grew by the river-side, just by the place where the girl was lost, and one day a man climbed up this to collect palm wine.

Now beneath the water was the house of a were-crocodile, and she it was who had seized the girl, and kept her all this while as a slave. When the man began to climb the palm tree the crocodile was angry. So she took an axe and put it into the girl's hand and said, "Go up to the top of the water and throw this axe at the man, that he may leave my palm tree and go back whence he came."

The girl did as she was bidden, but threw the axe so as not to hit the man. As it struck the tree the climber looked down and saw her. He therefore went back to his town with all haste, and told her father what had happened.

The latter wondered, and went before the chief and said, "This man says that he saw my daughter who died two years ago in the great river."

The chief was angry because he thought that the man was lying. So he ordered that chains should be brought and put upon him. The man, however, begged that they would take him to the place where he had seen the girl, and watch while he climbed the palm tree. To this the chief consented, and sent him, with three men, to the river. With them also went Uponnsoraw. The man climbed the tree and struck it with his matchet. No sooner did the girl hear than she rose to the surface, covered with ornaments, but sank down again almost at once. On this all the men ran back to the chief to tell him that the man had spoken truth, for they also had seen the girl.

The whole town set forth to fetch the Diviner, and asked him to practise the charm. This he did, and told them they must bring a black cock, an egg, a piece of white cloth, a ball of red cam wood dye, and some of the yellow 'ogokk' powder; also they must bring the great nets which are used in hunting. All these things, save the red powder, they must sacrifice to the crocodile, but the nets they must hold ready in their hands.

As soon as they threw the offering into the river the girl rose to the surface. When she appeared they cast the nets and caught her like a fish. Then they drew her to land and washed her with the red powder and with sand, and carried her in triumph to the house of the chief.

The cruel witch-wife came out to salute her, but no sooner did the girl hear her voice than she said:

"I will not see her at all. Crocodile told me a story about her. It was she who stole the goat." Then she said to her father, "Call all the people. I wish to say something."

When the townsfolk had come together they carried the girl before the Egbo house, where she stood up and said:

"Here I am. It was the new wife of my father who stole the goat that she might destroy me, lest I should be counted more beautiful than herself. Then she made a strong magic, so that the rope might bear her across the river, but break when I tried to pass over. Therefore all the people thought that I was guilty of the theft. Judge now, oh ye people, between her and me."

Then the Head Chief said, "Let the town give judgment"; and they cried in a great shout:

"The witch shall die for her crime." Then they set up two great posts, and from these hanged the woman by the very cord which by her magic she had caused to break beneath the feet of the innocent girl. Thus died the witch in the sight of all men.

From that day forward a law was made, "If anyone is proved guilty of the death of another, he shall surely die."

That is the reason why if anyone kills another they must hang.

Abundance: A Play on the Meaning of a Word
(From the Fang and Bulu peoples, Cameroon)

Ф

There was a certain Man who was very poor; he had no goods with which to buy a wife. He went one day into the forest to set snares. On the morrow, he went off to examine them; and found a Wild-Goat caught in the snares. He rejoiced and said, "I must eat Mbindi today!"

But the Wild-Goat said to that Man, "Let me alone, Bwinge is coming after awhile."

So, the Man, thinking that 'Bwinge' was the name of some other and more desirable animal, at once let the Wild-Goat loose, and went off to his town. On the next day, the Man went to examine the snare, to see whether Bwinge was there, and found Hog caught fast in the net. And he exclaimed, "I must eat Ngweya today!"

But the Hog said, "Let me go. Bwinge is coming." The man at once left the Hog, (still thinking that many more were coming); and it went away.

The Man wondered, and said to himself, "What Thing is it that is named 'Bwinge'?"

On another day, he went to set his snare. He found there a dwarf child of a Human Being; and, in anger, he said, "You are the one who has caused me to send away the beasts? Is it possible that you are he who is 'Bwinge'? I shall kill you." But the dwarf said, "No! don't kill me. I will call Ungumba for you." So, the Man said, "Call in a hurry!"

The Dwarf ordered, "Let guns come!" And they at once came. (This was done by the Dwarf's Magic-Power.) The Man again said, "Call, in a hurry!" The Dwarf called for women; and they came. The Man again said to him, "Call for Goats, in a hurry!" And they came, with abundance of other things.

Then the Man freed him, and said to him, "Go!"

The Man also went his way with his riches. And he became a great man. This was because of his patient waiting.

FLAME TREE PUBLISHING

In the same series:
MYTHS & LEGENDS

Also available:
EPIC TALES DELUXE EDITIONS